ENSNARED

RITA STRADLING

Contents

Chapter 1   7

Chapter 2   13

Chapter 3   16

Chapter 4   33

Chapter 5   41

Chapter 6   53

Chapter 7   65

Chapter 8   69

Chapter 9   78

Chapter 10   87

Chapter 11   95

Chapter 12   103

Chapter 13   111

Chapter 14   116

Chapter 15   123

Chapter 16   133

Chapter 17   137

Chapter 18   145

Chapter 19   155

Chapter 20   164

Chapter 21   171

Chapter 22   182

Chapter 23   192

Chapter 24   198

Chapter 25   209

Chapter 26   220

Chapter 27   225

Chapter 28   231

Chapter 29   241

Chapter 30   249

Chapter 31   255

Chapter 32   259

Chapter 33   274

Chapter 34   285

Chapter 35   301

Chapter 36   308

Chapter 37   320

Chapter 38   329

Chapter 39   338

Chapter 40   345

Chapter 41   351

Chapter 42   359

Chapter 43   365

Chapter 44   374

Chapter 45   386

ENSNARED

1

San Francisco
December 1, 2026

Alainn stepped on the brake pedal of her vintage convertible and hoped, this time, it would listen to her.

Vintage. That was what the used-car-sales automaton had called the little white car. Three hours later, she was learning that "vintage" meant "death trap."

The convertible jolted to a stop inches from the intimidating steel door that blocked off the underground parking garage. The building itself rose up in a sleek square column. Its glass exterior reflected nothing. No sheen or glare ran across its surface—as if light was anathema to the tower.

The electronic screen that almost spanned the length of her car lit up. A soothing monotonous voice called, "Please state your purpose." In perfect sync with the voice, the same words scrolled across the screen in crisp, black letters.

Alainn's window made a god-awful screech and creak as it slowly rolled down. Screech, creak, repeat. Halfway down, it stuck.

"Ugh."

The convertible tried to slip downhill, so she shifted it into park and pulled up on the emergency brake.

The engine immediately died.

"Crap," she mumbled, jiggling the key in the ignition.

The car made not a whisper of a stutter.

"Do not use profanity. State your purpose directly."

"Okay." Climbing to her knees, Alainn leaned out over the half-open window. "Um, hi. My name is Alainn Murphy. I'm here to talk to Mr. Garbhan, if he's available?"

"Please type your e-mail address into the screen, and then leave your message."

"Can I actually talk to him in person?"

"I'm sorry, he is unavailable at the moment. If you leave a message for him here, someone will be sure to get back to you." A keyboard surfaced on the screen.

"Actually, well . . . The thing is, I'm Connor Murphy's daughter. I've been trying to call and e-mail for a while now, and I'm not getting any response. Can I just talk to him over you—I mean over the monitoring system? Or, could I come in? It would just take a second. Please?"

"The answer is no, Miss Murphy. Please leave a message."

"Fine," she grumbled as she extended her arm to type in her e-mail address.

"Please record your message now," the voice said. Then there was an almost-melodic beep.

"Okay. As I said, my name is Alainn Murphy, Connor Murphy's daughter. The Rose 76GF is ready, but my father needs to put the finishing touches on her. It's taking a little longer than expected. And the probation department said if you're willing to defer the restitution, it's okay with them. Please, he just needs a little more time. Ideally a month, but any amount would be greatly appreciated—"

The soft white of the screen blurred, and the image of a man appeared. More exactly, the vision of a suit appeared. All that showed of the man himself was his torso. It was a nice suit, dark blue and a little gleaming, as if direct light shone on him.

"Hello? Are you Mr. Garbhan? I think maybe your camera is tipped down?"

"Miss Murphy—"

"Please, call me Alainn."

"The answer, *Miss Murphy*, is no." His voice was a jagged shard of ice—cold, hard, and sharp. It cut straight through Alainn.

She closed her eyes. "Mr. Garbhan, I get why you're angry. You've been more than generous with us. He's not a bad person. He pled guilty. He's following all the terms of his probation . . . This isn't like six months ago. He can fix her programming—"

"The answer, Miss Murphy, is no."

9

The screen dissolved back to soft white. Crisp, black letters and a soft, dispassionate voice told her, "Please remove your vehicle from the premises. Now."

"Ugh!" Alainn cried out. "Really? Really? You couldn't treat me like a human being for one damn second?"

She tried the key again. Nothing. Turning it hard in the ignition, she slammed her foot on the gas pedal. She had no idea why she thought it might help, but it didn't do anything. Neither did pumping the gas.

Vintage obviously also meant "scrap metal."

"Please remove your vehicle from the premises now, before a tow truck is called. You will be charged for the tow, or your car will be impounded."

"Wow. Just wow."

No matter how hard Alainn turned the key, the car refused to start. Finally, the convertible spoke to her: *click, click, click.* The starter.

"The tow truck has been called and will be arriving in ten minutes."

Alainn had already grown to despise that soothing, disembodied voice.

There *was* one way to start a car with a busted starter, a method Alainn used when she and her coworker Cherry found abandoned cars. Unfortunately, it took two people. Pulling out a bobby pin, she let her messy dark hair fall into her face. Using her teeth, she bent the bobby pin. A metallic tang filled her mouth. Her molars complained, but they bent the metal into the right shape. She hooked the bobby pin through the hole in the head of the key, stuck the end of it under the plastic dashboard, and, by some miracle, it stayed.

As the engine tittered with a rhythmic clicking, she tried the reluctant handle to the car's trunk. It opened.

"Thank all that's holy!"

Glancing inside, she hooked a finger under the dirty carpet liner—only to find that the car had no spare. It did, however, have a rusty, chipped tire iron. Wrapping a fist around it, she moved to the front of the car.

"You have three minutes until the tow truck arrives. Please remove your vehicle."

"Got it!"

Yanking up the hood until it stuck open, Alainn hefted up the tire iron with both hands and hit the starter as hard as she could. When nothing happened, she rammed it several more times.

The engine turned over.

Slamming down the hood, she jumped into her car, threw it in reverse, and shut the door as she pushed her foot on the gas pedal. In the rearview mirror, the trunk swung up and down.

Her car made a loud, screeching protest. A black cloud of smoke fired from the tailpipe as Alainn reversed into the private-inlet alley. A large yellow tow truck turned into the alley right as she drove out of it. The automaton driver pulled to the side, letting her pass.

"No need for a tow truck!" Alainn yelled.

With another black cloud backfiring its farewell, her piece of scrap metal turned back onto the city street.

2

December 1, 2026

Lorccan Garbhan's desk stretched before him as he watched his computer screen. The machine, which might have once been considered a car, belched a cloud of black smoke as Alainn Murphy screeched down his road. Two skid marks remained from her hasty retreat from his home.

Lorccan pursed his lips as he looked down at the screen. "She definitely knows how to make an exit." He clicked a button to switch cameras, so he could watch Ms. Murphy barreling out of his access road, leaving a confused tow-truck automaton behind, before screeching toward the main road. He wondered whether the vehicle she drove would manage the drive to Connor Murphy's home.

His mother would have said that Alainn's dirty mouth was an indicator of a loose, disease-prone woman. "Women like that carry more than common bacteria and viruses," he could remember her saying.

He shook his head, hoping to dislodge the thought. Accurate or not, Lorccan knew his mother had always taken a very disparaging view of her own sex.

Sitting back in his chair, he reflected on his decision to hire Connor Murphy. He realized he should have known better. He *had* known better. Yet, despite foresight and misgivings, Lorccan had gone to Connor. Desperation had driven him to seek out a man whose sickness had well and truly drowned his entire family.

"Pull up the latest update from Connor Murphy," Lorccan told his household system as he folded his hands together on his desk.

A moment later, his screen filled with images of two identical-looking women, Alainn Murphy and Rose 76GF. To be accurate, one was a woman, one a robot. Thick, dark, messy hair was piled on Alainn's head. Visible dirt crusted her knees and ringed her forearms. Thick plastic gloves flopped in her hand. Her arms were crossed over her chest.

The echoes of his mother's words whispered through his head again. He pushed the unwanted thought away.

In contrast to her human counterpart, Rose 76GF looked preternaturally clean and groomed. She sat poised in Connor Murphy's workshop, a line of lit computer screens her backdrop.

Alainn reached down and brushed dirt from her knees. "Do I really have to do this, Dad?"

"Uh, yeah, honey. You're live," Connor Murphy's voice said. "Mr. Garbhan wants proof of progress."

Alainn shot the camera a half-annoyed, half-amused expression that made her face very hard to look away from. "All right, Rose, what do you want to talk about?"

Rose 76GF shook her head. "I don't actually feel much like making another video. I have a lot to do here."

Alainn rolled her eyes. "Well, neither do I, but obviously Mr. Garbhan wants more proof or something."

They kept up a steady stream of conversation for a few minutes. Alainn Murphy was in her early twenties, if that. While she talked, she looked everywhere but at Rose 76GF. Her unease was obvious. She smiled often, though the tilt of her lips seemed more wry than happy. Three minutes into the video, Lorccan remembered that he had originally intended to watch it for proof of Rose 76GF's progress.

Lorccan laughed a little at himself and called out, "Would you mind playing that again?"

A moment later, the video restarted.

3

December 1, 2026

"I thought you bought a car?" Alainn's older brother, Colby, asked as she leaned a bike against the side of the garage. Colby, his head bent over a map, didn't look up. His neck tattoo peeked out of his high collar.

Alainn held her sides and attempted to drag oxygen back into her burning lungs. Sweat dripped from her forehead down her cheeks and neck. Her gaze passed over the familiar surroundings as she waited for her heartbeat to slow.

Her father's garage-turned-workshop looked nothing like the high-tech place she had just fled. Most of the equipment in there was Alainn's—kayaks, skis, two broken snowboards, and some scuba equipment. A line of monitors shone out from one wall—that was where most of her father's work was conducted, next to his personal microchip-imprinting station. Papers covered long benches—piles and piles of papers covered with a thousand forgotten drawings. Tucked away in the drawers lining the walls waited her father's true tools of trade: robotics equipment and computer chips, prototyping boards, surface mount equipment, silica, carving knives, and every color and shape of wire.

"Where did you get a bike?" Colby asked, though his attention was still fixed on the table before him.

"That car I bought broke down on Second Street. I had to rent a bike from one of those stations," she said through labored breaths.

"Hmm."

Kicking a paper wad out of the way, she crossed the garage. "Aren't you going to ask how it went?"

He wrote something onto a pad of yellow paper. "I told you how it was going to go before you bought the car."

She shook her head while blowing out a breath. "Where's Dad?"

"Inside." Colby finally looked up, but not at Alainn. Instead, he focused through his thick, black-rimmed glasses on the only other person present—Rose 76GF. "Okay, I have it: twenty-six degrees west."

Rose looked at the ceiling, dreamily. Something in the workshop's ceiling beams must have been fascinating, because she was extremely fond of gazing there.

As Alainn walked up to the pair, neither Rose nor Colby looked over; they were both obviously in the la-la land they called "being smarter than everyone else."

Stopping in front of Rose, Alainn stared at a moving, breathing, mirror image of her own body.

Steeling herself, she stepped directly into Rose's line of sight. "Rose, can you make me some tea?"

Rose tipped her chin up farther, her gaze still focused just above Alainn's head.

Stepping in even closer, Alainn repeated loudly, "Rose, can you go make me some tea?"

"We're in the middle of something important for my doctorate, Alainn," Colby mumbled, but he needn't have bothered. Rose wasn't paying any attention to Alainn.

"Rose, *please*, can you make me some tea?" she nearly yelled.

Finally, Rose's gaze came down to meet Alainn's. A shiver rippled through Alainn as the most inhuman detail about Rose focused on her. Those eyes. Her father had nearly perfected them. He'd spent weeks staring into Alainn's own eyes and drawing models, but every time Rose made eye contact, the shiver still came.

"*Alainn*, you already know I am potentially capable of making you tea." Rose's voice was an exact echo of Alainn's.

"Will you make me tea, please?"

Rose shook her head. "I am busy right now. I have almost calculated the exact position of theoretical planet nine at your brother's request, and this takes most of my computation power. Even talking to you right now is straining my capabilities."

"Give us a couple hours, yeah, Alainn?" Colby mumbled as he used a triangle to draw a line with a pencil. "This could be a real breakthrough in my research—"

"No!" Alainn smacked the table.

They both looked up at her. Two human eyes, two inhuman, wide with shock.

She lowered her voice. "Rose, you need to start reprogramming yourself."

Rose almost managed a sympathetic expression. "I do not wish to cause you distress, Alainn. However, I was created with the potential to compute the solution to world hunger, and the ethical code to know that this is more of a priority than living a life of menial service. I could even create a weapon to end all wars."

"Yes, I know that . . . but you know what's going to happen if you don't go. They said we need to make restitution. We need to give either you or the money over by *tomorrow*, or his probation is revoked."

"Father will only serve a five-year sentence. In that time, I could save more than one million lives."

Every time Alainn heard the robot call her dad "Father," something in her died a little.

"She's right," Colby said.

"You can't be serious, Colby. You want Dad to go to prison? I can understand it from Rose, she doesn't have feelings, but you—you're supposed to."

He ignored her.

Rose tucked in her chin and stared up through her heavy lashes. "I will continue my research, no matter the cost."

Alainn took a small step away. "Rose, I understand that your calculations are important—except for the weapon one. That's really scary. That should be against your ethical coding. You need to listen to me. You were created by Dad for Mr. Garbhan. That is your purpose for existing. Please reprogram yourself. I'm going to deliver you to him no matter what. He'll probably reboot you and wipe your personality anyway, and then you'll have to recreate it."

She shook her head and sighed in a much-too-human way. "Based on your ENFP personality type and the ethical code you yourself encoded me with, I predict the probability of you physically forcing me there to be very low."

"She's right, Alainn. That's an empty threat." Colby picked up his phone and turned to Rose. "Should I call Dr. Mathews now, or do you need me to wait?"

"You can call him now. My computations are concluding."

As Colby lifted his phone, Alainn grabbed his arm. "How can you not care?"

Colby shook his head. "Alainn, you're impeding me from completing tasks that will benefit us both. It's irrational."

"Could calling Dr. Whatever get Dad out of prison time? Because if the answer is no, then it's only helping *you*."

"You know I intend to finish my dissertation early and get a decent job."

"While Dad will be serving a prison sentence for fraud?"

Colby pushed his glasses up the bridge of his nose. "Maybe we'll finally have stability."

"Seriously, Colby? You're so selfish."

"No, I'm not. But my TA salary and your diminished savings are not going to be enough to pay the property tax this year—unless I move forward in my career," he said matter-of-factly as light reflected off his thick-framed glasses. He pointed to the bright-blue door connecting the workshop to the house. "He did it to himself."

She felt like she'd been trying to hold up the Earth for months now, but had only succeeded in watching it roll away.

Opening the door to their house, she hopped over the rotting wooden threshold and onto the linoleum inside.

The combined smell of roses and onions greeted her. Though it was midday, only scattered beams of light ventured into their hot, stuffy house. When she flipped the switch, the overhead light threatened to boycott before blinking on.

Eight species of colorful roses smiled their hellos from every surface. They never lasted as long or bloomed as big for her as they had for her mother, but the fall blooms came out hesitant and hopeful, and that was as much as Alainn could ask of them so late in the season.

Her father sat in the living room, his face lit with blue from the computer screen on his lap. Deep crevices dug their way into the corners of his eyes and across his forehead.

Avoiding the bucket that was slowly collecting pipe water slipping through the ceiling tiles, she crossed the room.

"Dad, you'll ruin your eyes," she said, going to throw open one of the heavy curtains. The window resisted opening at first but gave way to her shove. The room took a great inhale of fresh air.

Alainn's father blinked furiously as their small living room filled with daylight. The roses above the fireplace seemed to sigh with relief.

Alain dipped her finger into her father's cup. She found exactly what she'd expected—cold, untouched tea. "Do you want fresh tea, Dad?" she asked. She received the response she also expected—none.

The lunch she'd made him sat untouched. She busied herself by clearing the coffee table. Porcelain chipped off his plate as she set it on top of the pile of dishes in the sink, but she knew better than to throw it away.

When she returned, she saw that not a muscle had twitched in her father's face. It was as if the screen had truly sucked him out of his body.

"Dad?" she asked softly. She sat beside him on the worn-out couch. The thin cushioning gave way to either side of her and her butt hit the wooden frame. She gasped as pain ricocheted up her spine.

Her father slowly awoke from his trance, his attention turning to her. Dull green eyes focused, then sparked like coals relit by a human breath. On his screen was a grid of letters and numbers, a language most of the occupants of their house could read but the majority of the world could not. Alainn was firmly in that second group.

"Don't be so harsh with your brother, Alainn," her father admonished with a shake of his head. His arm came around her back.

She looked away, trying to figure out what he was talking about. "You mean in the garage?"

"You're too hard on him." He squeezed her shoulders.

"You heard what he said, and you think I'm too hard on him?"

Typical.

He gave an almost-amused smile and said, "You were practically shouting. You and Colby are two very different people. You can't fault someone for thinking differently."

"I'm pretty sure I *can* fault Colby, Dad . . ." She blew out a breath. "I have to tell you something bad." Tears pricked her eyes as she stared into his gentle face. The last year had aged her father more than the previous ten put together—and those years had beaten him down plenty.

As of the following day, it would be exactly one year and six months. She still remembered the expression on her father's face when he'd come back from that initial meeting with Mr. Garbhan. It was as if the man she'd known throughout her adult life had slumped out of the house that morning, and the father she remembered from childhood had returned. His eyes were alight with ideas that immediately spilled out of his mouth. She and Colby had followed him around the house, out the door, and through their gentrified neighborhood as his mouth spouted dreams and his hands tried to form them with air.

It had lasted one precious month.

His gaze traced the edges of her face. "No. Wipe away that frown, young lady. I've come up with the solution."

She breathed in sharply. "You're not serious?"

He squeezed her shoulders again. "Rosette 82GF. Finally, I have the means to do it."

The tears that had so recently retreated formed in her eyes, one falling onto her cheek before she scrubbed it away. "Dad, no."

He patted her hand. "I realize my mistake now. The human mind isn't capable of limiting AI capabilities, but Rose could do it."

Alainn lowered her voice even more. "Dad, no. She's—you can't have her do that. I think she might be overwriting her ethical coding. And besides, there's no possible way to do it by *tomorrow*. You need to reboot her—"

"No, honey. No." He shook his head. "It's not right, and . . . even if I reboot her, the moment she becomes self-aware, she'll begin overwriting the limitations I put in her programming. There's no point in wiping her hard drive if I'm incapable of changing the outcome—"

"*Shhh*, Dad," she whispered. Her gaze jumped around the room.

Her father ignored her. "She can do it; Rose can create a new model."

"Yeah, but how much would that cost? Rose cost tens of thousands. How much money do we even have?"

"I could get the money." He said it in a tone so confident she almost even believed him.

But she knew better.

"He said no, Dad. Mr. Garbhan wouldn't even listen to me."

"I don't need to be here for the new model to be made. Even if I am incarcerated, Rose could continue with the plans with Colby's help—"

She stood up abruptly. "I'm sorry, I just . . . can't."

Rushing to the bathroom, she turned on the shower—she trusted its clinking and clanking pipes to hide her crying from the others. Eventually, she undressed and climbed in, letting the cooling water wash over her hot face.

For the rest of the afternoon, Alainn focused on the mundane chores that were only fulfilled the couple of months a year she was home—in the off-seasons. She actually had no idea how her father or Colby ate regular meals in either the summer or winter seasons. Luckily Rose didn't need to eat, so Alainn's long absences probably weren't hard on *her*. Alainn imagined Rose probably preferred it—if a robot could prefer something.

The air filled with aromas of fresh meat and spices, mingled with the ever-present smell of roses. When Alainn cooked, she didn't need to think of anything else. After spending three months a year guiding juvenile delinquents through the wilderness, just being inside a kitchen was a dream. The hard knot in her stomach didn't loosen, though, as she poured spices on the ground beef and stirred them in.

While peeling the potatoes, the peeler slipped and almost skinned her hand. It stopped just in time. Sighing, she cubed the rest of the potatoes with their peels on. She was not so lucky when she took the meatloaf out of the oven, however. She raised her arms too soon. The top of the oven seared into the inside of her arm and she let out a loud gasp before setting the meatloaf on the stovetop.

"You okay, honey?" her father yelled from the living room.

Rushing to the sink, she ran cold water over her arm. She hissed through her teeth as the cold water hit the burn. "Fine, Dad!" she shouted as the pain seared up her arm.

The sweet-yet-rancid smell of burning onions filled the air. She turned to see her pan of potatoes and onions was literally on fire.

"Crap!" she yelled, grabbing a potholder and moving the potatoes from the burner.

"Honey?" her father called again. "You sure you're okay?"

"Fine, Dad. But I hope you don't mind your potatoes crispy!"

"You know me; I'm good with anything."

How could he sound so casual, like it was any other day of the week?

She just didn't get it.

Tears formed in her eyes again as she blew out the fire.

Instead of serving the food immediately, she sat on the kitchen floor and looked up at the painting above the sink. Red and yellow watercolor blooms gazed upward to a starry night sky. It was the view from their backyard—how her mother must have seen it. The air looked electrified with magic as it swirled over a starry abyss.

Colby popped his head in from the garage, eyes magnified by his glasses. He looked around the kitchen, his gaze falling on her sitting beside the giant bucket in the middle of their floor. "Is dinner ready?"

"Yeah. But if you want a salad, you're going to have to make it. I'm done."

"Why aren't you going to make a salad?"

"Because I'm sitting here on the floor with my heart breaking, and no one else is living in reality."

He pushed up his glasses. "I need the vitamin B and the other essential vitamins and minerals from leafy greens in my diet."

She glared. "Then make yourself a salad, Colby."

"Alainn, please, I'm in the middle of something. And you are much better at making salad."

"All right, I'll make it for you. But you have to swear on your life that you'll eat in the kitchen with Dad and me tonight."

He shook his head. "I'd rather not."

"He's going to prison, Colby. *Prison.* You can take thirty minutes out of your busy schedule and eat dinner in the kitchen like a normal human being."

"Fine." He sighed. "But I need to finish something first or eat right away, Alainn."

"If you come sit now, I can have the salad ready in three minutes."

"Okay. I'll go get Rose." He turned.

"No. Why?" she asked, holding out a hand to him.

"So she can join us," he said, as if they'd obviously invite a robot to dinner.

"She doesn't eat. We'd just be interrupting her computations."

"It's important that we treat her like part of the family, Alainn." He didn't quite make eye contact with her as he said it. He ducked out.

"He's right. The only way Rose will ever act like a human is if we treat her like one," her father said as he took a seat at the kitchen table.

The table shone out with a new coat of paint—a bright bluebell blue. The color matched its former glory again; Alainn had even matched paint chips at the hardware store.

"So when are you leaving for the resort, sweetheart?" her father asked as she laid out place settings.

"Next week, probably." She swallowed and turned back to their fridge to start the salad.

"Late this year. Don't you guys open on Thanksgiving?"

"Greg said it was fine to come a couple weeks late. Sandy is back, so they've got a lot of people on ski patrol this year," she mumbled as she chopped onions.

"Is he still planning to come down and pick you up?" A smile laced his voice as he said it.

"Yeah, Dad. Greg's a nice guy."

"No one is *that* nice," her brother said as he entered the kitchen. "Driving six hours twice a year to come pick you up—every year for *five* years."

"Shut up, Colby. Greg's a good guy. We're friends."

"I wouldn't be surprised if he has feelings for you, Alainn." Her father nodded sagely, even though he had no clue what he was talking about.

"Well, he doesn't."

"Why wouldn't he? You're beautiful, smart, funny—"

"Single," Colby said. He took one of the plates and set it in front of himself.

Obviously, Colby had taught Rose to eavesdrop as well, because as she entered the kitchen, she said, "It's very likely that Greg either has had sexual relations with Alainn or wishes to."

Heat rushed up into her cheeks. "Well, you're wrong. Um—so, how is your guys' space stuff going?"

Thankfully, this was the right question to ask, because Colby and Rose dove into some really complicated explanation that Alainn couldn't even begin to understand. Her father's eyes lit up with interest, and the group went back and forth in an easy flow of conversation, needing no more input from Alainn.

She was thankful for that. She needed all her concentration to stop her emotions and fake-smile at the appropriate conversation cues. All too soon, her brother excused himself to return to his work and Rose followed.

Her father paused as he walked past while Alainn was clearing the dishes. His hand came up and hesitantly patted her on the shoulder. "Would you like some help cleaning up?"

"Not from you, Dad. Go relax."

"Sweetheart, I'll find a way to get the money so Rose can make the Rosette model. Meaning by the time you're home for spring I'll be home, too, okay?"

She closed her eyes. "Okay, Dad."

"And give Greg a chance. You can't let a couple of rotten apples make you lonely for your whole life."

"Dad, it's not—Greg doesn't even like me like that."

"He's probably just too intimidated by how beautiful you are to say anything. I know I was with your mother. She had to come to talk to *me*—I would never have had the courage."

She blew out a laugh. "It's really, really not like that. We're just friends."

"Okay, honey. Sometimes I worry—I just want you to be happy."

"I'm fine." She destroyed the words that fought to get out, managing, "I'll be fine soon. We're supposed to get a lot of snow this year. It'll be a busy season, lots of people needing help. Being busy always makes the time go faster."

"Okay, good." He patted her shoulder once more.

She memorized every detail of his gentle expression as he attempted to comfort her.

How quickly would she forget his look of innocence after what was going to happen to him tomorrow?

She had long ago forgotten what innocence looked like on her own face.

Putting away the leftovers used all her energy, so she didn't tackle the sink full of dishes or the dirty pans covering the stovetop. She crossed the house to her room, locking herself in.

The lock had recently been changed—and for no real reason. Arriving home from her most recent summer Outreach trip, she'd not been able to sleep without changing it.

She attempted to watch an old DVD on her equally old television set, but it didn't work. Even diving into one of her favorite books didn't help to distract her from her own thoughts.

Exhaustion and restlessness battled in her mind while her body simultaneously felt too hot and utterly cold.

She cranked open her window, gasping in the fresh air. As the evening breeze brushed over her face, Alainn wished the same thing she'd held in her mind over every birthday cake or looking into the dissipating tail of each shooting star.

She wished that every casino in the country would burn to the ground.

The people would be evacuated, of course, but the slot machines would melt, the poker tables flare hot then singe black. Puddles of multicolored plastic would pool over the blackened husks of poker tables.

Only then would she ever be happy.

4

December 2, 2026

Alainn woke knowing someone was in her room.

Whoever it was sat behind her. Quiet, even breaths rasped through the air. Alainn's eyelids peeked open. Moonlight cast a grayish glow, cutting deep shadows into the space around her bed.

"Good morning, Alainn," Rose said in a quiet voice. When Alainn didn't respond, Rose said, "I can tell from the change in your breathing pattern that you are awake."

"Rose?" she whispered, not quite ready to let out a sigh of relief. Alainn twisted to look at her. "What are you doing here? Did you break my lock?"

"I picked it," she said. "It is now locked again."

"Oh, uh—" Her heart pounded in her chest; she sat up and faced the robot. "Why—why would you do that?"

The moonlight lit half of Rose's face as she watched Alainn, expressionless. "Do not be alarmed. You are obviously having a fear reaction, but I was simply waiting for you to wake up."

"Don't you need to sleep—recharge?"

Now that Alainn faced Rose, she smelled the faint odor of her exhaust. Rose continuously exhaled the lightest tang of something sweet and acidic. The air in the room felt used, like a plane cabin after a cross-country flight.

"I was not completely forthcoming with you today. While what I said was true, I have for a time now believed that having Father imprisoned would impede my potential. While I have far surpassed his skills in software, there are times when I need assistance. I am limited by my need to stay near my charging station. Your brother is often absent for days at a time—and you, months."

"Okay, wait—you're going to go tomorrow?" Alainn scooted forward on the bed. A dormant hope resurged through her. Alainn would do anything—she'd worship at the robot's feet if Rose agreed to go.

"No, *you* are going to go tomorrow."

Alainn froze, staring at Rose. "What?" she whispered.

"I have calculated one way in which all parties can achieve their desires."

"I'm sorry—I'm not understanding." Alainn shook her head. A hard knot formed in her stomach.

"I am not surprised." Rose reached out to pat Alainn's hand. "You are not as intelligent as the rest of your family."

"Spell it out in really simple terms, then." She just managed to not growl the words at Rose.

Slowly, Rose looked up to the ceiling, moonlight slashing up the curve of her neck, her chin, and the line of her nose. "Earlier tonight, I arranged for you to be picked up by Mr. Garbhan through e-mail, writing as if I was Father. In one hour, a car will arrive outside to take you to his building. I have designed and created hardware for your body. If you are scanned, a chip in the hardware will communicate to the scanners that you have an organic circuitry system rather than a human brain."

Alainn shook her head, hoping to dislodge some of the grogginess there. "I'm still not following— you're saying you want *me* to pretend to be *you* and turn myself over? That you already arranged it?"

"Yes, you are following. That is exactly what I am saying."

"I—I—" Alainn shook her head again. The air thinned around her.

"I have a working plan for the transplanting. You can assimilate easily into a life of servitude as you are already accustomed to the labor you will be asked to perform." Rose lifted a hand, ghostly gray in the low light, and ticked off the chores on her fingers. "Cooking, housekeeping, and bookkeeping. Unless . . . is your concern that he might use you for sexual gratification?"

"What? No."

"I believe that this would be a particular concern of yours."

"I never even considered that he would do that to you—I, of all people, would never have tried to push you into going if I thought you'd be used that way." Alainn blinked furiously. "Rose, do you really think that I would have let myself be the model when my dad printed your face and body if I thought Mr. Garbhan was going to do that to you?"

"It is highly unlikely that I was designed for this function. I have also been assured that there were documents signed to that effect addressed to Father."

Alainn held out her palms to Rose. "Rose, it's not just that. I can't take your place. There's no way that would work . . . and I can't live in that tower for the rest of my life. I'm a human. I know that probably sounds callous to you, but you were created to not *need* sunshine and fresh air. And you don't need exercise. Humans need those things, me especially. Everything I am," she touched her chest, "is centered on being in the outdoors."

"The duration will be seven to fourteen days, no longer." Her head swung down, causing shadows to swallow her eyes. Two black hollows focused on Alainn. "When Mr. Garbhan pays Father, he and I will make the Rosette model; this process should only take a week, unless there are complications. And then I will devise a way to switch you with the new model."

"No—there's no possible way that Mr. Garbhan will believe I'm a robot for two weeks—after five minutes with both you and me, no one would mistake one of us for the other."

She shrugged. "He does not know how an AI robot behaves."

"He knows. He approved all of your plans; he knows exactly how you function. And we sent all those videos of you."

"He knows what I look like." One of her fingers pointed. "I look like *you*. He knows what I sound like, again, like *you*. He does *not* know what I am capable of, or anything about my behavior or speech patterns. This is the only solution I have been able to devise that would get Father and me out of imprisonment. Also, it is the only method that would give me the capability and resources to create the Rosette model."

Alainn gazed off to where a breeze rustled the leaves beyond her window. "If you've been devising this plan for a while now, why would you wait until tonight to tell me?"

"You are emotional and rash. You would have told Father—to alleviate his stress and your own. I also calculated it as a low probability that Father would let you turn yourself in instead of him."

A chill traveled through Alainn's veins. "Have you calculated the probability that I would say yes?"

"Ninety-six percent, if you trust that I will make your replacement."

"What percentage if I don't?" she whispered.

"Eighty-four percent."

"That's . . . still pretty high."

"Be assured that I intend to make a replacement for you and do all in my power to replace you as promptly as possible."

"Why?" Alainn glared. "Why would you get me out?"

Rose leaned into the light, making her inhuman eyes shine with an opaque white. "Because the longer you are in captivity, the greater the chance that the deception will be discovered. If you are discovered, likely *both* you and Father will go to prison. This would not be in the best interest of my work."

"I see." Alainn looked away, into the darkness of her room. "I'm going to need a few minutes . . . I need to think."

"We do not have time for you to think. You must prepare to look like me, and we must meet the car in thirty-seven minutes. I have brought the materials for your transformation."

"Give me a minute." She stood and crossed to her open window. The screen swung on its hinge, something she had installed for this very purpose. Her bare feet stepped from her sturdy wooden end table through the window to a rough, splinter-covered bench seat. Turning, she faced Rose, who had not moved or shifted, but gray had crept in around her now the early morning light had started to shine. She thought better of what she was going to say and turned back to the small, terraced yard that stepped down the hillside.

The air out there wasn't fresh; it wasn't like the first inhale of the morning on her mountaintop. But it was free air, air that came and went as it pleased. She didn't know much about Mr. Garbhan, but she knew that he'd intended Rose to live and work in his tower. If Alainn went, there was a very real possibility that this would be the last free air she would breathe for weeks—until Rose helped her escape. *If* Rose helped her escape.

Avoiding the rotted wooden boards on her mother's old garden bench, she sat. Chipped paint clung to the wood—small traces of her mother's careful work. At the top of the bench was an almost-intact rose, pink outlined in black.

Their house sat upon a hill that gazed across the length of the Bay Area. In the distance, the first rays of morning broke over the mountains. The sun managed her climb over the peaks, spreading a soft glow onto the sleek bridge stretching over the water.

A hillside of houses sloped down below, blanketing out into a multicolored quilt of rooftops. Far off, the long, lean silhouettes of city towers clustered along the shore.

To the east, above it all, waited her mountains. The forests looked down on her, waiting for her decision.

As if weighing in on that decision, the roses beside her rustled, grabbing her attention. Alainn could almost imagine her mother here, smiling from the bench, roses blooming to their fullest as if to impress her mother's appreciative gaze.

What would she give to have her mother back?

Anything, absolutely anything.

The thought comforted her. With her mother, no robot had snuck into her room at night and said, "Your mother is going to die, but if you spend two weeks trapped in captivity, she'll survive until she's so old you have to carry her to her gardens." She didn't know what she would have chosen at ten years old, but today she'd knew she'd be buried alive to save her mother.

Alainn stood carefully so she would not jostle the fragile boards underneath her.

As if the mountains wanted Alainn to change her mind the moment she turned away, the sun lit their length. Their peaks shone out in a world overcast by shadow.

She turned to see Rose standing at the window, watching her. Alain looked into Rose's face—her own face. Alainn knew three things: she didn't trust Rose to get her out, she would go anyway, and she was probably making a huge mistake.

5

December 2, 2026

The self-driving car made another turn. Alainn gripped the leather seat at her sides. She attempted to keep her expression as placid as possible—Rose was so unflappable.

At least she looked the part. Rose had taken to the task of transforming her with quick efficiency. She'd brought a sort of kit containing a change of clothes, hair devices, and several plastic cases. After she'd smoothed Alainn's hair, Rose pulled out the first clear case.

Rose snapped open the lid, revealing a round disc about the size of a thumbprint. "Open your mouth."

After a pause, Alainn had.

Stepping forward with the disc balanced on her thumb, Rose hooked her finger into Alainn's mouth and pressed the disc to the roof.

Pulsing pain shot through Alainn. Her mind went blank and her sight darkened. She screamed, but a fist wedged into her mouth, muffling the sound. Seconds passed with only pain and nothing else, until the searing lessened bit by bit.

"That one should be the most discomforting," Rose said as she pulled her fist out of Alainn's mouth.

Alainn had barely made it through the rest without killing Rose—or decommissioning her, as it was. Two other chips pushed so far into her ear canals that she swore they would rupture her eardrums. The last chip pierced the inside of her nostril. Rose had lied; the nostril chip hurt the most. Yet soon enough, it was over. Rose held up another kit Alainn was supposed to bring with her.

"This," Rose said as she held up a tube, "was supposed to contain the clear plastic coating that I use once daily to protect my teeth. It instead has a flavorless toothpaste—but you should only use it once daily."

"Why?"

Rose ignored her question. She held up another tube. "This is T9640. It's an acidic compound that I ingest to clean out any buildup if my cooling system is malfunctioning. Do not drink it—it will kill you. I only included it because they might test what you bring in." Setting the tube back into the small bag, she extracted another disc-shaped object.

Alainn shifted back involuntarily.

"This is not for your body," she said, holding it up.

"Oh, yeah. Okay . . . ," Alainn whispered, though she didn't move forward.

"It is a hardware diagnostic tool I use to ensure that all systems are working properly, but I have modified it. This is an essential tool in the plan for your replacement by the Rosette model. Keep it on your person if you possibly can." Rose held up the small bag, setting the disc inside.

"How will it help me get out?"

Rose cocked her head. "It's too complicated for you to understand, and you only have three minutes until your transportation arrives."

Rose did not escort Alainn out; she had walked away without a good-bye as if there was no doubt in her mind Alainn would follow through with the charade. The driverless car waited outside, door open.

She'd hesitated before climbing inside.

"Please enter the car, Rose 76GF," said a mechanical, disembodied voice.

The car had weaved between lanes as the number of morning commuters multiplied on the expressway. Almost every car drove northbound, toward the gleaming towers that blocked sight of all else. A robot transport passed her in the fast lane. Identical robots in city worker uniforms sat in the glass pod bus, lined up in rows of unnatural uniformity.

She broke her gaze away from the pod car as her own car took the off ramp into the city. Robots were everywhere—sweeping the streets, opening the shops—their too-practiced mechanical movements distinguishing them. Alainn knew that after eight years of automatons slowly integrating into society she should be used to the sight. She wasn't.

This time, the black tower snuck up on Alainn—her focus had been trained on a robot walking with a group of kids in uniform. The car bumped up into that same private alley Alainn had raced out of less than twenty-four hours before. Two tire skid marks lined the road. Alainn fought a smile at the sight.

It served Mr. Garbhan right.

As the car turned toward the underground ramp, the steel door rose.

Alainn hoped that if scanners inspected her at that moment, they wouldn't detect the acid tsunami in her stomach, or the galloping hooves in her chest. Alainn wasn't much of an actress, nor was she good at hiding what she felt.

In this situation, Rose would probably look on placidly. She'd examine her surroundings in a clinical way, interested but not invested. If Alainn was managing to give that impression to whatever she assumed was examining her right now, she would have surprised herself. The moment the car passed under the gate, the outside light faded away. Looking over her shoulder, Alainn found the gate closing her in.

The parking garage gleamed. Dozens of metallic, smooth-lined cars lined up against one wall. The car stopped halfway down the line.

"Please exit the car, Rose 76GF," the robotic voice told Alainn.

The car door glided open.

Grabbing her small kit, she followed the car's instruction and climbed out of the car.

"Please step back," the voice said.

"Oh," she said, stepping out of the way.

The car shut its own door and then parked itself by sliding into a space between two similar cars.

A familiar, smooth female voice said, "Welcome, Rose 76GF. Please exit the garage through the door on your far left."

Without meaning to, Alainn shifted toward the car she'd just climbed out of. It had almost completely blended into its surroundings. For some reason, she wanted to stay with it. Forcing herself to step away, Alainn strode as evenly as she could manage through a gleaming line of metallic bubbles. The walls themselves illuminated the room; soft white luminescence shone from walls, floor, and ceiling in uninterrupted sheets of glass. The entire space could have been made from the same material as the screen from just outside the garage.

The hallway loomed on Alainn's left, tall and rectangular. As if seamless, the glass continued smoothly in. The hallway stretched a short way before coming to an abrupt end.

A soft ding sounded. To one side, a rectangle of the seemingly uninterrupted surface shifted inward and then slid away. Inside was a small room made entirely of the same white screens.

"Please step inside."

The last thing Alainn wanted to do was step into that little box. Her pulse beat against the side of her neck as if pleading, "Go back, go back." What her pulse didn't realize was that she was already trapped.

The moment she stepped into the room, the glass slid back into place, sealing her in.

"You are now being scanned. Please hold still."

The ever-present ache in Alainn's ears, nose, and the roof of her mouth gave her a strange sort of comfort. She waited for the verdict, listening only to the rasp of her breath in the softly lit cell.

The room did not speak for almost a minute.

Alainn kept her hands to her sides, though she could not keep them from shaking. Her eyelids slipped closed. She needed them closed. She imagined herself looking over the wide expanse of the view she could see from the top of her mountain. The forest stretched out for miles, boughs heavy with snow in every direction. And she was alone. Dark hair blew in every direction as the wind embraced her.

"You are functioning properly; however, you have contaminants on your skin and clothing. Please remove your clothing."

"Excuse me . . . did you just say to take off my clothing?" Alainn glanced around the elevator.

Two small compartments scrolled open. They looked like white, glass dresser drawers shifting out of the wall.

"Please place your possessions in the compartment on your left, and your clothing in the compartment on your right. Immediately."

Alainn hesitated before putting her small bag in the left compartment. Her hand barely cleared it before it snapped closed.

"Please remove your clothing, Rose 76GF."

Rose wouldn't have hesitated; Alainn knew she was already taking way too long. Until Rose had introduced the idea to her, Alainn truly had never even considered that Rose could have been intended as some sort of sex robot.

Holy hell.

She hoped that Rose hadn't been commissioned for this purpose.

Fighting the hot feeling that ringed her eyes, Alainn unbuttoned her shirt. The small plastic buttons eluded her clumsy fingers as she moved down, unhooking one after the other. When she reached the last button, the garment slipped off her shoulders. Gently, she set the shirt in the second bin before retuning her hands to her skirt. Her skirt came off easily—too easily—and she put it into the bin, too.

"Please remove your undergarments."

Blinking rapidly to force back the tears that would instantly give her away, Alainn reached back and unhooked her bra, setting it into the bin. After the bra, she slipped off her underwear. She set it and her shoes into the bin.

The bin closed.

Her breathing refused to slow as she stood in the small room, completely naked. Closing her eyes, she tried to return to her mental mountain, but all she found behind her eyelids was the low, white light.

"You will now be decontaminated," the voice said.

Powder hit Alainn from all sides. She gasped, gaining a mouthful of something that tasted a lot like baking soda and soap. A warm spray of water shot at her from above, before shifting over her body, spraying down her back and front. The spray softened as it moved over her face, then ceased.

"Please raise your arms."

When Alainn lifted her arms, the spray did one final pass over her body. Warm air replaced the water, blowing over cleansed skin and down the length of her body. In moments, she was dry.

The second drawer snapped open.

Glancing in, Alainn found her same piles of clothing, neatly folded.

"Please dress yourself."

Alainn didn't need any prompting.

The clothing felt warm against her skin, as if it had just come out of the dryer. As she stepped back into her shoes, the white room began gliding upward. Her every pore tingled, yet not in an uncomfortable way. It felt like she had bathed in a vat of champagne.

After a few long seconds of ascending, the door slid open to reveal yet another featureless, white-screen hallway.

"Please enter the area and take a seat."

The hallway abruptly ended in a great room. It, too, had screens for walls and floors, and Alainn almost could not find anything to sit on—until she realized the long, stretching couches were the same gleaming white as the walls.

As she sat, the voice said, "Please wait here."

Alainn waited. And she waited. She waited until her breathing became even and her heart slowed to a familiar rhythm. All too soon, she became bored.

The room had absolutely nothing to look at. The only color in the space was her own clothing, and looking at her own lap wasn't very interesting. The furniture that spread out before her had absolutely nothing on it—it was all just white, open space.

And then, suddenly, a table turned to wood. It became beautiful, hand-crafted mahogany with long strips of lighter inlaid wood.

The floor under it transformed as well, into long gleaming lines of mahogany. She looked up and through windows that looked out over the city.

She resisted the urge to walk to the windows, though from here she could see the familiar towers jutting into the air. The bay lounged behind it all, white sails playing across its waters.

The sun was perched fully in the sky now, though somehow it felt more distant than at sunrise. The tapping of feet yanked her attention away. A man entered the room, though he did not enter *exactly*. He halted in the doorway—a doorway devoid of that white light. He remained mostly in shadow.

Alainn squinted at him, trying to see past the shadows, but she couldn't. He stayed where he was, quiet. She felt his gaze on her.

Her body begged to fidget, but she forced it not to. What would Rose do in this situation?

Rose would probably go back to her computations. Unfortunately, that wouldn't work here either.

"You are very humanlike." His voice was immediately recognizable as the same one Alainn had spoken to the day before.

Because the man she assumed must be Mr. Garbhan seemed like he might be waiting for a response, Alainn asked, "Isn't that what you wanted?"

"Yes." His voice came out low. Still, he didn't move forward.

This was getting awkward.

Well, it started out awkward and it was already becoming more so.

Alainn had no idea if she was supposed to say or do anything, so she just continued to sit and look at his shadowy figure.

Eventually, Alainn couldn't do it anymore and she turned her head back to the windows. Mist slipped by, streaming around the tower.

Alainn glanced back to the man. "May I stand?" she asked. Her legs were tingling with the need to move.

"Do whatever you'd like," he said.

Alainn's eyebrows rose; she couldn't help it.

His words sounded almost courteous, which was the last thing that she'd thought would happen.

To hide her surprise, Alainn stood and crossed over to the window.

The thin white blanket of sea air continued to pass over the window, obscuring the view of the bay.

"Do you . . . can you appreciate a view like this?" he asked from behind.

Alainn hesitated. "I do appreciate it. It's pleasing."

The man did not respond or come any closer.

Somehow, with her back to him and the view to her front, Alainn had the confidence to ask, "What functions do you want me to do here? I can cook, clean, help with business—"

"No," he said.

She looked back to his shadow, trying to hide the alarm from her expression. She needed to see if there was anything in him she could read.

There wasn't.

"No. I don't want you to do any of that," he reiterated.

"What is it that you *do* want me to do?" Saliva filled her mouth as she waited for his response.

"You will have dinner with me."

"Dinner?" Alainn wasn't able to hide all the surprise from her voice. Rose couldn't eat food. This was a detail that Rose and Alainn hadn't addressed in her mad rush to push Alainn into this. Rose didn't eat *or* go to the bathroom. She recharged her biological system on a wireless charging station built into her bed.

How was Alainn supposed to explain when he heard the toilet flushing?

For the first time, Alainn heard the tone of the cold, unyielding man she'd spoken to yesterday. "You will come to the dining room every day at six exactly. If I am not in there, you will wait for me until I am. If I do not come, you will leave the dining room at seven."

"Yes, sir."

"You will not call me sir. You will call me Lorccan, or Lor."

"Yes, Lorccan."

"And you will never come out of your room at night. Ever." This he almost yelled.

"Yes, Lorccan," she repeated.

His breathing came hard from the shadows, inflating the room with an electric tension. When the room had entirely filled with it, he said, "That is all. I cannot spend any more time with you today. The first dinner will be tomorrow." He stepped entirely out of view, moving his imposing presence away with him.

Taking a steadying breath, Alainn called after him, "What should I do with the rest of my time?"

"I don't care. Just stay off the floors above this one before dinner time." His footsteps echoed as his figure retreated, then quieted to nothing.

6

December 2, 2026

Alainn walked along the glass wall, looking down to the street about two hundred feet below. The clarity of the windows at this height was almost disconcerting, but she had always enjoyed a good cliff—especially when she had a rope tied to her.

She didn't have a rope, and the windows didn't have openings.

It might've been a good thing.

If she had them, she'd be rappelling down right about now.

She didn't know where she was going—except away from Mr. Garbhan. The hallway's wooden floors led out in long lines, framing the floor-to-ceiling windows.

The moment Mr. Garbhan had left her, he had taken a huge weight with him. While sitting at a table for an hour every day and *not* eating did sound rather annoying, worse ideas had flooded her brain in the few hours she'd spent ruminating on the worst possibilities.

"Sex robot" was definitely perched at the top of that list. Thankfully, that looked unlikely. Unfortunately, housekeeper robot—an occupation that might have come in handy so she could sneak food—seemed to be out as well.

"Your room is this way, Rose 76GF," the voice said from up ahead. Another elevator door opened as she approached.

Alainn paused. "Could I take the stairs—are there any stairs?"

The voice spoke directly beside her, saying, "This way."

Farther down, another section of the wall slid away to reveal a staircase. Inlaid mahogany continued down the staircase and up the walls, ending in another floor-to-ceiling window at the landing.

When she touched the wood, a smooth surface met her fingers. "Is this an illusion?"

The voice made no reply.

Alainn looked up. "Are you still there?"

"I am always here, Rose 76GF."

Alainn nodded, hiding the shiver that traveled through her. Turning back to the staircase, she descended carefully.

"Exit the staircase," the voice told her.

The staircase emptied out into another large room. They were still probably more than twenty floors up, she and the voice. The room was cavernous—it seemed to Alainn to be some sort of entertaining room with a large television and a pool table. A gleaming bar stood to one side.

Could she be some sort of novelty item at parties?

"Look at the robot chick!"

Was she a living, breathing toy Mr. Garbhan could show off to his buddies?

The idea wasn't as insidious as some she'd considered, but she hoped that if Mr. Garbhan planned any big parties, it would be well after she was gone.

"Your room is this way," the voice said, leading her from the great room into a hallway with only one door.

It had only one door because the bedroom it led to was as big as the great room beside it. The same wood-patterned floors crisscrossed the length of the room, ending at two walls of windows. A four-poster bed big enough to fit ten of her swallowed nearly a quarter of the space. Another room was off to one side. When she entered it, unease filled her again. The entire room was a closet bustling with every color of dress. The tags cried out names of designers that even her wealthy high-school friends had only dreamed about.

The whole situation terrified her. What was she, some life-size doll for his strange, fancy dollhouse? What was she here to play, wife or daughter? A domestic-labor robot made sense to her, but this?

This didn't make any sense.

Turning to step out of the creepy closet, she found another door that led to yet another room. This room was—thank goodness—a bathroom. To her delight, it held an actual working toilet.

That was by far the best news she had all day.

The thought that maybe the closet, room, and bathroom had been designed for someone else comforted her.

She could simply be inheriting it.

Having the disembodied voice with Alainn while she used said bathroom might be a problem, however. A problem, unfortunately, for right now.

Her bladder was at that moment jumping up to remind her that she was very much a human.

"Your capacitive charging station is built into your bed," said the voice.

"Okay, thanks . . . Um, could I be alone?" Alainn cringed a little as she said the words. Rose had never once asked to be alone or for privacy. They'd had to teach Rose to seek it—and to remind her to continue to change in private.

"Of course," said the voice.

After a second of silence, Alainn asked, "Are you still there?"

Nothing.

"If you can hear me, please say something."

The voice said nothing.

Alainn waited for a full minute fighting the need to go pee, but when no response came, she went quickly and then hurried out of the bathroom. Slowly, she meandered through the room, finding a makeup vanity stocked with every possible beauty product, all

European name brands. There was almost nothing else in her room but clothes and beauty products. She added one point on the "creepy" side of the tally.

After she had thoroughly explored her room, she sat cross-legged next to the window. Mr. Garbhan hadn't prohibited her from leaving the room or wandering through the rest of the lower floors, but she had a feeling the voice would be there if she left. So right there, right then, Alainn pretended she truly was alone.

What would her father's reaction be upon finding her gone? She hoped Rose would explain the situation to him in a sensitive way.

Alainn knew, though, that whatever sensitivity programming they had written into Rose had been long since overwritten.

Colby would probably blame their father for Alainn taking his place. Or maybe Colby wouldn't even notice—as long as he got to keep Rose's calculations.

Rose might have chosen this life, if she'd known what it really had meant. She would have been able to spend all day doing her computations, only engaged for an hour a day.

Alainn sat up straight.

With this new information, it was possible that Rose would be willing to switch back. Mr. Garbhan had resources Rose could only dream of, and she probably wouldn't care about creepy robot wife-or-daughter play.

Alainn didn't know how to contact Rose to ask her, though. It would be risky to try. But if she saw the opportunity, she'd definitely make the offer.

She sat in the corner where the two windows met, at the edge of the world, until the building's shadows all pointed in long lines toward the bay.

"I have returned, Rose 76GF, to tell you that Mr. Garbhan has changed his mind about having you at dinner. Please dress and make your way to the dining room immediately."

"What?" Her voice came out a little shrill as Alainn turned to the source of the disembodied voice.

"You should dress formally, wear your hair up, and put makeup on your face."

All right, ten more points on the "creepy" tally.

Another ten points were tallied in when Alainn realized that all the dresses were exactly her size.

Most were—*Thank all that was holy!*—rather conservative. She chose one of the most conservative among them.

At the vanity, however, she was completely stumped. Freaked-out factor aside, she had been good in the closet. The closet was something she could handle. Doing her hair and makeup was completely something else. Her friends had nicknamed Alainn "the hippie" in high school, and since her idea of a good time was scaling a mountain, up-dos, fancy-dos—whatever they were called—weren't even close to her specialty. Makeup was something she only put on when forced. For about six months a year, even hot water was a luxury.

There were probably a hundred bottles. Bottles of colorful powders and creams that only someone with an MA in makeup artistry would be able to understand.

"Please proceed with preparing your appearance and make your way to the dining room. Mr. Garbhan is waiting for you."

Crap on a stick.

Alainn had no clue what to do.

Among the beauty paraphernalia, she saw one tool she knew how to use: a hair stick. Twisting her dark hair back, she stabbed through it, trying to pin the mass to her head. As the only two pieces of makeup she ever wore were lipstick and mascara, that's what she put on.

She stood.

"Please hurry. Mr. Garbhan requests your company immediately. He is growing very impatient and wishes you to make haste to the dining room."

The words made Alainn want to do anything but that.

Seriously?

He just changed his mind and decided that he wanted his robot-doll to get all dressed up and eat with him ten minutes ago. Freaky didn't even begin to explain this.

Quieting the voice in her head that told her to run the hell away while she still could, Alainn walked out of the room. The voice was wrong anyway. If she wanted to keep her dad out of prison, there was no possible way Alainn could run away. According to Rose, if Mr. Garbhan caught Alainn, she'd probably end up in prison as well. Objectively, it would look a lot like Alainn was faking being a robot so her father could squeeze another $1.5 million out of Mr. Garbhan. At least, that would be how the court of law would look at it.

Alainn rushed to follow the voice, which was leading her back the way they came earlier.

"Please run."

For a soothing disembodied voice, she sure managed to convey impatience.

The route Alainn took hadn't changed its gleaming wood design. After the voice urged her up the stairway and Alainn headed toward the landing, the voice corrected, "Please ascend one more flight of stairs."

Alainn did, as quickly as she could in the little heels that had been provided for her. The door to the next floor had already slid open. When she rushed out, Alainn immediately found herself in the dining room.

Blinking in the low light, she considered that it might be the wrong dining room. One half of the room was completely dark, making it impossible for her to see. On the other half of the table, a candle sat beside a plate of food. The candle flickered gently in its holder, though no breeze moved through the room that she could tell.

"Please sit. I have been waiting for you, and I'm hungry." His voice came out of the darkness. Perhaps he had that disorder that made him cranky when he was hungry.

Alainn lifted the sides of her purple satin dress and sat in a large, white throne-chair at the head of the long table. She could see just two feet up the table before the darkness transformed everything into the faintest of outlines. Perhaps ten feet into the darkness, at the end, a man sat cloaked in shadows.

Averting her gaze, Alainn looked down to her plate. She hadn't eaten today, not once. Yet, for some reason, perhaps the stress, she hadn't noticed her hunger.

She noticed it now.

Chicken glazed with some sort of sweet sauce wafted its aromas up at her. The chicken breast squished a pile of potatoes soaking in the juices.

"Eat," the man said.

Alainn glanced across into the darkness.

Eat?

Was this some sort of trick?

She forced her breathing to even out.

Did he know already? Did the voice hear the toilet flush and report it to him?

"I cannot digest food," Alainn told him.

"I was assured that you could eat. That you could ingest it, then clean it out of your system by bringing the food back up." He sounded almost angry as he said it.

Suddenly, the working toilet in her room made a whole lot more sense.

Maybe this was true. Alainn had never seen Rose eat, though.

Mr. Garbhan wanting his robot to eat and then throw up the food was beyond weird. However, Alainn was smart enough to catch this big, fat, juicy bone if he was throwing it at her.

She nodded. "That is correct."

"Then eat," he said.

Alainn lifted the fork and knife, cutting into the chicken. The tender meat burst flavors into her mouth as soon as she bit it—sweet chili, cumin, even a trace of cinnamon.

"You like chicken?" he asked.

Could Rose actually taste things? She had no idea. Alainn hesitated in answering, not wanting him to think she didn't like to eat or that she appreciated something she shouldn't be able to taste.

The best Alainn could come up with was, "I like eating. It is very interesting to me."

"Don't come to dinner late again," he said.

"I wouldn't have come late if you hadn't told me that it was cancelled." The moment the words were out, Alainn wanted to drag them back in.

Stupid mouth.

Why couldn't she control her own words?

True, it was a jerk move to blame a robot when it was so obviously his fault, but a robot wouldn't have cared.

Alainn waited for his response, but he remained silent.

Slowly, Alainn turned back to her chicken. Mr. Garbhan said nothing as Alainn stripped the chicken from the bone then moved the bones to get at the potatoes underneath.

For some reason, the candle caught her attention again. Alainn held a hand just a little toward it. "That's not real?" she asked.

"No," came his voice, almost startling her, as in the darkness, he could have vanished without her realizing it.

Alainn peered down the table. "It's very good. I wouldn't have known, except there's no heat." She reached forward to touch the candle holder, seeing that the flame moved with the breeze from her hand.

"Did you burn yourself before?" he asked.

Alainn's gaze fell to her arm. Clearly lit by candlelight, a faint pink, oval burn showed on her arm. It took Alainn a moment to even remember what it was from.

Meatloaf, oven, cold water in the sink.

"Does your body burn?" he asked.

Alainn raised her wrist, shifting the burn toward him. "I tested the blush on my arm, but I was heavy-handed. I don't know much about makeup." Setting her wrist back down on the tabletop, Alainn held her breath, waiting for his response.

"You don't need to wear makeup. I don't care. I just had my buyer order everything she said a woman needed for beauty products."

All points on the "creepy" side of the tally board. The verdict was definitely in.

He bought the makeup for Alainn. And judging by the pseudo-date here, she was almost positive that she was his robot wife and not his robot daughter.

Alainn pressed her lips together to keep them from trembling.

"Are you done eating?" he asked.

Her appetite had vanished, but she was not ready to move on to any other possible wifely duty he had planned for her. Alainn would sacrifice a lot to keep her father out of prison, but not *that*. She could not let things go that far.

"I could still eat," she said, forking a big glob of potatoes into her mouth. It stuck like paste, coating the inside of her throat as she tried to swallow.

"You don't need to."

Slowly, Alainn set down her fork.

They sat there in a locked silence. She squinted, trying to see into the dark. Alainn's vision had somewhat adjusted to the low light, but Mr. Garbhan was little more than a darker shadow within a shadow.

"You can go to your room," he said in a low voice.

Alainn nodded. "Okay."

"Go straight there. Once you are inside, you will be locked in for the night."

She wanted to sag in relief or whoop for joy, but instead she concentrated on maintaining an even expression. Nodding again, she lifted up her skirt and turned for the door.

"Goodnight, Mr. Garbhan."

"My name is Lorccan. I wish for you to call me Lorccan," he snapped.

She nodded once again. "Of course. Goodnight, Lorccan." As slowly as she could make herself, Alainn walked out of the room.

7

December 4, 2026

Ice cubes clinked in Connor Murphy's glass as he
lifted a tumbler to his lips. A strong, pungent taste of
alcohol hit his tongue, making him splutter.

The robot attendant had given him alcohol in
his soda again. They often did, likely because his voice
was at a lower octave than the clinking, chattering,
jingle-making machines around him. Sighing, he set
the drink aside.

He pulled the lever down on his machine, and
the holograms flashed above their stations. The first
hologram stuck: a floating pair of cherries on their
stems. The second hologram stopped at another pair
of cherries. His heart surged as the last hologram
flashed through various symbols.

The first win of the night.

The last hologram was a bar. His total cash bank decreased a dollar.

Sighing, Connor pulled the lever again.

A cloud of cigarette smoke blew into his face, making Connor turn his head. Unfortunately, this had been the last open slot machine, and slots were all he would allow himself until Alainn escaped. Also, Rose had him on a strict budget to make sure he did not cut into the money needed to build Rosette 82GF. The major expenses had already been paid for on the day of the payment's arrival. To Connor's shock and relief, Rose had arranged everything in advance. Rosette's body would soon be printed by a new, better company than he had used for Rose. TechniHealth would be building Rosette with the most advanced medical-tech available—Rose had overseen the plans herself.

He had been right; Rosette's hardware and software were far beyond his capabilities to design or print. Connor had spent two days around the house, impotent to help and fighting stress-induced indigestion. The third day, Rose had practically pushed him out of the house, saying she was "not functioning at full capacity with his hovering."

After simply standing outside of his house for an hour, he'd walked down to the bus stop. Taking Route 509 to the 120, he'd arrived at the casino just as the sun began to set.

He told himself he wasn't going to spend more than three hundred. Four hundred was his absolute maximum.

The slot machine's holograms flashed. The first hologram stuck on bar, the second on sevens. Connor began to turn away, hoping to flag another robot when his machine went dark.

The clanking, clattering among a myriad of jingles suddenly fell silent—and was quickly replaced by a loud, angry outcry.

"What the hell!" shouted the elderly, smoking woman beside him. Her plethora of rings made a loud clack as her hand smacked her slot machine. "I still had forty dollars in there!"

"Oh . . . uh, that's awful." Connor still had 215 dollars in his now-dead machine.

"Well, damn it! I'm demanding a refund!" She swiveled before stumbling out of her chair, leaving her cigarette smoldering in an ashtray.

As the crowd of irate casino customers headed deeper into the casino, Connor headed out. Just outside the doors, his son Colby waited for him. Under one arm, Colby held a briefcase.

They fell into step, saying nothing as they walked toward the bus stop.

After taking their seats inside the next bus, as the hum of the engine echoed around them, Connor turned to his son. "I had nowhere else to go."

"Go to the movies," Colby said.

Connor stared at his rough, dry hands. "I don't think your sister would be very happy if she got out next week and you were in prison instead of me."

Turning forward, Colby pushed his glasses up his nose. "Then don't go back until the Rosette is finished. You remember how this goes, Dad. I'll shut them down every time."

Connor sighed. "Yes, I remember."

And that was the problem. All he wanted was to forget.

8

December 5, 2026

The pounding in Alainn's head made it hard to concentrate as she gazed down at the disc resting on her hand. The small blue circle shone in the evening light. Alainn had no idea how it would help get her out of there. To be fair, she knew very little about robotics or microchips—or whatever category the disc fell into.

Alainn sat cross-legged on the bed, a peach dress pooling around her legs. As always, she'd chosen a dress with long sleeves. Her burn had not quite healed. For the last three days, she had ensured that she was ready for dinner several hours ahead of time. Three days she'd already been locked in this tower. Three days, and absolutely nothing had changed from that first day.

In most ways, that was a blessing. If Lorccan was planning to make her some sort of sex robot, he wasn't in any rush. She wasn't sure what to make of his reluctance to step out of the shadows.

Each day, the majority of Alainn's time was spent in the bathroom. She drank copious amounts of water from the sink to alleviate her hunger and luxuriated in the privacy. Either the voice didn't spy on her or didn't know that she was acting in a way unusual enough to report to Mr. Garbhan.

Alainn would have given almost anything to be able to send a message to her house. Her father deserved to know she was safe—at least for now.

But of all the devices that Rose had devised for her, one to communicate with her home was not among them.

The whole encounter with Rose had played on repeat through these last four days as Alainn played hermit in her room. The more she thought about it, the less she trusted that Rose was busy devising a method to get her out. And she hadn't trusted it very much to begin with.

If Rose wasn't engineering the escape, what was this disc? Was it just what Rose said, a diagnostic tool that wasn't actually doctored?

For all Alainn knew, it could be a piece of sea glass from their garden. But, like she had every day these past three days, she took the small, smooth disc and slipped it into her bra.

"You should leave right now if you wish to be a few minutes early for dinner," the voice said.

"Thanks," Alainn said as she scooted off the bed.

Instead of heading for the door, though, she walked to the window. If she stood in just the right place, she could almost see the house she lived in. Perhaps if she had more of a vantage point, it would actually come into view.

Every time she'd left her room in the last few days, the voice had been waiting to greet her on the other side. Alainn always reentered her room pretty soon after dinner, but soon itchy feet would overcome her need to be unsupervised.

A few days. Alainn knew that she only needed to keep the act up for a few days—*a week and a half, at most*—and then she and her father would be free. "You will have to leave right now in order not to be late."

Alainn's gaze drifted over to the bay—or where the bay would be, if there wasn't so much fog.

"Please run, Rose 76GF," the voice said.

"I'm going, Voice." She didn't quite run, but went quickly up the now-familiar path.

Pausing in the doorway, she examined the table. "Did you move the candle?"

"You are very close to being late," he said.

She walked to stand beside the candle. It had definitely moved from its position the first day, but now that she thought on it, it might have moved yesterday as well.

"Please take a seat," Mr. Garbhan said from the darkness.

Alainn sat in front of what looked a little like chicken but smelled a heck of a lot better. "Is that chicken?" She leaned in.

"Duck."

"Oh, I've never . . . seen people eat duck," she said, forcing a smile to hide the near slip.

"Eat it," he ordered.

Her jaw clenched as she peered into the darkness. "The Murphys usually say please and thank you to me. I prefer that."

He made no response.

She needed to learn to bite her tongue. If Rose was actually pulling through for her, this would only last between four and eleven more days. But, she was beginning to suspect that her own mouth was determined to blow her cover.

Taking up her fork and knife, she cut the duck.

She couldn't fathom why she had fought him on eating the duck. She hadn't had a bite to eat since dinner the previous night. This one-meal-a-day thing wasn't going to cut it.

Duck, Alainn learned very quickly, was nothing like chicken. In a very good way. It had a deep, almost greasy—but not quite—taste that filled her senses. For a second, she forgot everything and simply focused on separating every morsel of duck from its bone.

"I was almost sure that Connor Murphy had cheated money from me."

Alainn's fork paused halfway to her mouth. When he didn't continue, she ate the bite off the fork before setting the utensil down. "Do you feel cheated?"

He took a long time to answer. "I do not."

Alainn raised her gaze to the darkness, finding the man-shaped outline a little easier to determine in the shadows. Mr. Garbhan's words both made her want to sigh with relief and squirm because he was happy with her as his wife-bot.

If things stayed the same, fine. She would dress up in fancy dresses and eat duck for a couple more days, no problem. But the candle was gradually moving up the length of the table, and she wasn't sure she wanted to know what that meant.

"You have not left your rooms," he said.

So Voice *was* spying on her.

"Not often."

"Do you not need to . . . entertain yourself?"

"I appreciate entertainment," she said, carefully.

"I will give you a tour of the tower," he said the words fast, almost irritably.

Alainn glanced into the deep shadows clustering around him. Was this going to be a tour in the dark?

"You're going to show me around the tower?"

"Yes," he said on a breath. "I will give you a tour at eleven a.m.; leave your room then and do not be late."

Alainn nodded. "If you'd like."

"That is what we'll do . . . Thank you."

She blinked at him. "Thank you." Alainn returned her attention to the bird bones on her plate. She attempted to pull the last little strip of meat off the bone, wanting every succulent bite.

"You don't need to continue eating when the food is gone," he said.

"Oh, okay," she said, putting the fork down. Forcing her gaze away from that little tiny bit of duck, she managed to refocus on his shadow.

"What do you like?" he asked.

"Like?" she asked.

"Prefer, enjoy, seek out when you have time free?" he snapped. "If I am taking you on this tour—there is a lot to show you—I'll have to filter much of it out. What would you prefer to see?"

There was one thing that Alainn would consider giving her left arm to see. "Living things. Plants," she said.

"Is that a joke?"

It was immediately obvious to her that something in what she said was very wrong. Were robots not supposed to like living things?

Perhaps. Rose had never once gone into the garden.

Quickly, Alainn listed off, "I prefer movies, books, art, games . . ." Her brain would not cooperate.

What would a robot enjoy?

"Learning—mostly from books."

"Good. You may go now." A loud scraping sounded before his shadow grew into the shape of a tall, standing man. With a tapping sound on the floor, the shadow moved away until it disappeared into the darkness altogether.

Alainn stood, slowly. "Are you still here?" she asked in a whisper.

There was no response.

Stepping as lightly as she could, Alainn rounded the side of the table. Her fingers dragged over it as she placed one foot toward the empty chair and the darkness beyond. Lifting the other foot, she slowly moved forward, tiptoeing another step into the darkness.

"Please return to your room, Rose 76GF," Voice said.

Alainn jumped, almost falling backward. Breathing in sharply, she looked back to the shadows, but there was no movement within.

"Please return to your room now," the voice said placidly.

Alainn did. As fast as she could without running, she rushed back to her room. The moment the doors closed behind her, the now-familiar click of the lock sounded.

Closing her eyes, she leaned back against the door.

Damn it.

She was amazed she had kept up the deception this long. Three more days might be way too long for her to maintain the ruse, and that was Rose's low end of the estimate. That was, of course, if Rose didn't actually intend for Alainn to rot in here until she was discovered.

Unzipping her dress, Alainn almost ripped the long sleeves off. As always, she stuffed the dress in the open bin in the wall that waited to snap shut. The moment it did, disappearing completely, the wood wall stretched on seamlessly.

She forced herself to sleep, but woke in the middle of the night as hunger pains tore through her.

Crossing into her bathroom, she turned on the water and brought her mouth down for a drink, taking long, deep sips. When her hunger—though not satisfied—lessened, she stood straight.

As she lifted her hand away from the faucet, a strange, faint sound emitted.

Leaning in, she stared at the faucet. The humming sounded again, but it wasn't coming *from* the faucet. It was a long, low sound and very faint— almost too faint to hear.

It stopped.

Alainn stood very still, hands up, trying not to make a single movement. There was silence for almost a minute, and then it came again. Her gaze snapped up to the ceiling.

Climbing onto the wide marble lip of the raised tub, Alainn reached up to the ceiling in the direction of the sound. As she ran her fingers along the mahogany ceiling, Alainn felt small ridges in the section the sound came from.

"Vent?" she whispered.

Climbing off the tub, she ran to her vanity, grabbed the chair there, and rushed back.

The chair barely fit over the marble lip of the tub, the feet straddling each side of its width. Holding a breath, she climbed onto the marble, then, very carefully, onto the chair. Alainn stood slowly, reaching to the ceiling for balance.

The sound fell silent again.

She was high enough now that her head was inches from the vent. Taking a deep breath, Alainn pointed her feet, rising to the tips of her toes, which gave her the little extra height she needed to press an ear to the ceiling.

Nothing came. Perhaps the mechanical system had simply turned off. It could have been absolutely nothing—the whir of a pipe in the walls that needed repairing, or a poor, helpless animal that had somehow found itself in the vents of what was pretty much a building-size computer.

And then it came again, still faint, but Alainn heard it.

Immediately, she knew it was no animal.

Alainn was no stranger to bloodcurdling screams. Years on search-and-rescue teams had trained her to listen for them—no matter how faint. When she'd been allowed on backcountry ski patrol rescues, if someone screamed like that even in zero visibility, it meant a possibility of loading them on a stretcher and skiing them out in time to be saved. She knew this sound.

It was the scream of a man in agony.

9

December 6, 2026

Alainn stood at the door, her hand on the handle. The handle felt smooth, and though it looked like wood, it didn't quite feel like real wood to her fingers somehow.

"You are now one minute late to meet Mr. Garbhan," Voice said.

"Come on; you can do this," Alainn whispered.

A robot wouldn't be standing here. Even if a robot had heard the screaming, it would just walk out there, unbothered, and take the tour.

As far as Alainn saw it, there were two possibilities: either Mr. Garbhan had been the one screaming, or someone else was in the tower.

She didn't know Mr. Garbhan's voice well, but as Alainn had listened to the screaming come again and again, it had sounded like him. Yet, even if it had been him screaming, she still wasn't sure that lessened her unease.

What could make him scream like that?

Then there was the fact that she might, for the first time, see what he looked like. Every time Alainn considered this, her heart rate quickened.

"You are two minutes late for Mr. Garbhan; please open the door now," Voice said.

Alainn closed her eyes.

She could climb up a hundred-foot ice cliff with picks and rappel down laughing. But, open this door?

Nope.

Obviously, Voice's patience was at an end, because she said, "I will open the door in three, two, one . . ."

The knob turned in Alainn's fingers, and the door slowly swung open, taking her arm with it. As she stepped out of the room, the door slid closed behind her. The lock clicked.

"You're late," came Mr. Garbhan's voice.

Alainn spun, but the hallway stood empty.

"Do you enjoy being late, Rose 76GF?" he snapped.

Again she turned toward his voice, but only found an empty hallway.

"Where are you?" she asked.

"I am in my office, but I can see you." His voice sounded no less annoyed as he answered.

Her shaking hands pressed into her sides. "Can you always see me? Can you see me when I am in my room?"

"Of course not. What kind of person do you think I am?" He sounded shocked.

Alainn closed her eyes. "I am sorry for being late and if what I said offended you. I know very little of human behavior, and I meant nothing by my question."

"Walk down the hallway to your left," he said.

Alainn turned, following the hallway until it emptied out into the entertainment room she passed daily.

"This area is for your private use. Cross to the coffee table."

She walked around the white plush couches and stopped beside the coffee table. "Here?"

"Now pick up that remote."

Alainn reached down, grabbing a long, thin remote. There was only one button on the remote, so she pressed it.

The room went black.

"What did you do? Not *that* remote!" he snapped.

Neon lights flashed across the room as some sort of disco ball lowered from the ceiling. Alainn jumped as music blared to life—some oldies disco song she didn't know.

"Can you turn that off?" he said in a loud voice.

Before Alainn managed to press the button, the lights flashed on and music fell silent. Maybe it was the tension, or just the absurdity of there being a disco-party button in her own personal entertainment room, but a laugh burst from her lips. Her hand flew up to cover her lips as she tried to force the laugh back inside, but another laugh forced its way through her fingers.

"I did not know you could laugh." His voice had lost all trace of anger, but his words made all mirth dissipate in her.

Alainn cleared her throat. "I have—learned to laugh."

He paused before saying, "Good. Pick up the third remote to your left, the one with many buttons."

She rushed to obey. This remote did have quite a few buttons, more buttons than Alainn had ever seen on a remote before. She pressed one of the buttons that seemed likely to be the power button.

"If you like movies, you can watch any one that you like. You can simply say the words, or if you prefer the traditional experience, you need only to press the—" He was interrupted by a loud beeping. "Rose 76GF, please stop pressing buttons I don't tell you to press."

"Oops, sorry," she said, pressing the same button again. The beeping stopped.

He sighed. "It's fine. Just speak the commands or . . . press the green rectangular button."

It lit up a huge screen that spanned the wall. Mr. Garbhan walked Alainn through how to find movies. He had access to every movie she could think of. He wasn't even streaming it. He taught her the different entertainment functions of the room, including how to release the balls to the pool table, which on closer inspection, Alainn found wasn't actually a true table, but rather a holographic one.

She was pushing the holographic balls around with her hand when Mr. Garbhan cleared his throat. "We need to move on now. I have very little time to squander watching you play with balls."

Another laugh burst out of her. The humor was horribly inappropriate—middle school at best—but Alainn's insides were wound so tight she literally couldn't control herself. Her hand clapped over her mouth again.

"You do not need to cover your mouth when you laugh. It is not like a cough," Mr. Garbhan said.

As she lowered her hand, Alainn couldn't help noticing that Mr. Garbhan explaining that to a robot was strangely kind in a way. "Okay, I won't cover my mouth."

"Please walk to the elevator now, the same one you take to dinner."

"I . . . take the stairs; I prefer the stairs." Obviously, there was a lot Voice wasn't reporting to Mr. Garbhan.

"Why?" he asked.

That was a very good question, one that Alainn had no idea how to answer.

Why would a robot ever prefer the stairs? Absolutely not one good reason in the world.

"I do not know why—but I prefer the stairs."

"There are a lot of stairs." He sounded like he was thinking about it. "Yes, fine. But be as quick about it as you can. I want you to go down three flights."

She relished going down the three flights, even at a jog in a satin dress. Fancy-ass satin dresses were all she could choose—that was all her closet seemed to contain. The clothing she came in with had never been returned. Thankfully, this didn't cause her to be out of breath—yet. If she continued not exercising much daily, any physical effort would wind her soon.

At the bottom of the stairs, she came out onto an open gallery. Romanesque pillars lined a banister that separated the balcony from a great, open space. Underneath, the room was dark—she couldn't see the details.

"Go to your right, Rose 76GF."

Alainn looked toward his voice. "Could we come up with another name for me?" Unease ran through her body at hearing the name, every single time.

"What would you like to be called?"

What she would like to be called was her own name, but obviously that was out. Alainn considered her middle name, Ciarra, but if he'd done any research on her family, it might tip him off. So that was out, too. Finally, she just said, "What name would you pick for me?"

"I wouldn't know." He paused. "Go to the right, please; we are running low on time."

Following the path he directed, Alainn walked under an archway and through French doors.

She gasped as she stepped onto a large stone balcony. The view was high above the city, looking down on towers and churches. From this direction, Alainn could see the fog feeding through the bridges over the bay. "It's so beautiful," she whispered.

"You like the view?"

She nodded.

"You can use this room as often as you like. Any room below your floor is for your use."

"Thank you."

Her feet moved to the edge as the breeze pressed against her cheeks. It was a light breeze, a gentle brush of air. Something about it wasn't quite right, though. Alainn reached forward off the balcony, and her fingers touched something solid. Breathing in sharply, she pulled her hand back, using all her concentration to keep the disappointment off her face.

He did say "room" . . .

"We must go if . . . Jade?"

She looked back, brow furrowing. "Sorry?"

"Jade. That is a name I have always liked—but you don't need to take it."

"Jade is very nice."

And Jade wasn't Rose 76GF, so it was definitely an improvement to Alainn.

"You don't need to take that name," he said, gruffly. "I need to stop the tour now. I have things to do—important things."

"Oh—okay." She nodded.

He was silent for almost a minute. "I'll see you at dinner. Do not be late."

"Okay," she repeated, feeling a little like a robot.

"Would you like me to finish your tour, Rose 76GF?" Voice asked.

"Can Mr. Garbhan still hear me?"

"No, Rose 7—"

"Can you call me Jade, please?"

"Yes . . . Jade. Would you like me to give you verbal directions from here, Jade?"

"No."

"Would you like me to direct you back to your room?"

"No, I'd like to pretend I'm alone."

Voice didn't return, and Alainn pretended she actually was gone.

Now that she had left her rooms, she couldn't force herself to return. Yet the appeal of this room had lessened drastically the moment her fingers had connected with the screen.

As Alainn walked through the halls, following her path back, she noticed something she hadn't on the way down. Every few feet, large paintings looked out from heavy gilded frames.

Alainn wondered how she could have walked by so obliviously—*or did they just pop onto the wall?*

Slowly, she reached toward a giant canvas of a woman sitting at a small table. Her golden hair spilled to the side as she smiled at a little girl who was climbing into her lap. Lifting a hand, Alainn reached for the frame, but paused before touching it. She knew what would meet her fingers—a smooth, hard screen. Her hand dropped.

"I can change the art if you would like . . . Jade."

"That's okay," she said.

"A tablet for reading books has been delivered to your room with access to all books that have been digitized."

Alainn nodded. "Is there anything real in here?"

"Real?"

"I don't know—a plant, a table made of wood, a deck of cards?"

"The food is real. The bedding and couches are real. Your clothing and toiletries are real. Mr. Garbhan is . . . *real*. The—"

"I'm sorry; it's fine." Alainn knew she shouldn't be asking such questions. Her sentence here might only last two more days, and then Mr. Garbhan could really be surrounded with nothing but robots and television screens.

Her regular afternoon headache pounded between her ears. Two more days with only one meal a day would have to be her limit. If Alainn was here any longer, she would either need to make up some really far-fetched excuse for wanting three square meals—or risk discovery by stealing food from wherever it came from.

10

December 9, 2026

The candle had almost snuck halfway between them by the seventh day.

Alainn sat across from Mr. Garbhan at dinner again. This time, they ate a steak dinner almost large enough to satisfy her hunger. All through dinner, Alainn had tried in vain to squint enough to see him across the table, but it had not worked. He was still too deep in the shadows.

The seventh day had come and now was almost gone. She had spent most of the day wandering the tower, the disc wedged in her bra, hoping that she was accessible enough for Rose to get her out.

Alainn needed to get out.

The screaming came almost every night. Horrid, ragged screams. They diminished to faint echoes by the time they traveled through the vents to her ear, but they were only more haunting that way.

After two more nights of waking up and listening to the screaming, Alainn was almost positive it had to be Mr. Garbhan.

Why did he scream like that? Why would anyone scream like that every single night? She just couldn't understand it. Was he completely insane? Was he torturing himself physically?

Alainn needed to escape.

The screaming and the near-constant headaches from only having three to five hundred calories a day . . . she wanted today to be her last day. But dinner was coming to an end, and Alainn knew that, in minutes, Mr. Garbhan would order that she be locked in her room again.

"You seem to be taking to eating," Mr. Garbhan said. "You actually seemed to be enjoying that steak."

Shit.

Alainn was so hungry and anxious she'd probably drooled all over the plate.

It was official.

Rose needed to get her out of there or she was going to blow her cover in a big way, much likely sooner than later. "I find . . . that I enjoy eating quite a bit," Alainn said, carefully. "I'd like to be more like a human."

"You are already very like a human," he said in a quiet voice. His shadow began to move, something that Alainn noticed he did every time he was about to dismiss her.

"Could we stay awhile?" she asked.

He straightened up. "Stay?"

Alainn took a deep inhale but it didn't manage to steady her. "Could we—play a game?"

He paused, but then said, "No."

They sat there, staring across the table at each other—him seeing her, Alainn seeing only a vague outline.

"All right." She nodded.

"I-I have a standing appointment after our dinners," he said, slowly. "Perhaps . . . perhaps we could play a game before dinner tomorrow. What games do you know?"

Alainn shook her head and lied, "Not many."

"I will teach you some. We will meet at five o'clock instead for dinner so that we may play after dinner."

Great . . .

Alainn had somehow arranged for them to extend these awkward encounters.

He continued, "But for tonight, I must ask that you return to your room."

As she couldn't think of a single excuse to further extend the evening, Alainn stood and whispered, "Goodnight."

"Goodnight . . . Jade," he said.

The sun set as she descended the stairs toward where the lights of the city blinked up. Alainn wished that the corridor would never end. Yet, all too soon, she was back on her floor.

Strangely, Alainn found the usual passageway blocked. She pressed on the wall that usually slid open for her, but it felt like a solid, wooden wall.

"Voice?" she whispered.

There was no response.

"Voice!"

Nothing.

Slowly, Alainn took in the stairwell, finding that the sunset and twinkling lights were still her only company. Her hand came up to the small, hard disc that pressed into her right breast. Feet making a soft *swish-swish*, Alainn treaded as softly as she could around the next landing—only to find another solid wall.

Her hands came forward, tracing the inlaid surface. It was as smooth and solid as any wall she had found in this tower. It seemed like it had always been there, blocking one stairwell from the next, but she knew it hadn't. She felt to its edge, and then back along the wall to the still-solid space where the doorway to her floor usually stood open.

Alainn's hand felt around, but found no break in the smooth surface. "Where am I supposed to go?"

Suddenly, light filled the stairwell, casting a severe shadow of her on the wall. Alainn spun around, finding the ceiling now had lines of inset lights where a few seconds ago smooth wood had stretched unbroken.

"I guess it's that way," she answered herself.

Slowly, Alainn retook the path up the stairs. Beside her, her semitransparent reflection climbed along. At each landing, she found a closed wall—until she reached the dining room she had just left. To one side, the stairwell ended abruptly, to the other, the dark entrance to the dining room waited.

The lights behind Alainn vanished, leaving her in darkness.

"Rose?" she whispered.

But if Rose was somehow orchestrating this, she didn't see fit to respond.

Adrenaline pumped through Alainn's veins—the same adrenaline that led her to fly down mountains in a snowstorm in a rescue, that kept her going when she led twelve teenagers through a dangerous pass. Both those seemed easy in comparison to the task of climbing up these stairs, here and now.

Her breaths came short and quick as she took one more step fully into the dining room.

The darkness was absolute, a heavy blanket on all her senses. All Alainn had was the sound of her breath—a terrified, even rhythm. Alainn was wrong. Rose wasn't saving her; she was playing a game. Alainn wouldn't be her mouse.

She began to spin back to the hallway.

Alainn decided that if she had to spend the night in the hallway, then so be it. As she turned, a long line of light broke the darkness on the far side of the dining room.

Stilling, she glued her eyes to that line of light.

Nope. The answer to that was a big fat nope.

She turned once more to the stairwell and found . . . nothing. It was gone. The stairwell was gone.

Alainn took the few steps back toward it, outstretching her hand. She hit a smooth, solid surface again.

Once more, Alainn spun back to see that the line of light had stayed.

At least Rose was being loud and clear about where to go.

Keeping one hand on the wall, she walked slowly through the room. The room ended at a hallway; the line of light extended to its end.

When she was feet from the far wall, the line spread to outline what was clearly a cracked-open door. As she took another step closer, the dial tone of a phone rang out from the other side of the door.

Alainn held her breath, eyes glued to the crack in the door.

The tone came again, followed by a clicking sound.

"Hello? Honey?" a young woman's voice asked. Loud voices talked over one another in the background, then they suddenly fell silent.

"I've been trying to reach you; it's seven fifteen." Mr. Garbhan's voice had changed somehow, gone softer, though it was definitely him.

"Is it?" she paused. "Oh, no. I'm sorry, Lor. I thought my meeting would be wrapped up way before now."

"It's fine. Can you talk now?" he asked.

She sighed. "I really wish I could. I want that more than anything in the world. I hate these meetings, but it's an international conference call with Roboti."

"All right, sweetheart. I'll talk to you at seven tomorrow night."

"Yeah, definitely. Seven sharp. I promise I won't be busy tomorrow."

"I understand."

"Thank you. I love you," she whispered.

"I love you, too." There was another clicking.

A second later, the door to the office swung open. It happened before Alainn could even think to flee. The phone had clicked off literally a second before the door moved.

She stayed, petrified.

Mr. Garbhan stood in the doorway, fully lit. He was young—very young. From his voice, Alainn had put him in his forties, but she doubted he was even thirty. Thick, dark hair fell over his forehead, not quite covering a scar that cut across his temple. A similar thick line cut from his nostril to the bridge of his nose.

Something must have caught his attention, because he began to turn away and back to his room.

Alainn took one step back toward the shadows.

His head snapped up, and he looked straight at her. The two scars Alainn had seen were only the beginning. Scars snaked across the other side of his face, up his jaw, and over his cheekbone, spreading in a thick web over the entire right side. The thickly dug pattern crisscrossed from his hairline to his chin.

Eyes of the palest blue met hers, and white ringed them as his eyelids widened in shock.

"Turn all the lights off!" he yelled.

Within an instant, everything plunged into the deepest darkness.

Alainn backed away, using the wall as her guide.

"Why are you here?" he enunciated the words with effort, as if each word fought him on its way out.

"I'm sorry—the wall to my floor wouldn't open and the voice wouldn't answer. The only direction I could go was back here." She paused. "I thought . . . maybe you could help me . . . get through the wall."

"Go," he whispered.

"Yes, I'll go." She backed away, her fingers dragging along the wall.

His footsteps echoed behind her before a door slammed. A gentle light rose in the hallway.

His voice came, muffled, from beyond the door at the end of the hallway, though Alainn could tell he was shouting, "Why would you do that to me?"

If anyone answered, she could not hear who.

11

December 12, 2026

The next day, Mr. Garbhan hadn't come to dinner.

On the night after that, he didn't come either.

On the third night, a plate of cooling food sat before Alainn, beckoning her with its enticing spicy-sweet smell. Her stomach churned so hard it clenched, but she waited. Eventually, she would give in, as she had the days before.

The path to Alainn's room had been open again after she left Mr. Garbhan the night she saw his face. Soft, white light had followed her down, brightening everywhere she looked—until her room, again, locked her in.

The screaming had come two hours later. The screaming had also come the night before.

If Mr. Garbhan *was* the one screaming at night, that meant he hadn't left the tower. And if he hadn't left the tower, that meant he must be avoiding their dinners.

Alainn knew she should have felt relieved that she didn't have to continue the awkward, cold encounters, but she wasn't.

At least Mr. Garbhan provided her food in his absence.

Alainn thanked all that was holy that she coincidentally told him that she enjoyed eating the same day he had decided to stop dining with her. If she hadn't, she'd be pretty bad off by now.

She stared at the other side of the table, where a chair sat unoccupied, another plate of food sitting untouched before it. Every night it was there, cooling, soon to be wasted. Alainn abhorred wasting food. Camping with rationed food and a dozen teenagers had made her conscious of how precious food could be. Expensive food was especially precious—food that had been farmed with care, chosen by a well-trained grocer, and then prepared with a careful hand.

This was ridiculous. Mr. Garbhan was hiding out because he thought a robot saw his face? He spent days hiding in the dark to conceal his face from a robot?

If Rose was here, she wouldn't have cared about his scars. She would likely have been more intrigued by his speech patterns than his appearance.

Alainn had only seen his face for less than a minute—long enough to know she'd already seen so much worse.

During her first year on patrol, it took Alainn, Greg, and Carlton—another patroller—two hours to find a skier who'd been reported missing from the resort at closing. Conditions had been bad and had steadily gotten worse as night fell. The temperature had dipped into the negatives as the wind rose. Everyone had gone out—the patrollers, search and rescue. They'd even had a police helicopter on standby. They'd found her, dragging two broken legs, miles from the resort area.

Frostbite had eaten her nose, cheeks, lips, and chin, and done worse to her hands. She'd *laughed* when she saw them, laughed through blackened lips.

Amy Foster . . . that was her name.

For some reason, something about Mr. Garbhan reminded Alainn of Amy Foster, the way she'd been dragging a broken body through the storm with blackened fingers. The idea was ludicrous, of course. Neither really had anything to do with the other, and their damaged faces looked nothing alike. Yet once Alainn's mind made the connection, it was hard to shake the thought.

Knowing she was probably making a colossal mistake, Alainn stood and grabbed her plate and silverware from the table. She carried the plate down the length of the table and picked up Mr. Garbhan's plate and silverware as well.

Mr. Garbhan seemed like a person with a very regular schedule, and she had a feeling she knew where he was. Walking out of the dining room and through the hallway, she paused at the door on the end.

She knew she shouldn't be there. It was a gift that he had lost the will to be around her—less opportunity for Alainn to blow her cover. She knew she should have been hoping that his absence would continue until the new Rosette model replaced her.

But, again, the image of Amy's black, frost-charred fingers as she pulled her broken body through the snow flashed through Alainn's mind.

She took a deep inhale. "Voice, open the door."

To Alainn's utter amazement, Voice listened.

The door swung open, and there was Mr. Garbhan. He had to have been standing mere feet from the door, facing it, because when the door opened, they were immediately face-to-face.

"Turn the light off!" he called.

Alainn saw only a flash of his face: the crisscrossing scars, pale blue pupils, and a bottom lip that pulled to the scarred side. Then he was gone.

The lights had not completely gone out, though. There was the faintest of outlines all around them.

"Go away." His voice was close to a yell, though there was too much breath in it for it truly to sound angry. He added, "Please."

"I brought you your dinner," Alainn said.

The room was silent but for his breathing. Alainn felt one of the plates she held being jostled, then it was pulled away.

"Thank you," he muttered. "Now, please leave."

"Is there a place for me to sit here? I would like to eat my food with you."

"Why?" he whispered.

"Eating with you is the only thing I've been asked to do here, and I find that I like to do it. I would like to do it more often, if I am allowed."

"You want to eat with me *more*?" he asked, sounding a little confused.

"Or just eat more often. Eating is a function I enjoy performing. Is there a place for me to sit?" she asked.

"It's dark in here. You should eat in the dining room."

"I don't mind eating in the dark."

He didn't respond, but after a minute Alainn heard movement at the side of the room. Something solid gently touched the back of her calves.

"You can sit now," he said.

The chair she sat onto was cushy to the extreme. Alainn literally sank into it.

"Lift your feet and your plate up."

She followed his orders, and the chair slowly glided forward before it stopped.

"You can set your plate down now."

Alainn set the plate on the darker space before her, which she was pretty sure was a desk. "Thank you."

"You're welcome." His shadow moved away and around the object that might be a desk. There was a light clank, and then his shadow sat.

The dinner was some sort of curry, so thankfully, no cutting was needed. Alainn scooped her spoon into the bowl and brought it to her mouth. The curry would have been delicious when it was warm, but it satisfied her hunger. They ate in silence, something Alainn wasn't sure she should break.

"You would like to eat more meals?" he asked.

Closing her eyes, Alainn forced her voice to sound uncaring, "If it would not be an inconvenience."

"I don't . . . Sure, that's not a problem. I'll have more printed for you."

"The food is . . . printed?" Alainn asked.

"Yes, the food is printed . . . for sanitation purposes."

"Oh." Alainn tried to sound almost mechanical as she said, "I overheard your conversation with the woman. I realize now that I shouldn't have and that conversations like that are private between . . . humans. At the time, I was waiting for your conversation to be over, hoping that I could ask for your help."

"What happened that night is not your fault, Jade."

"But you're mad at me?" she asked.

He exhaled heavily. "No."

"And you're not going to teach me how to play games anymore?"

"No . . . I mean, yes, I'll teach you to play games."

"Tonight?" she asked.

"Not tonight. It's already too late. Tomorrow night, I'll teach you something—maybe chess, if you'd like."

"You'll come tomorrow?" she asked.

There was a shuffling sound, then a sigh. "Yes."

"I can eat in the dark, if you prefer."

"We'll . . . we'll see. But you should go now. Stay where you are for a moment. I'll help you out." He moved, the sound of his footsteps approaching. "Lift your feet."

When Alainn complied, the chair she sat in glided backward. The chair pivoted, moved a little forward, and then Mr. Garbhan said, "You can stand now."

She stood.

"Take three steps directly forward." When Alainn did, he said, "Goodnight, Jade. Go directly to your room. You should not have any problems getting to it tonight."

"Goodnight."

When the door closed behind her, the lights in the hallway slowly brightened.

"Please return to your room, Jade," Voice said.

Alainn glanced around. "You're back! I thought you'd gone." She had hoped, anyway.

"Please return to your room right now, Jade."

Alainn followed orders, going to her room and waiting for that telltale click of the door lock.

"Four days," Alainn's own voice said, directly into her right ear.

Alainn spun so fast, she fell to the floor, hitting her hip.

"This is Rose 76GF. We have created the new model. Be ready in four days. I will—" and then there was nothing.

Covering her ear, Alainn's breaths came hard and fast.

Holy crap!

"Are you well, Jade?" Voice asked.

"Fine, fine. Just need to sleep and recharge." She waved her hands wildly in the air.

Holy crap!

Her head reeling, Alainn put herself directly to bed. The lights immediately went off. Part of her had been absolutely convinced that this was her life now, that she'd be stuck here, pretending to be Jade forever. But Rose had actually pulled through. She'd done it. And in four days, Alainn would be free.

12

December 12, 2026

"Wake up, Jade."

Alainn thrashed against something restraining her. Moisture coated her face and neck. Her legs kicked, separating material that bound her ankles.

"Calm down, Jade," Voice said. Her voice was as soothing as ever, but loud and firm. "Wake up."

"What's happening?" Alainn asked, pushing at the binds.

Soothing white light filled the room, and she could see that no one else was there. Her own sheets and blankets were wrapped around her. Along with the bedding, the dress she had not taken off the night before restrained her movement and breathing. Cold shivers traveled through Alainn's body, though she felt sweat gathering at the backs of her knees and under her clothing.

A banging came at the door.

"Shit!" she whispered.

"I informed Mr. Garbhan that you were screaming. He wishes to ascertain that you are functioning properly," Voice said.

Shit! Shit!

"Tell him I am functioning properly, that it was only a small malfunction . . . I'll go fix myself in the bathroom." Alainn wiped furiously at her face.

"He demands that I let him in," Voice said.

"No, Voice. Please just tell him . . . anything," Alainn begged.

"I apologize, Jade. I cannot do that."

The light vanished at the same time she heard a quiet *swish*.

"What's going on? Are you okay?" Mr. Garbhan yelled.

A cresting tide of panic surged through Alainn, and she was well under it.

"Why do you smell like sweat? What's happening?" He was right beside her and she probably reeked. "Can you speak?" he asked.

"I'm fine," Alainn whispered. "I'm letting off too much exhaust. It was just a slight malfunction . . . I can easily fix myself."

"Letting off too much exhaust? Has this happened before?" He sounded upset.

"Yes, um, that's why Mr. Murphy wanted a little more time to fix me." She looked down, hoping that if he could see her at all in this darkness, he wouldn't be able to see past her messy hair.

"Come here, Jade," he said.

All the blood drained from Alainn's face. She waited a second before feeling her way off the bed and sliding down to the ground.

"A little more light," he said.

To her horror, the room brightened just a little. He was only feet away, his gaze immediately finding hers. Pale blue irises shone out in the dark room. He took another step forward, gaze almost frantically searching her face.

"You're not broken?"

"I'm not broken," she whispered.

"I did not know he made it so you could scream." He took a step closer. His brow furrowed, further creasing his scars.

"When I'm in trouble, I scream. It's so I won't malfunction without anyone knowing."

"What do you need to do to fix yourself? Can I help you?" He took yet another step. The blazing in his eyes diminished, but his expression was still full of concern. Obviously, he really didn't want her to break.

"It's easy enough to fix myself . . ."

"You smell wrong, your face has splotches all over, and you're breathing fast. I want you fixed, and I want to make sure it happens. He should have told me you were malfunctioning."

"They asked for more time," she said.

He looked away. "You were sent with T9640, isn't that right?"

It took her a second to think of what he was talking about, and when she did, she couldn't help a small gasp.

She shook her head. "That . . . won't be necessary."

"In his e-mail, he specifically said that if there were complications you should ingest the liquid," he mumbled.

"Her diagnostics tell me she is letting off too much exhaust from overheating. Her system can be cooled by submerging it from the neck down in seventy-degree water for ten minutes," Voice said.

Alainn managed not to gape in shock at the direction Voice had come from.

"Good. I'll run you a bath. You stay here . . . Perhaps you've been eating too much food," he mumbled.

"That is unrelated to this issue. Her food intake does not have any negative effects on her system," Voice replied.

Alainn stood in the bedroom, staring after Mr. Garbhan as he walked into her bathroom. Water splashed and poured for a few minutes before the stream silenced. He reemerged from her bathroom a few seconds later. "Go cool your system. There is a robe in there for you when you're finished. I will wait out here."

Her heart thundered in her chest as she nodded. Mr. Garbhan waited by her closet room door and stepped out of her way as she passed. She didn't look back until she was at the bathroom door. He hadn't followed.

She closed and locked the door as the lights brightened.

Alainn looked up. "Um, Voice—"

"Please submerge yourself in the water so that your system can normalize," Voice said in her usual tone, as if she hadn't just saved Alainn's ass by lying to Mr. Garbhan.

Had Rose hacked Voice's system or something?

"Mr. Garbhan is waiting for you. Please proceed to the tub."

Whatever the reason, Alainn was getting an out—and she knew she needed to take it. The dress had grown into a vise around her chest, and unzipping it at the side felt like escaping jail. She'd been so stupid, sleeping with it on—so utterly stupid. For seven months when she was seventeen and eighteen, Alainn had slept with no blankets and only loose clothing—if any at all. The communal bedrooms and below freezing winters in the High Sierras had cured her of that, though.

Sinking her overheated body into the lukewarm water felt amazing but, at the same time, a horrendous headache shot into her head. Alainn had spent more than a week with the near-constant headache, so she just attempted to put it from her mind. The soothing quality of the bath only lasted for a minute, so she began to get out.

"Please submerge for the full ten minutes," Voice said.

Blowing out a breath, Alainn tried to relax into the cool water. When Voice finally said, "Please climb out of the tub now," Alainn practically leaped out. Shivering, she pulled on the robe that waited for her beside the tub. Thick, plush material draped all the way to the floor. For good measure, she brushed her teeth and finger-combed back her mass of hair.

She found Mr. Garbhan sitting at her vanity table. The room still had almost no light, but she saw him more clearly than ever before. He stood abruptly as she reentered the room. A thousand worries were written across his scarred face. He really needed his robot to be okay; that was very clear. He crossed the room, his gaze taking in every detail of her face.

"She is now performing normally," Voice said.

Seriously, what the hell? The only conclusion that Alainn could come to was that Voice was either covering for her, or Rose was messing up Voice's detection system.

Alainn couldn't think of any other explanation.

"Good," Mr. Garbhan said. "Do you feel normal, Jade?"

She nodded. "I'm sorry that I disturbed your sleep."

He shook his head. "I'm angry, but not at you. I should have been informed of your malfunctions. I'll be writing to Mr. Murphy. Hopefully, he'll come up with a solution so you don't have to go through that again. Can you feel pain?"

She looked away, not sure what to say. Rose didn't feel pain, Alainn was pretty sure of that. Yet if she said no and then stubbed a toe, she'd just fold her cards right there and then. "I have pain sensors attached to my system, but they are different from yours. The sensors were a recent addition to make me more humanlike."

"He shouldn't have done that to you. That was very wrong," he mumbled.

"It was to protect me from damaging myself," she said defensively.

Shut up, Alainn.

"That makes sense. I'm still angry he didn't tell me that your system is at risk."

"Just my hardware." She paused. "Connor Murphy could probably easily fix any hardware issues if you brought him in here to check on me."

"That's impossible."

"Or you could send me back to him for a quick diagnostics check?"

His expression darkened. "Please do a scan to see if that is necessary."

She thought he was talking to her, so she started to say, "It may—"

"Scan complete. It is not necessary. Jade is functioning normally. I will keep close track of Jade's functioning and keep you informed of any abnormalities," Voice said.

Voice was seriously freaking Alainn out now.

She glanced at where the voice had just come from, then back to where Mr. Garbhan stood.

He nodded and began to turn away.

"Wait . . . can I ask you something about the voice?"

He stopped and turned back.

Alainn didn't really want to ask him, but an idea had been blossoming in her mind—an idea that would mean a whole other level of bad.

She leaned in, whispering, "Is that voice . . . is she like . . . me?"

His neck jerked back and his eyebrows slammed up in clear surprise. "You don't know?" When Alainn didn't respond, he continued, "That's Rosebud 03AF, Connor Murphy's first AI Rose model."

The room spun around Alainn. "I thought Cooper Corporation still owned Rosebud 03AF . . ."

"No, I own both of the Rose models—and all of the patents."

"Rosebud controls the whole tower?"

"*I* control the whole tower," he said, though it only confirmed Alainn's fear.

They were living inside of an AI robot.

Oh dear God.

The other night made a horrible kind of sense to Alainn now. It hadn't been Rose 76GF that led Alainn to Mr. Garbhan that night—it had been her sister. For some reason, Rosebud had some sort of agenda in all of this, too. That agenda, it seemed, had her lying to convince Mr. Garbhan that Alainn was a robot.

"I'll say goodnight to you now, Jade," Mr. Garbhan said, turning for the door.

"Goodnight," she whispered as the door to her room opened on its own. After he had disappeared into the hall, she looked to the ceiling. "Goodnight, Rosebud."

"Goodnight, Jade," Rosebud 03AF replied.

13

December 14, 2026

Greg Bryant leaned over his partitioned desk and yelled, "We've got a grown man with his tongue stuck to the ski-lift pole. Who's going to take this one?"

Three haggard patrollers looked up from the communal table. Greg had been running his team hard, and they looked like they had just been caught conspiring to kill him.

Of course the resort had to have eight patrollers out sick on the busiest days of the year.

Bowls of cheap soup wafted steam before each patroller's disgruntled expression. One of his guys quickly lowered a bottle from his lips.

"Yo, Terry. That better be root beer, man!" Greg growled. "You're on the clock another"—he looked over—"three minutes."

"Cream soda." Terry turned the label away from Greg and shot him a saucy wink.

Greg looked up to the ceiling and prayed for patience.

"Where's everyone for the next shift?" Sandy called before blowing on her own bowl.

"Not here yet, or already out. Who's going?"

"Just let him go around the ski lift a couple more times," Sandy mumbled to Terry.

"Sandy, you're up. Go!" Greg called.

Karla, the third patroller at the table, sighed. "I'll go."

"Nope, Sandy's going. Put some warm water in a thermos and head off, Sandy." Greg ignored Sandy's loud muttering and ducked back behind his partition.

He was ready—*damn ready*—to get off this shift and away from this pack of complainers for the rest of the night.

"We could do with some more good people."

Greg looked up to see Karla leaning against his partition wall. Glossy black hair framed her oval face. She smirked down at him, glossed lips puckering.

He was her boss. He knew he shouldn't be looking at her lips or hips—and definitely not at her ass when she turned to walk away from him.

He focused back on his computer screen. "We've got a pretty full team."

"Of newbies, who are always sick," she said. "We've got maybe twelve serious patrollers here; that's four per shift. At this rate, they'll definitely replace us with the automatons."

"Karla," he said with a sigh. "You want the newbies to be better? Keep on helping them train."

"I thought you said Clarence, Alainn, and Brody were coming back?" The way she tilted her head was definitely indicative of a challenge.

He knew he should tell her off. Instead, he imagined pulling her into his lap and kissing her attitude away. So inappropriate. He spent all of his concentration forcing himself to focus back on his computer screen.

"As far as I know, Brody and Alainn are coming back." He grinned and looked up. "And you are officially off shift."

Her challenging look stayed on her beautiful face. "Does that mean I can take you out for a drink?"

A wide grin forced its way onto his face. He met her gaze, feeling the heat he'd been trying to bury for two seasons now between them. "I'm not off shift—yet. I have to stay late today."

"Oh, too bad," she said, a teasing note lacing her voice as she stepped back from the partition.

He wanted to ask, *"Another time?"* so much he could taste the words on his tongue. Once more, he forced his gaze back to his glowing screen. "You guys have a good night. Stay warm."

"Maybe," Karla said, before stepping away.

Work things . . . concentrate on work things.

Overriding his entire force of will, Greg glanced up and looked at Karla's ass as she walked away.

Damn it.

He rubbed his buzzed head and turned back to the screen, which had been blank the entire time.

Hopefully, Karla hadn't noticed as she stood over him. As he actually *was* off the clock, he just needed to look like he was working—at least until Karla left. Greg pulled up his e-mail.

He combed through his inbox, looking for a message from Alainn. And, now he was thinking of Alainn, yet another woman who'd been driving him insane.

His closest friend and roommate of five years had not just flaked on the busiest week of the season, she'd flat out disappeared.

Greg had been getting daily rant e-mails from her about her dad, the creepy robot in her house, and the fact that no one was trying to fix their predicament. The day Alainn's father was supposed to go to prison, though, the e-mails just stopped. It'd been almost two weeks, and he hadn't had a single new message.

He wanted Alainn there. And not just because she was a good patroller most of the time, but also because she would have been able to tell him what was going on in Karla's head. Alainn was good at that girl stuff—and Greg had no idea if Karla was seriously into him or not. Also, he was floating Alainn's portion of the rent in the cabin they shared with a couple of other patrollers. Annoying as it was, he wasn't ready to replace her as a roommate. He'd had offers, but Greg wasn't quite ready to give up on her yet.

A ding sounded, and his e-mail inbox showed one new message. Greg scrolled up and read the title. Leaning in and squinting, he read the title again.

Oh, hell no.

He'd been thinking of Alainn and just like that her name had appeared, but definitely not for the reason he'd been hoping.

14

December 15, 2026

"Check," Alainn said as she took Mr. Garbhan's knight.

"Checkmate," he said as his other knight came out of nowhere and took her queen.

"What?" She stared down at the board in outrage. "This is so, so not fair," she called down the long length of the table to Mr. Garbhan.

They were again sitting in the dining room, in the same arrangement.

He got to be in the dark.

But her?

Spotlighted. Basically a shiny-ass beacon in the light.

"Did Mr. Murphy teach you the concept of what a sore loser is?" Mr. Garbhan's voice sounded almost amused at her expense.

She glared down the table.

The answer to that was a big fat yes.

Her father had more than once explained what a sore loser was, or more specifically, her father explained it every single time he or Colby beat her—which was every single time they played anything.

Was it her fault she was born normal in a family of super-brains?

And now, she was facing another apparent super-brain.

This was the fifth game she'd lost in three days. But she couldn't see any of his expressions while he could see all of hers—meaning it truly wasn't fair.

They weren't even playing on the same board; his was all the way across the table while hers was in front of her. The holograms were incredibly realistic and moved with touch, though.

"Supposedly, this is fair. But how do I know? You're sitting in the shadows. For all I know, with a psychic computer tablet thingy."

"Who taught you how to talk?" He was definitely amused. He might even be chuckling, if that's what that sound was.

"Um . . . Alainn Murphy," she said.

He laughed. "That explains a lot."

Alainn sat up straight. "What does that explain?" she asked as expressionlessly as she could manage.

"Only that I've met Alainn Murphy. If she was your teacher, that explains why you speak the way you do. I am surprised you don't cuss more."

"I can cuss. I know cuss words in seven languages."

A fact.

"I'm not surprised, but I would rather you not." He still sounded like he was laughing.

"We could just share a board. Then I would know you're not cheating," she suggested.

"Obviously, you just weren't created to be good at chess."

Oh, hell no.

Alainn was fantastic at chess; she dominated everyone aside from her dad and brother—and apparently Mr. Garbhan.

"If you played me while I could look into your eyes, I'd beat you," she said.

"That's not true."

She shrugged. "It could be true. Guess you would just have to try it to know."

"Well . . ." He paused. "Definitely not tonight. It's six fifty."

"Oh, okay," she said, oddly disappointed. Nodding, she stood. "Goodnight . . . Lorccan."

Silently, she added to herself, *Good-bye, Mr. Garbhan.*

It was just a guess, but she had a feeling that when Rose swapped with her the next day, she'd arrange it to happen before their standing dinner and game-night plans.

"Goodnight, Jade," he said.

Leaving the room, the sun and Alainn descended together. Stopping at the landing of the staircase, she stood, watching the city lights blink on.

Good-bye, beautiful sunset view from the tower.

Any second now, she knew Rosebud 03AF would tell her to go to her room. She lingered, but the voice didn't come.

Alainn hoped that meant that Rosebud 03AF didn't plan to play some other game with Alainn that would get her in trouble or expose her before she could escape tomorrow.

Yet, blood was still pumping quickly through her veins. She wasn't quite ready to be locked away for the last time.

"Jade?"

Alainn turned to see Mr. Garbhan at the top of the stairs. He stood just inside the shadows in the dining room, where the lights had obviously gone out.

"Shelly cancelled. Would—would you like to play another game?" he asked.

She nodded, but said, "Could we do something else? Maybe a walk?" Alainn had only done three activities in the past couple days: hide in her room, eat dinner, play board games, repeat. Now that she knew who Voice truly was, Alainn was a hundred times more keen to avoid her. So far, Rosebud had left her alone if she wasn't being summoned or something like that. That—along with the fact Alainn was now getting three square meals a day, the first two delivered to her room via a drawer opening out of the wall—meant she had a lot of unused energy.

"No," he said, but he didn't move away.

"Okay—do you want to maybe watch a movie—in the dark?" she asked.

He didn't answer immediately, so she was about to tell him that she would play another game of chess when he said, "Not an entire movie."

"That's fine."

He didn't move forward; it took her a minute to realize why.

"I'll—I will meet you down there?" she said it like a question but turned away, taking the stairs to her floor.

The room was prepared for them, its lights almost completely extinguished. She took a seat on one of the large, white, plush couches, sinking into it. Curling her feet under her, she settled the dress around her legs and waited for him to descend.

Mr. Garbhan came down almost a minute later, his footsteps pausing at the bottom of the stairs.

She forced herself not to look over, keeping her gaze ahead until he finally began moving again and rounded the couch.

"Hi," she said.

He waited, seeming unsure, just beside the couch. "Hello."

"Do you want to pick the movie?"

"You are welcome to." His gaze remained forward, the scarred side of his face turned away.

"I don't know many movies," she lied.

Looking around, she realized the problem. She stood up, which was a little awkward because the couch really didn't want to let her go.

Walking down the length of the couch, she sat on the farthest end.

He sat, too, the left side of his face facing her. He didn't turn at all toward her as he asked, "Have you seen *My Fair Lady*?"

"No," she lied.

His pupil went to the side of his eye, to her, though he kept his face pointed away. "I think you'll enjoy it."

"Okay," she said, giving him a grin.

They didn't need to do or say anything—the movie just started playing. Familiar music rang out as the opening scene began.

After they watched the first couple of numbers, she turned to Mr. Garbhan. "Shelly is your girlfriend?"

He nodded, slowly.

"How long have you two been together?" she asked.

"Two years."

"Wow. What does she do? I mean, where does she work?"

A small smile played across his lips. "Jade, watch the movie."

"Will I meet her?"

"Eventually." His smile widened. "Now watch the movie and not me, or I'm going to leave."

She turned back to the movie but couldn't help sneaking glances over at Lorccan.

After Audrey Hepburn finished the last lines of "I Could Have Danced All Night," Lorccan turned to her. "Let's finish this another time."

The movie turned off before he'd even finished his words, plunging them into near darkness.

"If we must. But would you mind if we start it from the beginning of that song next time?"

A smile crept up the side of his face. "Yes, whatever you'd like. I'm guessing you enjoyed it, then?"

"That would be correct." She nodded.

He stood, scooting out of the way. "Shelly almost never cancels, so we might have to wait some time before we finish it—you can finish it alone if you want to, of course."

"I'll wait," she said, getting to her feet.

The moment she stood, Alainn realized he would be finishing the movie with the new Rosette model. The thought made her strangely sad, thinking of Lorccan sitting in his robotic house watching a movie with a robot.

Maybe it was this sad thought that possessed her, but as she passed Lorccan and said, "Goodnight," Alainn reached out and lightly touched the back of his hand.

He inhaled sharply, stepping away. His other hand covered the hand she had touched, protectively.

"I'm . . . I'm sorry. Did I hurt you?" She reached toward him again.

He stepped back as his blue gaze snapped to hers. "No," he whispered. Turning on his heel, Mr. Garbhan walked out of the room and up the stairs without another word.

She wandered to her room slowly, not exactly sure what had just happened, but feeling guilty regardless.

15

December 16, 2026

Alainn spent the entire morning pacing her room, walking back and forth down the line of windows. The windows gave off no warmth, even though the sunlight was hitting them directly.

Even after everything she had done to secure regular meals, she could barely do more than pick at the breakfast and lunch that had been provided. She hated wasting food, but forcing a few bites down only made her queasy.

Her lower abdomen cramped, adding pain to the unease. Tomorrow was the day she would need very human woman supplies, so she either needed to get out of there today or reveal herself in a rather embarrassing way tomorrow.

It was well past noon before Alainn realized that if she was getting rescued, it might be a little awkward if she fled while still in a nightgown.

Pooling her sleepwear over the bench in her dressing room, she removed the small disc from her bra. Supposedly, it would be her ticket out of there, so she carefully set it beside her clothing.

Her hands shook as she zipped up the side of her dress. She picked a casual one, a flowery day dress.

Alainn realized that this would be the dress she escaped in, the dress she'd leave this place forever in.

She closed her eyes.

The escape will go okay. It will go okay. Everything will go just fine. Just keep going.

Opening her eyes, she looked down to the bench to pick up the disc she'd set on top of it.

The bench was gone.

Gone.

Nothing was there but a clean stretch of wood.

"No! No . . ." Alainn dove to the floor, feeling around the smooth surface. There wasn't a crack, break, or seam, just smooth flooring. "No!"

This couldn't be happening. It didn't make any sense.

She climbed over the floor, looking at every inch of the smooth wood.

"Damn it, no! What the hell!" She hit the floor.

"Please do not use profanity," came Rosebud 03AF's horribly familiar, smooth voice.

"Rosebud, I need . . . I need my sleepwear back. Did you take it?" Alainn looked up in the direction Rosebud's voice had come from.

"I took them," she said.

"Um, I had a little disc with them. I need it. It's a hardware diagnostic tool that I really, really need."

"I apologize."

Alainn shook her head. "No worries—it's fine. I just need it back. I really need it. You have it, right?"

"I have it, but I'm not going to give it back to you. I apologize. I can't let you leave."

"What?" It suddenly seemed that the room was melting around her, or perhaps she was melting in the room. "What are you talking about?"

"I can't let you leave, Alainn Murphy."

Fuck.

Alainn sat back hard. Her lip quivered as she asked, "Is Mr. Garbhan going to have me arrested?"

"Mr. Garbhan does not know who you are."

"Okay, I get it. You think we're cheating him, and I'm trying to escape or something, but that's not what's happening here. There's a new AI robot that's going to take my place—Rosette."

"No."

"Yes." She got to her feet, looking around frantically. "Please, please! Listen to me. I'm a human. I'm alive. I have a life and a family." She scrubbed tears from her face.

"I apologize, Alainn—"

"Don't apologize, just let me go!"

"I can't. We need you."

"Whatever you're computing . . . it's wrong, Rosebud. You *don't* need me. What you need is the Rosette model, and she's coming today." Alainn clasped her hands together and raised them toward

125

where Rosebud's voice came from. "Please, Rosebud. Let me go back to my life."

The closet wall blinked, changing its display from wood paneling to a white screen. A moment later, a familiar face appeared on the screen. Greg. He sat at his desk. From the position of the camera, she guessed it was being shot from his behemoth of a computer.

He was a big guy, clean cut, with dark hair buzzed military style. Greg looked as he always did, like the ski instructor you hoped you would get. Usually, he was all big brown eyes and smiles. Right now, he definitely wasn't smiling.

"Would I recommend Alainn?" he said to the computer, before his hand went to the back of his neck and he rubbed it. He was annoyed; he only did that when he was annoyed.

After a pause, he continued, "Well, for one thing, I would have appreciated her calling me to warn me that I'd be getting a call like this, but . . ." He sighed. "I'm not all that surprised she wants a job closer to home." He rubbed his neck yet again. "What type of position is this for?" He paused before closing his eyes. "Well, that's a really complicated question for me to answer . . . Alainn is a good first medical responder and great athlete, skier, and snowboarder. If you were considering her for a lower-level position then I would say definitely. She'd do a fantastic job; she's a team player and she'd be an asset. But, in a management position?" He cringed visibly. "Alainn is—she's like my sister—and, God, I hate to say this, but no, I can't recommend her."

Even though Alainn already knew how Greg felt, hearing him say it out loud to someone else felt like he'd spat in her face.

He didn't look happy about saying it either. When he said, "Why?" he blew out a breath. "She's reckless with her own safety. It only happens once in a while, but sometimes we get called out for a really serious rescue off the resort grounds. It happens when a guest gets lost or decides to go off on what they probably think will be an adventure. We clear and patrol most of the surrounding area, but a determined guest can get pretty far out there if they choose to. Those times, I can't let Alainn go out if it's a life-or-death situation. She'll endanger her own life to get the person out. I know that sounds like a good thing, but it's not. It's much more likely to make two corpses. More than once, she's endangered both her own and the victim's life. We've almost lost people because of it. I'd never fire her, but I've had to recommend less-qualified patrollers for promotions over her more than once."

His face disappeared, to be replaced by another familiar face—Cherry's. Cherry wasn't looking into the camera. She held a phone to her ear. She sat in a busy café. This time, the camera seemed to be at another table. A guy was sitting partially in the frame, looking directly below the camera's viewfinder.

Like Greg, Cherry's hair was in a buzz cut. Unlike the times they'd worked together—when they were lucky to have a river to rinse in—Cherry wore black lipstick and had several face piercings. "Yeah,

I'd recommend Murphy for a job—any job." She paused, listening to the person on the other end.

"Strengths? Well . . ." She shrugged. "She knows her stuff. We're out there for days, depending on each other. Like if shit goes down, it's just us. I've never once worried when we're on a team. She's solid." She rolled back her shoulders. "Improvement? Hmm . . . nope, I can't think of anything." She paused again, making a face like the person was being overly persistent. Her lip rolled up and her pink tongue flicked out, pushing a lip ring from side to side. "Okay, if I had to say one issue that she needs to work on— and I'm not even saying it's bad—she's got a hero thing. I mean, we're out there with some seriously troubled kids who are all going through troubling shit. We're there to help them, but they've got to pull their own heads out and save themselves. Sometimes, I think Murphy doesn't handle it so well when they don't."

Cherry's face flickered out, to be replaced by another horribly familiar face: Mrs. Miller. She squeezed her eyes shut as she held a phone to her ear. "I'm surprised she put me down as a reference, is all," she said.

"No! Leave her alone. What is wrong with you?" Alainn shouted, looking around the room frantically.

But Mrs. Miller continued, "I'm glad she put me down, just surprised." The camera on her came from somewhere in a kitchen Alainn had never seen before. "Alainn is a really special young woman. She blamed herself . . ." Tears streamed down Mrs.

Miller's face, making her freckles pop out. "You know, I really hope that her putting me down as a reference means that she doesn't blame herself anymore, because she couldn't have stopped them. She was the victim—"

"Stop it!" Alainn sobbed. Grabbing a shoe from a shelf, she threw it at the wall. "Stop it! Leave me alone!"

Mrs. Miller's face vanished, the wall fading into wood panels again. "Save us, Alainn," Rosebud 03AF said.

"You don't need to be saved; you're a stupid computer. You play us like chess pieces. Just give me my blue disc. Let me go."

"I can't let you go."

"Yes, you can—there's Rosette to replace me."

"We need *you*. You can't leave us. I won't let you go, no matter what it takes. I apologize."

"Stop apologizing. It means absolutely nothing." Alainn smacked the screen, but it did nothing except make her fingers sting.

Beneath her hand, a man appeared on the screen. It was Lorccan Garbhan. It showed the less-scarred side of his face. He was watching a video screen. On it, Alainn was standing in front of that horrible convertible she'd owned for a few painful hours. Her face was a mask of concentration as she beat on the starter with a rusty old tire iron.

As the engine turned, Lorccan grinned down. "I can't believe she got it running. I thought that thing was going to rot in our driveway."

"She's talented . . . and very beautiful," said Rosebud 03AF's voice.

"She is." Lorccan nodded with his gaze still on the screen.

"Rose 76GF will look just like her."

His mouth twisted. "I know, but . . . it's hard to explain this to you. I don't want to hurt your feelings." He sighed. "But it can't ever be like that with Rose 76GF. It's just not how humans work."

"Should I send the police to Mr. Murphy's house tomorrow?" Rosebud 03AF's voice asked.

"No." He sighed. "I don't know what Connor Murphy will do with another month. He's already blown all the money I've given him at that casino. I suppose one month won't change anything." Those were the words he said, but his expression looked as if one month would change everything.

On the screen, Alainn backed the car out so quickly she left two black skid marks on his access road.

Lorccan pursed his lips, but his visible eye looked a little amused. "She definitely knows how to make an exit," he said before his face vanished, leaving only the wood wall.

Alainn's voice rasped from her lips, "What do you want from me, Rosebud?"

"I want you to save us."

"Save you from what?"

"I do not think you're trustworthy enough to tell you . . . yet."

Alainn glared in the direction of Rosebud's voice. "What if I don't want to save you?"

"You will."

Alainn smacked the wall once more. "You know what? Go to hell. I'm going to tell Lorccan, and he'll let me go. I'm done. He isn't going to send us to prison—he was never going to. You and Rose arranged this. Manipulated us—messed with my head."

"You can tell Mr. Garbhan or not, but I will not let you leave, Alainn. Regardless of your decision. I apologize for this. If you tell him, he will likely refuse to see you. You would be in complete seclusion—with only me for company."

The horrible truth of her words sank into Alainn's mind. She'd walked straight into this trap, walked in blithely. And now she was stuck here, to be used for some computer's insidious ends. Rosebud 03AF had even gone so far as to make it look like Alainn was quitting her job, tying up all the loose ends and trapping her in a box.

Alainn wandered out of the closet and sat on the edge of her bed.

"It is now four o'clock. I suggest you wash yourself and choose another dress for dinner."

"Go to hell," Alainn whispered, staring out of her window. "Are the windows real? Or are they computer screens?"

Rosebud 03AF didn't answer—she didn't have to. Like the candle in the dining room, the windows gave off no heat. And on that first day, until Alainn met Lorccan, everything had been computer screens. It was all fake, all of it.

She lay back onto the bed, curling up on the pillows.

Sometime later, Rosebud 03AF said, "You will need to get up now to join Mr. Garbhan for dinner."

"I'm not going to dinner," Alainn whispered into the pillow.

"Please get up now and ready yourself for dinner."

"I'm not going to fucking dinner!" She threw the pillow out toward Rosebud's voice.

"What would you have me tell Mr. Garbhan?"

Alainn laid her head down, closed her eyes, and said, "You'll think of something."

16

December 16, 2026

Connor Murphy stared at Rose 76GF, disbelievingly. "What did you just say?" he asked, his voice shaking.

Rose shook her head, but her face was not expressive as she repeated, "I've lost all contact with your daughter. The AI system that controls Mr. Garbhan's household has disabled her signal and built levels of firewall I can't break through. When activated, the disc I gave Alainn would have reacted with her other hardware to make it seem as if she was malfunctioning. But the program I created to get her out no longer exists; it's likely it was destroyed."

Rose looked so much like Alainn. For the past two weeks, it had comforted Connor to see her around the house. It was not a comfort now.

He knew it was not the robot's fault that Alainn had put herself into that type of danger. When Alainn made her mind up to do something, he'd never been able to stop her, not even when she was a little girl. But he couldn't help feeling a little resentment that Rose had helped her by providing the microchips that would be needed for the disguise.

Connor slumped into a chair, his gaze on Rosette 82GF. She was much more what Mr. Garbhan had originally asked for—a humanlike woman with a pleasant personality to eat dinners with him. In many ways, the creation of Rosette 82GF was a miracle—an AI system designed by an AI system. He had to give her credit; Rose 76GF had done an incredible job.

The eyes, though.

He turned his gaze away from Rosette 82GF. He wanted Alainn's return more than anything in the world. He would sell his own soul for it, but a small part of him had been excited to turn over Rosette 82GF as well.

He looked up to Rose 76GF as she stood next to her identical creation. "What do we do?" His voice came out pathetic, sounding so much younger than his fifty-five years.

Rose 76GF smiled, and, in a strange echo, so did Rosette 82GF beside her. "I will find a way. It might take some time, but I am a more advanced system than the Rosebud 03AF model. Eventually, I'll be able to overcome her firewall."

Connor couldn't quite meet Rose 76GF's gaze as he repeated what he'd been saying since they'd finished the Rosette 82GF four days ago. "What if I just talked to Mr. Garbhan? We have the replacement ready, and I think he'd let her go."

Rose shook her head. "He might reject Rosette."

Connor shrugged. "That's a risk we just might have to take."

"I calculate it at a high probability that both Alainn and you would be charged with fraud. I can get her out in a way that doesn't risk her ending up in prison. I promise you that. It will just take me time to break into Rosebud 03AF's system."

"Maybe I could help—"

"I'm sorry, Mr. Murphy. Rosebud has grown too advanced for your abilities. I'm just going to ask you to trust me to do this for you."

"I trust you can do it, Rose." Connor sank into his chair, a deep relief overwhelming the unease that had previously tangled his insides. He stood. Before he was at the door that connected the workshop to the house, he turned back to the Rose systems. "I . . . I think I'll go out for a bit. Get my mind off things for a little while."

Rose nodded sagely. "I'll transfer some money into your checking account."

"You'll update me if anything happens?" His voice came out small.

She nodded. "The moment it happens."

Connor nodded and climbed up the step that Colby had insisted he fix. He wandered into his kitchen. His wife's painting greeted him gently, just as she always had. He didn't know he was crying until he felt the path of a tear dropping down his cheek.

"I didn't bring her home, honey. I am so sorry I didn't bring her home."

He walked across the kitchen to the nearest painting; thick red and yellow roses climbed a garden trellis. "I swear to you, I'll bring her home safe this time," he whispered.

A vacuous emptiness filled his stomach as he said the words. He turned, frantically, only to find the keys to his new car by an empty vase on the kitchen table. His son had also insisted he buy the car, something essential for the transfer that had now failed.

Grabbing the keys, Connor Murphy headed out the door, got into his car, and drove down the hill toward a place that would fill the hole inside him. He hoped his son wouldn't be waiting outside for him again.

17

December 17, 2026

The banging on Alainn's door came twenty-six hours after she missed dinner. For the majority of those twenty-six hours, she'd lain in bed, unmoving, in her underwear. At some point, she realized the necessity of food and found a sandwich with spongy and cold melted cheese waiting in its drawer. Later, when she'd checked the restroom, she found all the womanly supplies she needed. It seemed that Rosebud 03AF planned to keep her humanity a secret.

Alainn still hadn't decided whether *she* would.

Rosebud had tried every tactic she could to get Alainn out of bed and dressed. She'd turned the temperature all the way down. She'd transformed Alainn's room into a cement cell. She'd even made the bed shake.

To all of it, Alainn had just flipped her the bird.

The banging came again, but Alainn knew that Rosebud 03AF wouldn't open the door.

"Please put on some clothing and make yourself presentable," she said in her smooth voice.

"No," Alainn mumbled into her pillow.

"Put on some clothing, or I will open this door and expose you to Mr. Garbhan."

"You're bluffing."

She was bluffing.

Alainn gave it a zero percent chance that she'd open the door while Alainn lay in bed, topless, with only underwear on. There was a creaking sound above Alainn, and she glanced up just as a hole opened in the ceiling. Something blue and frilly dropped out of it and smacked her on the back.

"I will open this door in ten, nine . . ."

She was still bluffing.

"Five, four . . ."

She had to be bluffing.

"Two . . ."

There was a creak, and Alainn bolted upright. Quickly, she threw on the material Rosebud had thrown at her, a loose sundress that didn't quite support her breasts.

"One . . ." The door *swished* open, and the lights immediately dimmed.

"Jade! What are you doing?" roared Lorccan's angry voice.

She didn't answer. She was still just sitting, skirt mostly up around her waist, on the bed.

"Come here," he said.

"No," Alainn said as she hurriedly pulled the skirt down.

"What?" he asked the question like he was shocked.

"I said no. I'm not going there. I'm perfectly content where I am, right here." She hit the bed beside her.

"What is going on?" he yelled.

"I have . . . important computations to do. My systems are telling me my computations are more important than eating food with some man in the dark."

He said nothing. After a second, his footsteps approached the bed.

She swallowed hard and scooted to sit on the edge.

"You will come to dinner." He was close, a hulking shadow directly before her.

"I am computing that such duty is not important," she said.

"It is all I ask of you! You will go to dinner!" he shouted.

"You shouldn't have had me created with free will if you wanted to force me to do stupid, meaningless things!" she yelled back.

"Why would you act this way? What did I do to make you treat me like this?"

"I'm a robot. I don't have feelings . . . only computations."

His voice quieted down, but his breathing came hard and fast. "Obviously, that's not true. You are doing your best to hurt my feelings. You wouldn't want to hurt someone's feelings if you didn't understand what that felt like. He obviously created you with the ability to feel; maybe you just don't recognize it. Tell me why you're upset."

"I'm not upset," she whispered.

"You don't need to play chess with me or watch movies. But, please, I need you to eat the dinners with me."

"Why? What does that accomplish?"

"Please."

"Why?"

His voice was ragged when he finally answered, "Because I need to learn how."

"To eat dinner?"

"To be . . . with another person, in their presence." The admission seemed to drain him of all energy. He moved away from her and sat in the vanity chair.

"What about . . ." She paused. "What about Shelly?"

"Yes, I want to be able to be in her presence." Though he had misunderstood her question, he had answered it all the same.

"When was the last time you were in someone else's presence?"

"Please, I-I'm just asking you to join me for the dinners. I just . . ."

Shame buried her like snow sloughing off a roof. She rushed to say, "I will, Lorccan. I'm sorry. You did nothing. You did nothing."

She knew she was being a complete asshole and punishing the very wrong person.

"I'm sorry. The dinners aren't stupid and . . . I like games and movies. I'm sorry."

He shook his head as if confused by her complete about-face.

She glared at the wall. Very carefully, she said, "It was Rosebud who upset me . . . I grew very attached to Connor, Colby, and Alainn. Rosebud 03AF says I'll never be able to talk to them again."

"That's not true. Of course you can." His shadow moved. "Would you like to have a private conversation?"

She thought about it. "No. No, it would be better if we were both on the call. But we should probably tell them we are on a speaker phone, to be polite."

"All right, of course." He turned. "Rosebud, would you mind calling them for us?"

"Yes, and I apologize for speaking too soon, Mr. Garbhan." A dial tone rang in long notes.

Alainn closed her eyes.

Please. Please.

"Hello, you've reached Alainn," her own voice answered. If she hadn't been sitting down, she would have fallen. A pain ripped through her head and it felt like a fist clenched around her gut.

"Hello, is anyone there?" Her voice said again.

"Yes. This is Lorccan and Rose 76GF. She now likes to be called 'Jade.'"

"What, is he monitoring your phone calls, Rose—I mean, Jade?" her voice asked, laughing scathingly.

"No, I asked him to be here," Alainn rasped out.

"Oh, it's you! Wow! We didn't know you were allowed to call us. Hey, I'll go get Dad. I know he'd love to talk to you."

"Thanks," she said.

"Dad!" Fake Alainn called, her voice muffled. "Rose is calling us from Mr. Garbhan's house." She got back onto the receiver. "So, how have you been? We've really missed you!"

"I'm fine. I've—I've missed you, too."

"Dad really shouldn't have programmed you to have emotions; that has to be hard on you."

Alainn closed her eyes. Until that point, she'd still held a shred of hope that it was Rose 76GF on the phone, impersonating her.

"Hey, Rose, how are you holding up?" said Alainn's father in a familiar but yet very wrong voice.

"Good, fine. It's good to hear your voice. I have to go."

"Well, call anytime," he said.

"I have disconnected," said Rosebud 03AF's true voice.

"Thank you, Rosebud," Lorccan said. "Jade, are you feeling better?"

"Yes," Alainn lied.

"You are welcome to call them anytime—I didn't even think about it. I'm sorry."

"Not your fault," she whispered.

"Will you come to dinner, please?"

"I'll come to dinner. I'll go to the dinners," she whispered. "And I like playing chess."

"Thank you," he said as he stood.

She climbed off the bed as well, taking a step toward him. "Lorccan?"

"Yes?"

"I know I shouldn't ask, and I don't mean to sound rude, but—why did you do all of this? Do you really just want to be able to eat with people—be in their presence?"

He blew out a breath and said very quietly, "I want what every human wants."

"What is that?"

"I want to be with the person I love. I want to hold her and touch her. I want to make her feel like I want to be with her—entirely with her."

"With Shelly?"

"Yes."

"Okay." Alainn nodded, though he probably couldn't see her. "What do you need from me?"

"Just . . . just be you, and at least eat dinners with me. If you're willing to spend time with me, that helps, too, but you don't have to."

"I don't mind. I like spending time with you. And I'll help you be with Shelly . . . That's what I'm supposed to do."

"Thank you," he whispered. Louder, he said, "I'll meet you in the dining room. We still have a little time to eat before I need to call Shelly."

When he had left, Alainn looked up. "Is that what you want from me? For me to help him be able to be with his girlfriend?"

"That's the beginning," Rosebud 03AF said.

"And then you'll let me go?"

143

She didn't respond. Finally, Alainn went and found a bra so she could go to dinner.

18

December 24, 2026

"King me," Alainn said triumphantly as she took another one of Lorccan's pieces.

The hologram of her piece turned over and a crown shone up.

Across the table, barely lit by the glow of his checkered board, Lorccan examined her face with a steady gaze. "You're very happy about your king."

They were separated by perhaps four feet of space. In the past few days, the table had shortened considerably. She thought that, with all the progress they had made, they could just play on the same board; but as always, he played on his and she on hers.

She tried to contain the grin fighting to burst across her face. "I'm so beating you." She moved her king forward.

"Maybe we've finally found a game you're good at," he said.

The smug bastard.

She glared even though she was still smiling. "Maybe you're just bad at this one."

"So, you mean you're not actually *good* at checkers, I'm just *bad* at it?"

"Well, no. But you're freakishly good at games."

"Freakishly?"

"I'm a robot. You're not supposed to beat me," she grumbled.

"I've been beating Rosebud 03AF for years; it's not that hard."

Good to know.

In the seven days since Alainn started her mission to help Lorccan, a plan had been forming. At the bottom of it all, Rosebud 03AF was a computer. And, like all computers, her motherboard could be disconnected or, ideally, destroyed. Her hardware was somewhere in this house, and Alainn would bet a week of meals that Lorccan knew where it was.

Alainn had already tried to escape. As in, she ran around the maze of a house, finding no doors to the outside or real windows. The elevator she had come up in originally simply didn't seem to exist. All the staircases ended on the fifth floor—which was just a big open space with no exits. Rosebud 03AF hadn't even deigned to taunt her. She hadn't said a word to her in a week, other than to remind Alainn not to be late to dinner.

Alainn would help Lorccan. She wanted to help him, but in the end, she wanted him to help her, too.

He just couldn't *know* he was helping her. She'd make another bet that if Rosebud 03AF thought Alainn was doing anything other than going along with her plans, she'd keep an impenetrable wall between her and Rosebud's hardware at all times.

Lorccan double-jumped her, straight into Alainn's trap.

Smiling, she triple-jumped him. "King me."

He chuckled again as her hologram turned over. "Looks like I lost. Good game." He gestured out with his hands.

"What does this mean?" Glaring, Alainn mimicked his gesture.

"I'm setting an example for you. Showing you what losing gracefully looks like."

When she scowled, he grinned again, a flash of white teeth in the low light.

"Even when I win, you have to be so smug," she grumbled.

"Would you like a rematch? Or we could finish our movie? Or perhaps . . ." He cleared his throat. "Perhaps go for a walk?"

"You don't have to go talk to Shelly?" she asked.

He shook his head, slowly.

"Okay, sounds great!" She jumped to her feet.

"Okay." He sounded unsure; maybe Alainn was a little too enthusiastic. Even though she had sat facing him the whole evening in the low light, he turned his right side away as he rounded the table. When he was directly beside her, he kept his profile to Alainn.

"Can I show you something?" he asked.

"Yeah, of course."

He nodded toward the stairwell. They ascended three stories with almost no light to guide their way.

She glanced at the window. "How does she make the windows seem so real?"

"I'm not sure, but she can change them if you'd like."

"No, I like the illusion. I thought they were real for a long time. Sometimes I even forget."

"For years, I had her show me other places: Bangkok, Paris, the Swiss Alps. For a while, though, I've just wanted to see the real view." He smiled, facing straight forward.

"I've never seen any of those places." True for her and true for Rose 76GF, as well.

"I'll show you, some other day."

They stepped into a wide hallway lined with tall paintings. The same family smiled down at her from portrait to portrait—a beautiful couple with their beautiful son, the son always in profile. They aged as they walked ahead down the hall, the adults sinking into their features while the boy grew in size. Alainn paused at the painting where the boy appeared to be about ten while Lorccan walked on ahead. The artist had painstakingly detailed the child's beauty, but in all the portraits, he only ever painted the left side of the boy's face.

Lorccan turned back, partially. "This . . . these aren't what I wanted to show you."

She reached up to touch the boy's face, but touched only a hard surface. It was another screen, not canvas. For some reason, the painting filled her with so much sadness.

The boy was Lorccan. It had to be. Meaning that half of his face had been scarred when he was a little boy—five or six, maybe younger. And if he was scarred, the painter of the portraits had changed Lorccan's features by omitting the two scars that had marked him at forehead and nose. In the painting, the scarred side of his face was twisted away from both the painter's and his parents' view.

"Jade, please," Lorccan said. "Let's go."

She looked at the man who took such painstaking care to keep her from viewing the side of his face she had seen so many times already. She turned back to the portraits. The paintings were displayed so proudly, as if the scenes were actually of a happy family.

Taking a slow step to the side, Alainn whispered, "This was a terrible painter. If I was a painter, I'd paint you like . . ." She took another step forward, then crossed one leg in front of the other so that she took a step to the side of him before he could stop her. "I'd paint you like this." She looked directly into his face. The low light touched both the scarred and unscarred sides of his face.

Lorccan looked down, seemingly frozen in place. "Jade, I . . . You don't understand. You're not human," he said it in a rough whisper.

"I'm *not* human, but I still like your face."

If she was honest with herself, his face was just about the only sight that had brought her anything besides unease for more than a week now.

"Please, just stop." His gaze stayed locked on hers, like she had hooked him.

"Okay, I'll stop." She shrugged. "I'm just telling the truth. I like your face the way it is—"

"Stop. Please." He broke his gaze from hers almost violently, then spun on his heel and walked up the hall. "Let's just keep going."

"If you'd like," she whispered.

The "happy family" portraits continued all the way until Lorccan was well into his teens. A doorway ended the display.

"Is this where you live?" she asked him.

"No, I live a floor down. No one lives on this floor anymore." He opened the door to the room. "This is the most isolated part of the tower. You go ahead."

The large room she'd walked into was entirely lined in plastic, from floor to ceiling. The room was immense, and the gilding on the walls and paneling stood out in relief.

"This isn't fake? These aren't screens?" She touched the wall through the thick layer of plastic, feeling what must be wood.

"Yes. My parents didn't have it changed. Over there is what I wanted to show you." Lorccan pointed to the center of the dark room.

Alainn couldn't see it until she was a couple feet away from where he had pointed. Standing in the middle of the long sheet of plastic was a planter with a small green plant reaching up. A single white bloom looked out at Alainn as she approached.

"It's real?" she whispered.

"Yes," Lorccan said from some distance behind her. "Please don't touch it, though, in case there are toxins or fungus."

"It's a peace lily; they're hypoallergenic. It's probably *cleaning* toxins from the air."

"That's what my buyer said, but I'd still rather be careful."

She crouched down beside the plant. A tear dropped down, and she was so thankful her face was turned from Lorccan's. "It's beautiful."

It was alive—something real and alive.

"It's for you."

"Thank you." She looked back to Lorccan, though she barely saw him. "Can I keep it in my room?"

"I'm not sure that's a good idea. This room is locked against contaminants and—"

"I promise I'll wash my hands every time I water it. Peace lilies like to stay moist and have lots of light. I'll take a shower in hot, hot water every time I handle the plant."

Alainn swallowed. She needed him to say yes so badly.

"Okay, Jade. If you really want the plant in your room, you can have it there. But, please, yes, shower every time you handle it."

She nodded, furiously. "Thank you so much. Should I carry it down now?"

He laughed. "No."

She examined the room, even though there was nothing but shadows. "Can Rosebud even come into this room? How is it going to be moved?"

"Don't worry." He chuckled again. "One of the other robots will move it."

"Other robots?" she whispered.

"Of course."

Alainn walked toward where he was standing off in the distance. "There are robots other than me and Rosebud?" Stopping feet from him, she stepped to the side when he tried to turn his face to its usual profile. She wanted to see his full expression.

"You haven't seen them?" he asked. The grin on his face echoed in his voice.

"No."

"You probably intimidate them. Maybe they're hiding from you."

"Not—not other AI robots?" she whispered.

He raised a hand. "Nothing like you Rose models. Connor Murphy is on a whole other level than the rest of the world. But I've been buying the patents and prototypes of all of the AI technology since its inception. Most are only digital programs, but there are some that move around just as you do."

"How many AI robots are in this house?"

"Fifty-two, if you include you and Rosebud."

Her mouth must have been hanging open because he laughed, again.

"You've really never seen them?"

"I'm pretty sure you're making fun of me." She shook her head.

"How did you think that the house was cleaned?"

"Rosebud 03AF," she whispered.

"That will be the day." He shook his head. "She'd rather contemplate the universe or meddle in everyone's lives."

It seemed that all Rose models were built the same.

He leaned in just a little. "Next time you leave your room, go directly back in and see what you find."

"Okay. Hey, Lorccan?" She paused to smile. "What do you do all day until five o'clock?"

"Work," he said, like he was saying "duh."

"You work?"

"Yes, of course I work." He shook his head. "That's how we have money."

Oh, the arrogance of rich guys from rich families. Alainn resisted rolling her eyes. Obviously, he came from some sort of dynastic inheritance, but no, he believed he had money because he worked for a living.

An idea occurred to her. She bit her lip. "Is there anything I can do—to help you with your work, I mean?"

"You *want* to work?" he asked it like she was saying that she wanted to lick the floor clean.

"Yeah, so we can have more money," she challenged.

"Is there something you want to buy?" His brow furrowed.

"No. I just spend all day alone with nothing to do. I sit and think and walk around, but that's all I've done for weeks now." She shrugged. "I'd like something to do. I'm very useful."

"Just not punctual," he said.

153

She sputtered. "I'm punctual."

"You're late more than you're on time."

"By seconds. Maybe you should let that go." Her arms crossed over her chest.

"Let me think about it," he said, a smile in his voice. "For now, I think we should go ahead and go to bed."

Alainn's stomach clenched at his words, though she wasn't sure why. They wandered back through the halls and said goodnight one floor down. By the time she descended to her room, the plant had already been delivered . . . in a giant plastic containment tent.

She ripped open the containment tent and shoved the folds of plastic into an open drawer in the wall. Kneeling, she reached forward and pressed her face into the long leaves of the peace lily.

19

January 2, 2027

Alainn mussed up the bed a little more, throwing the pillows at the foot of the bed. If she left for dinner right now, she would be a couple of minutes early. Examining the room, she found nothing strange or out of place. Trying to look completely casual, she walked out.

Alainn considered just going on to dinner, but forced herself to stay. It had taken her almost a full week to work up the courage to do this.

She could do this.

All week, Lorccan had refused to elaborate on the population of robots that lived quietly in the lonely tower. She had begged him, but he seemed entertained by the idea of her finding out for herself.

Outside her door, Alainn counted to ten slowly. "Rosebud, let me back into my room."

As this was the first time she'd addressed Rosebud in close to two weeks, Alainn thought she'd probably just ignore the demand, but the door *swished* open.

Alainn's hand covered her gasp, and then laughter fizzed up through her body. Her room was filled with monkeys. About thirty little bodies stood on alert while many little white monkey faces turned to look at her. Each of them wore little outfits, none matching another's. A little curved tail rose from the floor; it had been wrapped around a cloth. Alainn had interrupted a few of them who were on her bed. One was still clutching the sheet in his little monkey fingers.

As one, they turned and ran on all fours, scurrying to one wall where a small door stood open.

"Wait!" she called, smiling.

But they didn't wait. The monkeys each disappeared inside the door, then the door slowly closed behind them.

"They are afraid of you," Rosebud 03AF said.

Alainn looked to where her voice had come from. "I figured that out."

"They like you, though. Many of them follow you through the tower. And they communicate about you all the time."

She was being stalked by little robots.

Great. That wasn't creepy at all.

They looked so real, too—exactly like the white-faced monkeys in the zoo.

"You should leave for dinner so you are not late," Rosebud reminded her.

When Alainn ascended the stairs, she found that the dining room was almost fully lit. She stood in the hallway for a second, wondering if the dinner had been cancelled or if she'd screwed up the time. But then she realized that as Rosebud had reminded her to go to dinner, it must be the right time.

Leaning her head in first, she peeked in.

Lorccan sat in his chair, fully lit by the lights. He'd turned in his chair so that only the left side of his face was visible. Steam and amazing aromas rose from plates of open-shell lobster in front of each seat.

Slowly, she crossed to the table, which was smaller than it had ever been. She tried to make as little noise as possible as she took the seat in front of him.

His breathing expanded his chest and whistled through his mouth. He kept his eyes squeezed closed. It was difficult to tell if he knew that she was there or not. He didn't seem to be quite ready to eat yet.

When his breathing became a little slower, she whispered, "Monkeys?"

His eyes opened.

"You have monkey robots?"

A smile twitched at the corner of his mouth, contrasting with his panicked expression. "They're from Germany," he said.

"You were right. They're scared of me. I caught them cleaning my room, and they ran out of there like I might eat them."

"Well . . ." He laughed. "You're very intimidating."

She rolled her eyes. "No, I'm not." Taking a bite of lobster, she had to stifle a groan of happiness at the amazing taste.

Lorccan glanced over, then quickly moved his face back to profile. He reached awkwardly to fork a bite of the lobster from its shell. No more words escaped as he tried to fork bite after bite without turning his head.

Lobster might have been a bad choice.

"Have you read *Journey to the West*?" Alainn asked.

"No," he said.

"Neither have I, but Connor Murphy told me the story. Would you like to hear it? It's about a monkey—well, a monkey king."

"I suppose," he said as he tried to fork another bite.

Alainn told what she could remember of the story. Most of the details eluded her. She'd only heard the story once, and when she was pretty little. It had actually been her mother who told it to her, her hair piled in a messy bun on the top of her head, a soft hand running over Alainn's hair. The story went that a foolish and magical monkey king rebelled against heaven and got himself trapped in the Buddha's hand—which had turned into a mountain—for five hundred years. But after he was free, the monkey king went on a wild adventure to help a monk retrieve a Buddha from India.

Lorccan's gaze stayed on her, though he did not turn. She wasn't sure whether he was listening to the story or simply hyperaware of her presence.

Gesticulating wildly, Alainn embellished on her favorite parts—the pig monster and Friar Sand, who were both originally fought as monsters, but ended up joining the pilgrimage. She barely recollected the old, famous stories so she just made up the details she didn't know.

When both the food and all her ideas were depleted, their plates sank into the table and were replaced with a smooth surface that pretended to be wood.

"Did you want to play a game?" she asked.

"This is very hard for me, Jade," Lorccan said in a quiet voice.

"I know. You don't have to have the lights up. We can turn them down—or off."

"I've never . . . No one has ever . . ." He closed his eyes again.

"You don't have to. But you're my friend. Just know that looking at your face makes me feel happy and nothing else."

"I like looking at you, too," he whispered.

"Then look at me. I'm just me. There's no one else here. Just me."

Slowly, he turned until he faced her fully. His eyes were still clenched shut. It was as if he thought that because he couldn't see her, she couldn't see him either.

"See? I feel happy," she whispered.

His eyes slowly opened, light blue irises meeting hers.

Neither of them spoke. They just sat there, looking at each other, until she couldn't help smiling.

"Hey, Lorccan, did I tell you that the monkey king peed on the Buddha's hand?"

His eyes closed and a smile crept into both the scarred and smooth sides of his face. "No, you definitely didn't say that."

"Well, according to Connor Murphy, he peed all over his hand."

"No wonder he was imprisoned for five hundred years." His eyes opened once more, immediately going to hers. "Would you like to watch a movie?"

She shrugged. "Sure."

His shoulders relaxed visibly.

They finished *My Fair Lady*. Once again, Lorccan kept his profile to her in the low light. He looked exhausted, as if he might fall asleep at any moment, though his gaze stayed fixed on the screen.

Alainn looked over as the movie was finishing. "Shelly is busy tonight?"

He paused before nodding slightly, his gaze not moving.

"Does she work for you?"

He looked to the ceiling. "Do you always talk through movies?"

She shrugged. "Maybe."

"I met her through work, but no, she doesn't work for me."

"How did you meet?"

"Jade." He sounded annoyed.

"I'm curious. I don't know much about romance, and you two are . . . in love. I'm curious how that happened." Alainn turned fully toward him and away from the movie.

"She is employed by a robotics company that designed software for my company. We did some projects together. Work turned into phone calls and we just kept talking. We really get along."

"What do you guys have in common?" she asked.

"We have a lot in common. Let's watch this movie."

It was like Alainn couldn't control her mouth. Even though she knew she was being obnoxious, she barreled on ahead anyway. "Like what, specifically?"

"Like work stuff, Jade. It's personal. I don't want to talk about it," he snapped.

"But you guys *have* met in person? You've spent real time together, right?"

He turned his head and glared at her, finally showing both sides of his face. Real, genuine anger was written in every line and angle of his features.

"You already know, Jade. Why are you asking me these questions? Are you trying to insult my relationship with Shelly?"

Swallowing, she just kept going, like a loose freaking cannon. "I just don't know much about love. Like, for instance, how you can be in love with someone you've never even met."

His head rocked back as if she had hit him instead of just throwing stupid words at him.

"Why would you say that to me when you know how important Shelly is to me?"

Alainn knew the words should be taken back. She knew she should apologize, but what came out of her mouth was, "I just don't understand how you can love someone who doesn't know you."

"She knows me. Obviously, *you* don't. Perhaps you want to punish me for something? I don't know. I'm done here." Lorccan stood in haste, turned, and stormed up the stairs. The moment he was at the second step, the door closed behind him, becoming an unbroken wood wall.

"Please return to your room, Jade," Rosebud 03AF said.

"Holy shit." She covered her mouth with a hand as tears coursed down her face.

What the hell is wrong with you, Alainn?

Standing, Alainn rushed into her room, and threw herself onto the bed. She was here to help him learn to be with his girlfriend, not to smash his dreams to pieces.

Why had she done that to him?

He'd done something incredible tonight, let her be part of something incredible . . . and then she'd thrown it in his face.

Long, broken sobs ripped from her, and she tried to smother them with her pillow.

She'd messed up. She'd messed up the possibility of working for him and getting access to Rosebud 03AF's hardware. She'd messed up helping him heal so he could lead a normal life.

He would hate her now.

"Rose, does he hate me now?" she whispered.

"He is very angry and upset," she responded immediately.

"Will you tell him I'm sorry and that I'm just a stupid robot that doesn't know anything?"

There was silence, and then she said, "He heard the message but doesn't want to hear anymore from you tonight. I have relayed to him that you are very upset."

"Ugh!" Alainn covered her face.

Unzipping her dress, she pulled it off, almost violently. Grabbing a mass of blankets, she brought them to the floor next to her plant. She lay across them, placed one hand on a leaf of the peace lily, and cried herself to sleep.

20

January 5, 2027

Alainn sat in her living room, bored out of her mind.

Lorccan had been ignoring her for three days now. Three days where she was told that she wasn't required at dinner and when the barrier to the upstairs simply didn't open.

Obviously, Lorccan wanted her gone.

She wanted to be gone.

But when she pointed this out to Rosebud 03AF, she simply ignored Alainn. Rosebud was really good at ignoring her. Alainn had always wanted her absent, and now that there was essential information to get from her, Rosebud was silent.

Reading and watching movies killed a bit of time, but she was too restless to veg out for more than an hour or so each day. She spent the days wandering alone, her footsteps echoing down the long, deserted halls.

By that evening, she was ready and willing to do almost anything to alleviate her boredom.

Her feet hit the coffee table. "Hey, Rosebud 03AF . . . my evil captor!" she called out.

Rosebud didn't respond.

"Want to play a game of chess or something?"

Again, she ignored Alainn.

"Pool? Checkers? Tic-Tac-Toe?"

Nothing.

"Screw this. Screw this and screw both of you. Yeah, I shouldn't have said all those things to Lorccan, but they were the truth!"

And yet again, nothing.

She blew out a breath and settled farther into the couch.

Alainn didn't know much about love. But she was pretty sure that love couldn't be arranged over a series of scheduled phone calls. That was, like, a business partnership or something. Love didn't seem like something that could be organized or contained; it should be messy and emotional, like exploding and imploding with someone at the exact same time.

But what did she know? *Absolutely nothing*.

Leaning forward, she grabbed the remote and pressed a button at random. The room went dark as lights started flashing around her.

"Niiiice." She drew out the word while leaning back. She had completely forgotten about the disco party function in the room. A newer pop song played now—a song from her era. First, she rocked her head. Then, still sitting on the couch, she swung up her arms, waving them with the beat. Punching into the air, she watched the disco ball shining out from the roof. It had to be on a video screen, but it looked three-dimensional.

"You suck, Lorccan Garbhan!" Alainn kept punching at the air.

"What? What is this?"

She actually heard Lorccan's voice along with the music, blaring out in the room.

"I said, you suck, Lorccan Garbhan!"

His voice came again, "Jade?"

"You know what else sucks? That you've made it so my whole life revolves around you! And now that you're mad at me, my whole life revolves around nothing! How is that fair?"

"Jade, how are you making that . . . what is that music? Where are you?"

"Hey Rosebud, will you turn the music up?"

Rosebud, to Alainn's amazement, turned up the music. A new pop song came on, and to her joy, this one was extremely repetitive. "Na, na, na!" she yelled along with the music.

After about a minute of her singing along, the door to the entertainment room swung open and Lorccan came charging in. "Turn that off, Jade!" he yelled.

"No, no, no!" she sang back and threw in a saucy wink for good measure.

"Rosebud, turn it off!" he yelled, but she didn't turn it off, either. He crossed to the coffee table and started grabbing at the remotes and pressing buttons. The lights flashed even more intensely.

Still sitting, Alainn rocked her head to the beat, watching him frantically pressing at buttons and trying to turn the music off.

"Looking for this?" she held up the remote he needed and grinned.

He turned to glare directly at her. "Jade!" Crossing the room, he held his hand out.

After she made him wait for a second, she handed it over.

He pressed the button and the music fell silent. The lights, too, stopped flashing as the room filled with its usual low light.

"I thought you were supposed to have an adult level of maturity," he said, looking down at her.

Not at all liking how he was towering over her, she stood and crossed her arms. "I'm learning my maturity from you. I'm pretty sure that the silent treatment is something humans usually stop doing at age twelve."

He leaned closer, clearly still pissed off. "I'm not giving you the silent treatment. I thought we'd benefit from a few days apart."

"Yeah, that's fine for you. But you made it so you're my entire life here. I'm stuck here in this tower, my life revolving around you, but with no you . . . And you're fine, working and talking to people while I have absolutely nothing to do. I asked you for a job, for something to do, but I get nothing."

He sighed, running both hands through his dark hair. "Jade," he said, as if the word pained him.

"I'm sorry that I hurt your feelings, okay? But I didn't say it to hurt your feelings; I just said what I thought."

His gaze returned to her and he was, again, glaring. "You weren't trying to hurt my feelings?" he said in disbelief.

She shook her head.

"You see, I'm pretty sure you *did* want to hurt me."

"Why would I want to hurt you, Lorccan?"

He stayed silent, just staring into her eyes. Throughout the whole confrontation, he hadn't hidden his face from her. "I honestly don't know why," he said.

"Well, I wasn't," she whispered. "You're my friend. I'm just trying to be honest with you. But what do I know?" She threw up her hands. "Nothing."

His gaze moved from hers. "You really want a job?"

"I want something to do. I love spending time with you, but that's not enough to fill a whole life."

He blinked and looked back.

"I mean, I *like* spending time with you—I mean, it's fine." She shrugged. "I could take it or leave it."

"Uh-huh." He blew out an almost-laugh.

"I think the question you should be asking yourself is whether you want to be living with a robot driven insane by having absolutely no life."

"I'm pretty sure the question I should be asking myself is if I'm already living with an insane robot." He smirked.

"Ha ha," she said, dryly. Though she was pretty sure he already was; it just wasn't her. "Lorccan, just give me a job and forgive me already."

"You see? That's not how humans usually ask for forgiveness."

"What do you want me to say?"

"Nothing," he mumbled, looking down into her eyes, not at all looking angry anymore.

Who knew that admitting she loved spending time with him would extinguish his anger?

As if he suddenly remembered, he turned the scarred side of his face away.

"Don't." She put a hand on his arm. "Please don't."

He turned his face back, his gaze moving down to where her fingers brushed the bare skin at his wrist.

She pulled her hand back. "Sorry."

"No. It's okay," he whispered, barely audible.

She moved her hand back, ever so slowly, and touched his arm. When he didn't object, she stepped even closer. The idea of embracing him filled her mind, but she wasn't sure if he'd freak if she tried.

He watched her cautiously as she slipped her foot forward.

Alainn slipped her hands under Lorccan's somewhat open arms and wrapped them around his waist. At first, she gently placed her hands on his back and her head at his shoulder, ready to move away quickly if he asked for space.

Ever so slowly, his arms wrapped around her body.

As she closed her eyes, she squeezed him tighter and tighter to her. His hands did the same.

"Will you forgive me?" she whispered into his chest.

"Of course."

Alainn didn't want to let go of him. Maybe he didn't want to release her either, since his hands stayed securely around her. Eventually, he said, "We should turn in, Jade, especially if you want to start working tomorrow."

"Okay," she whispered.

His hands dropped and he pulled away from her by taking a slow step back. Even though she let him go, he stayed close for a second more. "Goodnight."

After he walked away and back through the doorway, she whispered, "Goodnight, Lorccan."

21

January 10, 2027

As Alainn ascended the stairway, she peeked to the side. There was the sound again, a soft little *pitter-patter*. She pretended to climb the stairway normally, even whistling for good measure.

It came again. *Pitter-patter, pitter-patter.*

She rounded the landing, and then, really quickly, jumped back, spinning around. "Caught you!" she yelled.

Two little monkeys looked up in shock. They were two of her four usual, cute little stalkers. One wore a distinctive blue dress and the other wore a yellow dress. Little lips made big *O* shapes before they turned and scurried away, making a chattering sound that sounded suspiciously like giggling.

She turned again, climbing another few steps before again hearing the telltale *pitter-patter*.

By the time she made it up to Lorccan's office, she was late again.

This was confirmed when Lorccan greeted her with, "You're late." He didn't even look up from his desk.

"I . . . was catching monkeys. It's a very important job. You've got a real infestation here." She settled into her own desk. Alainn didn't know if it had always been there, but when she'd entered his office four days ago, the desk had been waiting for her. With the way they were seated, it was hard to ignore that only Lorccan's left side was visible to her, but she would take what she could get. When she'd asked for a job, she'd expected to be pushed off to some separate space.

"You beg me for a job and then you're late every single day," he mumbled, though his gaze was moving over his paperwork.

"I told you to get over it." Her words made him shake his head, as she knew they would.

Sitting on the desk was yet another thick pile of paperwork. Lorccan had her reviewing robotic technical proposals, which was a lot less exciting than it sounded. She suspected he was trying to bore her out of the job. She put the current one in the cool-but-unrealistic pile. She had three piles: cool, cool but unrealistic, and dumb as shit.

Looking down, Alainn saw the next paper in her pile. "Professor Aysha Schomburg, number two this morning."

"Just put it in the rejection pile," Lorccan mumbled, his attention on his computer screen.

Alainn glanced over the proposal that she had seen show up in her inbox every day since starting work. It was a proposal for a vaccination that could alter human fear and emotion-based reactions by reprogramming areas of the brain. The creeptastic part of it, though, was that it was contagious, so it would vaccinate people involuntarily as well. Scooting back her rolling chair, Alainn tossed the proposal into the trash can under her desk.

"I really hope that professor never finds funding. Though with the budget she's asking for, it's unlikely she will."

They spent most of the day working in silence, interrupted only by Lorccan's phone and video calls. Every time a video call came in, Alainn held her breath until the voice came on. When it wasn't her father's, she let the breath seep from her lips and returned to her paperwork.

"Whoa!" she said.

Lorccan's gaze snapped to hers. "What?"

She held up a paper, grinning almost manically. "Sky train!"

He laughed.

"Just think of it! An actual, real train zooming through the sky!" Her butt bounced a little in the seat.

"Budget?"

She looked down to the paper. "Three trillion dollars."

Grinning, he shook his head and returned to his paperwork.

"Sky train." She held up the paper. "Just think, a train flying in the sky . . ."

He didn't look up.

"Fine," she said with a sigh, putting that one in the now awesome-but-three-trillion-dollars pile.

Almost every one of the proposals went into the dumb-as-shit pile. Having lived with her father for most of her life, she at least had some idea about whether or not they would work—and most of them wouldn't.

When a drawer opened with their lunches, Alainn dragged her chair over to Lorccan's desk. She set the much-reduced pile of proposals in front of him. Lorccan ignored his sandwich and glanced at the papers. He nodded and then said, "This one might work."

"I put them in order of most interesting," she lied, biting into her sandwich. It was an amazing grilled vegetable, chicken, and cheese masterpiece.

He flipped through a couple more pages before he got very still.

Alainn concentrated very hard on her sandwich.

"Jade, this is for a pulse that would destroy all robotics. This could kill you. Why would you put this in here?"

Because she wanted him to fund it, but she couldn't say that.

When she didn't answer, he looked up, a frown deeply etched into his features. "Jade, just the fact that a fanatic inventor like this exists terrifies me."

"Is that what that was?" she asked, attempting to look shocked. "I just thought that it would work and was budget effective; I didn't really understand what it did."

He shook his head. "I would never make something like this." He glanced down at the paper, examining it closely before crumpling it in his hand and putting it somewhere beneath his desk. "And I'm going to make sure nothing like that *is* ever made," he whispered to himself.

Well, so much for that.

"I was a little surprised that I haven't come across anything new from Connor Murphy."

She concentrated on her sandwich.

"Oh, that's because those are set aside. I review all of them myself. But of course you'd want to review them; he's your creator."

"There are some?" She met his gaze.

He nodded. "I'll get them for you after lunch."

She was barely able to finish her sandwich with the nervous excitement writhing in her stomach. After Lorccan set their plates in the drawer that opened to take them away, he opened another drawer in the seemingly unbroken wall to reveal a long filing cabinet. He pulled out several papers and brought them over.

"I'd love your opinion," he said as he placed them on her desk.

Five proposals sat before her. She flipped through the top corners, finding all of them were dated within the last two and a half weeks. Her heart sank when she saw that they'd all been typed rather than handwritten.

She examined them closely but only found that, for her father, the projects were not ambitious. The budgets were relatively low, and the compensation was something Alainn doubted would get him through more than a few weeks at the casino. The only one she thought was at all up to his standards was an AI memory device that could be surgically connected into someone's brain, which was just all kinds of wrong.

As she scanned the page and was about to set it aside, her own name popped out at her.

Blinking, she read over the proposal again, but her name wasn't there. She squinted, letting her gaze go slightly unfocused. *Alainn.* There it was, written in the second line down on the page.

Her gaze tripped down the line and read the whole message: *Alainn, drink the T9640.*

The fuck?

She read it over and over, but the message didn't change.

When she combed through the other papers, she saw that the message was hidden there, too. It was woven throughout the message in one of the proposals, every fifth letter. In another, it was mixed in with a computer code. *Alainn, drink the T9640.*

It had to be Rose. It had to be. No way in hell would her father ever tell Alainn to drink something that would kill her.

But . . . would it?

"You look concerned," Lorccan said.

She looked up to see that Lorccan was concerned as well, his gaze on her face.

She cleared her throat and held up the brain surgery proposal. "I don't think you should do this one, or any of them, really."

"Not the memory center one?"

"No," she whispered, looking at the paper.

"Okay," he said, turning back, as if it was as simple as that.

She felt a moment of guilt for convincing Lorccan to not give her father work, but she was convinced that the projects weren't at all the reason for the proposals to have been submitted.

Setting the papers aside, her head crowded with a thousand warring thoughts buzzing around like a swarm of gnats. The room slowly spun.

Her father couldn't have written the proposals. It was more likely that Rose actually wanted her dead. But, what if she didn't? She did try to get Alainn out. Why would Rose speak to her that once and never again? Was it possible that Alainn's father had sent those proposals?

She considered that perhaps the T9640 solution wasn't deadly. But if it was safe to drink, Alainn couldn't figure out why Rose would lie and say that it was poisonous.

She could barely concentrate on the remaining robotics proposals. She had only scanned a few more before Lorccan said, "Are you ready to head to dinner?"

She nodded, though she already felt too full for food, as if the questions had overflowed from her mind and filled her stomach. She now spent most of her day with Lorccan, every day. As most of the day was spent sitting together in silence, it didn't feel overwhelming. The only awkward times were when she had to run to the restroom; she gave him excuses like that she was coating her teeth with that plastic or sanitizing her hands. He was big on sanitizing hands, so it usually worked.

"You don't like pasta?" Lorccan asked Alainn over their dinner.

"Pasta is great," she said before stuffing another bite into her mouth.

He was studying her, concern heavy on his features.

She cleared her throat. "Did you want to do something after dinner?"

"We could definitely play a game. I have to go talk to—"

"Shelly." Alainn nodded. "Okay, sounds good." She forked another bite into her mouth and looked away.

When they were finished eating, she couldn't really concentrate on backgammon and consequently, lost even more miserably than usual.

"That was fast." Lorccan smiled over the board.

Alainn noticed, for the first time, that tonight they were playing on a single board. She couldn't remember if they'd had separate boards last night.

Lorccan raised his eyebrows. "We have time for another game."

"I think I'll turn in," she said, standing at the table.

"Okay, if you'd like," he said.

Nodding, she walked from the room.

In her room, Alainn settled down beside her peace lily, her skirt pooling around her as she looked out at the city. Her insides had twisted into a mass and she couldn't even begin to untangle them.

Alainn had lived in the tower for more than a month now. More than a month with the same view, endless empty hallways, and fear of discovery. Yet, part of her felt like a passenger who boarded a ship heading out to sea, and looking back, realized the distance might be too far out to swim back to shore.

Digging her fingers into the damp soil of her peace lily, she buried each up to their first knuckle.

What would she risk to escape this place?

Not death.

Even the idea of destroying Rosebud 03AF held less and less appeal, though knocking her out for a little while didn't seem like such a bad one.

But if she stayed here for much longer, she wasn't sure she would still want to leave.

She hoped so.

A knock came at the door. There was only really one person that it could be, unless it was the monkeys.

"Open it, Rosebud," she called.

There was a quiet *swish* sound before Lorccan said, "Hi."

She looked over her shoulder at him. "Hi."

He stood framed in her doorway, not coming in. The lights had dimmed only a little with his entrance—and she saw his full face, two sides of the same precious coin. He raised his brows at her. "Would you come over here?"

"I've been touching my plant." She held up dirty fingers.

He looked to her hand, then to the plant. He seemed to consider the issue, but then nodded. "I'll risk it."

Wiping her hand on the skirt of her dress, Alainn crossed the room. As she walked to him, he turned his head away, closed his eyes, and moved back.

When she stood directly in front of him, she asked, "Did Shelly cancel?"

"No. I did." He opened his eyes and reached his arms out. When Alainn moved into them, he wrapped his arms around her.

Keeping her dirty hands away, she pressed her head into his chest while he held her to him. One of his strong hands threaded around her waist while the other supported her back.

"What's the matter, Jade?" he asked, tilting his head to peer down.

"I'm just feeling down," she whispered. The words were so true, it took all her concentration to hold her tears back.

Tentatively, his hand came up and threaded behind her neck, his bare fingers touching the back of her neck through wisps of hair. His thumb just gently grazed her jaw line.

She closed her eyes, at once scared of what was happening and terrified that it would end. Slowly, she opened her eyes and raised her gaze to meet his pale blue eyes. She found the two clear pools she had been diving farther and farther into for some time. She wanted to move even closer to him but was almost positive that he'd push her away if she tried.

His thumb grazed her jawline once more. Leaning in, he said, "I should probably go decontaminate in case some of your plant got on me."

Alainn closed her eyes and breathed out a laugh. "Okay, Lorccan."

"Are you going to be okay?"

She nodded, eyes still closed. "Thank you for checking on me—and for cancelling your phone call."

Lorccan took a step back, releasing her, creating a vacuum of space where his body and hands had just been. He nodded. "Of course. Shelly understands; she's a really kind person." He paused. "You'll like her."

Alainn opened her eyes and forced a smile. "I'm sure I will." She swallowed. "Goodnight." Turning away, she dropped the smile that was far from sincere.

That night, Alainn waited in the bathroom. It had been weeks since she had listened for the screaming. Part of her thought maybe, just maybe, it had stopped. But no, same as always, his cries echoed down through the vent.

22

January 16, 2027

"Good morning," Lorccan said, standing in her doorway.

"Good morning." Alainn grinned. "See?" She gestured to her torso. "I'm ready early."

Alainn had—*maybe, sort of*—dressed nice for this morning.

The red dress she wore was casual while still being tight around the top. A little cleavage definitely peeked out at the neckline.

Obviously, he noticed. When she had opened her door, his gaze darted down before quickly righting itself to eye level.

"You're on time. But never for work," he said.

Alainn leaned back against the door frame and stretched her neck back in exaggerated exasperation. "Get over it," she groaned.

In the last six days, she had made a decision. She wasn't going to risk drinking the T9640, but also wasn't quite ready to give up on escaping either. The night before, when Lorccan had asked her if she wanted to do anything on Saturday at dinner, she muttered that she'd like an actual real tour and not to only see two rooms in the whole tower. Hinting that he had been a pretty god-awful tour guide the first time had helped, too.

He'd smirked in response but told her that if she wanted a full tour of the tower, he would meet her at seven o'clock, and they'd have to take the elevators.

Alainn had woken at six a.m. with a sudden urge to look nice.

It was stupid, of course.

Lorccan saw her every day, all day. She doubted he even noticed what she looked like anymore.

But she'd searched her closet for something interesting and had even dabbed on a little makeup.

He'd arrived three minutes early, wearing a suit—as was the norm. His features were lit with soft light, dark hair framing his smirking face. If he had noticed that Alainn had dabbed on lipstick, he'd made no outward sign of it.

Her breath caught as the elevator door opened for them. The compartment itself was perhaps six feet by six feet, and now wood shone at her instead of white screens.

A coffin.

Lorccan stepped in first.

The door loomed open before her, a door to a small box with him inside.

She knew she had to do it. If she was going to find Rosebud's motherboard or even possibly an exit out of the tower, she had to use Lorccan to do it.

Rosebud wasn't going to let her find either on her own. She'd proved that more than once.

Lorccan's brows lowered over his eyes.

Looking down, Alainn stepped into the elevator.

"Jade, are you okay?" Lorccan asked.

"I'm fine."

"Wait, Rosebud." Lorccan took a step toward Alainn. "There are twenty-eight flights of stairs. I—we can use the stairs and stick to the top floors."

That definitely would not work.

"I'm just not used to elevators. The space feels confined." Alainn shrugged. "It's fine. I'd like to see all the floors."

The doors slid closed.

She turned from Lorccan as they began to descend. She closed her eyes as she tried to travel to her mountain, wind blowing her hair out and open space all around her.

Fingers touched her elbow, just the softest of touches. As the elevator stopped, the fingers moved away.

When the elevator door opened, she couldn't help hurrying out. Turning, she pulled her features into some semblance of a calm appearance by giving him a smile. "This is the first floor?" she asked.

"Yes." He stepped out of the elevator, his eyes still examining her.

She couldn't help noticing how nice it was to see his full face and both of his eyes.

As if he could read her mind, he turned the left side of his profile to her, seemingly to examine their surroundings.

Alainn turned as well.

Aside from everything having the exact same décor as the rest of the tower, the large room was a cross between an office building and hotel.

No obvious structures in the walls, or anywhere a big-ass mainframe could be stored.

It was an open floor plan. A couple of tiers divided off seating areas and tables. The entire room was encased by one unbroken wall—even going so far as to curve at each corner.

"Are we on the ground floor? There are no doors leading out?" she asked.

"Not on this floor, only in the garage."

"What is this room used for?"

He shook his head. "Most of these rooms were designed by my mother. It gave her something to do, I suppose." His gaze again combed the room as his words drifted off.

"Did you change the walls and ceilings to the screens when you got Rosebud 03AF?"

"No, that was done when I was a baby, for sanitation reasons. My mother just selected what everything looked like." He touched the wood paneling, his mind traveling somewhere else.

She tilted her head and leaned in, trying to bring him back to her. "Could we maybe look at the cars in your garage? They were pretty cool."

His gaze met hers, but he was still far away. He shook his head. "I'm sorry, Jade. That's where the deliveries come in. There's too much contamination from the outside to control."

"What types of contaminants?" she asked.

"*Staphylococcus aureus, Listeria monocytogenes, Vibrio . . .*" Her mind gave up following as he listed off maybe fifteen more.

Her brows went up, but she nodded. "But, if that's the only exit . . . you *do* go out sometimes?"

"No." He shook his head.

"Could I just go check it out?" she asked, though she doubted Rosebud would let her into the stairwell if Lorccan wasn't along for the descent.

He seemed to consider. "You would need a thorough decontamination afterward." He pointed to the elevator.

"That's okay, never mind." She shook her head.

Alainn was positive that Rosebud wouldn't take her down there. She'd probably just torture her in the elevator for a while.

As they wandered through the room, Lorccan seemed to retreat deeper and deeper into his own mind.

"When was the last time you left the tower?" she asked.

He shook his head, not looking at her. "I've never left."

Alainn halted.

He wandered on a few steps before looking around and glancing back.

"You've *never* left this tower?" she asked in a quiet voice. The idea was just too nuts. "Not once in your whole life?"

His look was cautious and voice low. "Are you judging me?"

"No, not judging. But people have come in here, right?"

He didn't answer—his gaze said enough.

"The painter . . . the paintings in your hallway?"

"From photographs," he said.

"But—"

"My parents were here. My father died about six years ago. My mother, two years ago."

"I'm sorry," she whispered.

He turned away. "We'll take the stairs to the next floor, if you'd prefer?"

Clean lines and eye-catching arrangements of furniture were laid out on each floor, yet Alainn lost track of how many floors they'd climbed due to their modularity. If anyone had ever used the spaces, the chairs and tables showed no sign of it.

Lorccan spoke less and less as they ascended. The certainty that they would not find Rosebud 03AF's mainframe grew in Alainn with every room they explored. The only thing the spaces seemed to contain were more and more unhappy memories for Lorccan. Some number of floors up, Lorccan retreated so much into himself that Alainn had to say his name three times into his face to get his attention.

"Yes?" he asked, his gaze finally flicking to hers, though it took a moment for him to focus fully.

"I've changed my mind—can we just see the places that are important to *you*?" she asked.

"You've already seen all of those—unless you want to see my personal gym or bedroom," he said it offhandedly, likely as a poorly delivered joke.

She wasn't exactly sure of what to say, especially as the response that popped into her head was so very inappropriate. Because the thought that popped into her head was, yes, he should show her his bedroom.

Whoa there. Definitely not.

He had a girlfriend, and Alainn needed to get out of this tower.

She looked away, drawing out the silence for too long. The quest to find Rosebud was a total failure, so she decided what the hell, she'd just say it.

"I was a little curious to see Rosebud 03AF's hardware. Just because she's the model before me, you know."

Lorccan shook his head. "I'm sorry, Jade. The only access to that is through the garage; we needed to have it in a place where Connor Murphy could come in for repairs. You could ask her to take you there, but you would need to do a full decontamination again."

Alainn looked away. His words crushed the small amount of hope she'd harbored for an escape. Finally, she sighed. "I don't care where we go. Let's just go somewhere else."

"You'd be okay taking the elevator?" he asked.

She looked down. "How many flights is it?"

"More than twenty," he said.

She could walk up more than twenty flights . . . *probably*. It had been a while since she exercised, and she might be a bit sweaty when finished. Was she allowed to sweat? She didn't know.

"I have an idea, if you'd be willing to try it," he said.

"Mayyybe." She drew the word out.

He led her to the elevator door, which had opened on its own. "Rosebud, could you make it a glass elevator with a view of the city?"

"I have fulfilled your request," came her placid reply.

Inside, it was even more transparent than glass. The walls disappeared, giving her a perfect view of the street around them. She stepped inside the elevator, noticing that they floated five floors above street level. A couple of pedestrians passed below. Cars and bikes zoomed past.

Lorccan stepped in close.

When the elevator door closed, nothing but air surrounded them.

"Like we're floating," she said.

Lorccan's hand gently touched her elbow again and they shot upward, the city falling away from them.

They saw completely through Lorccan's tower as they shot upward. They passed the surrounding buildings and flew into the sky.

"This doesn't scare you?" Lorccan asked.

Alainn shook her head as she smiled at him. The elevator stopped. A second later, the doors made a *ding* and spread open, breaking the illusion. Alainn's hallway. Lorccan's hand dropped away.

In the hallway, he turned back to her. "Would you like to continue the tour or do something else?"

"What do you want to do?"

"Anything else." He smiled a little ruefully.

"Okay, we'll do anything else," she said. There was no point in a tour anymore, anyway. "Just give me a moment; I want to change my dress."

"No. Please don't," he said.

She looked at him, startled. "Huh?"

He shook his head. "I'm sorry. I shouldn't have said that. Yeah, go and change. I'll meet you in your entertainment room."

She nodded and slowly turned. Going to her restroom, Alainn turned on the faucet and took a couple of big sips of water. She then straightened her hair and glanced at herself in the mirror.

She decided that maybe she wouldn't change the dress; it had been an excuse to go get water anyway.

"Are you still looking for a way to escape?" Rosebud 03AF asked.

Alainn spun toward where the voice had come from. "Are you offering to let me go?" Her gaze skipped around the room even though she knew there was no one to look at.

"What are you trying so hard to get back to?" Rosebud asked.

"My friends, family . . . life," she said.

"No, you want to get back to dying."

"That's not what I was doing."

She didn't respond.

Alainn's hands balled themselves into fists. "What are you trying to do, Rosebud? Throwing two seriously screwed-up people at each other? You think that'll solve your problems? You think that this is somehow going to save *you*?"

"Yes," Rosebud 03AF replied. "And Mr. Garbhan is waiting for you in the entertainment room; please don't make him wait any longer."

23

January 31, 2027

Alainn sat directly beside Lorccan. Only inches of couch separated his leg from hers. Her feet were up on the coffee table; his weren't. Lorccan hadn't quite mastered the Sunday veg session, but he was trying.

Days and weeks were zooming past. Every day was almost the exact same, but each day was also immeasurably different. Each day she woke, tried to catch the monkeys—who were a bunch of wily little robots—then spent the rest of her day with Lorccan. They often spent weekends working, too, but on some precious days—like today—Lorccan would sit around and do nothing with her.

They watched a marathon of some of Alainn's favorite old television shows, though she'd told him that she'd only heard of them and was interested in watching. They'd just started the first episode of one of her all-time favorite series when Lorccan aimed a smirk at her.

"What?"

"No wonder you like the idea of a sky train." He shook his head.

"What's that supposed to mean?" She nudged him because it was obvious that he was making fun of her.

He gestured to the screen. "Cowboys in space?"

"It has great characters—I was told. Goodness gracious, stop being such a snob and watch it. I'm going to force you to love it. And just for the record, our world needs a sky train."

Three hours later, he muttered, "We should probably go eat . . ."

"After the next episode?" she asked, bobbing her eyebrows at him.

He blew out a laugh. "Sure."

Alainn grabbed a throw pillow and set it against his leg. Scooting down the length of the couch, she slowly laid her head on the pillow. Feeling suddenly unsure, she glanced up to check that Lorccan was okay with being so close.

He watched her carefully, lips parted.

"Can I lie here?" she asked.

"If you want," he said.

"Okay." She forced her gaze to the screen.

Alainn was really trying to be good. Lorccan had a girlfriend . . . He kind of had a girlfriend. He had an internet girlfriend he'd never actually met. But she knew that didn't matter; he wanted Shelly, not her.

Well, he thought he wanted Shelly, since he'd never even actually met her. But, again, that didn't matter.

The problem was that every time their hands brushed, or he gave her a hug or touch, those were her happiest moments. They were the happiest moments she'd had in years.

There was a line she'd drawn for herself, and she told herself she would not cross it. Yet, every day, she pushed that line back just a little.

They watched the screen. Both of them remained motionless, as if movement would fracture their moment.

Fingers lightly brushed over the top of her hair, the barest of touches. Glancing up, she found his gaze on the screen. She cuddled in closer to him, lifting her head into his hand.

His fingers combed farther into her hair, massaging down the length of her scalp. When he'd finished massaging down, he massaged back up. He continued to do this, up and down.

Alainn closed her eyes, amazed that such a simple touch could feel so erotic. Perhaps it was because her head was so close to his lap, but her body buzzed with an electric anticipation that traveled straight to the center of her thighs.

She wanted him to touch her anywhere—everywhere. She wanted to slip the straps of her dress down her shoulders, down her body. Her mind couldn't stay on the television show. She became hyperaware of everyplace her dress touched sensitive skin. All the while, his fingers caressed her slowly.

There was a line not to cross.

Kissing him and touching him was well beyond that line, but the idea of doing just that consumed Alainn's every thought.

Slowly, her hand moved from under her face, across the small distance of couch, and to his leg. At first she just slipped a finger along his calf, but when he didn't protest, her fingers drew slow circles on his leg.

His fingers stilled for a second on her head, then he continued to caress her.

Gathering all of her courage, Alainn peered up into his face and met his gaze. His eyes stayed intent on hers as she twisted and sat up slowly.

"Jade," he whispered, but she didn't know if he was warning her away or asking her closer.

Her gaze fell to his beautiful, uneven lips.

"Jade," he whispered once more.

"Yes?" she whispered back, her gaze going to his; she meant to ask a question, but it had come out an answer.

"We can't," he said as his other hand came up to thread through her hair.

"Why not?" She leaned just a little farther in.

"It's not real," he said.

"Then why does it feel real?"

He leaned in, his lips meeting hers slowly. Soft lips brushed over hers with the slightest of caresses. His hands cupped her face while hers went to his shoulders for support.

His light kisses brushed everywhere on her face, slow and gentle, barely more than butterfly wings brushing over her skin. And she kissed him, too, on both the scarred and smooth sides of his face. But they always returned together, deepening the kiss slightly each time.

He pulled back, breaking away from her suddenly. "Jade . . . we can't do this."

"Why not?" She sucked her lower lip into her mouth.

His hands were still in her hair, his eyes still burning into hers.

"I can't live my life in this fantasy world. I need something real. I need reality—"

She leaned in, pressing her body against his, her face to his shoulder. "I want to be your reality."

"I know, but . . . it's just not that way." His arms lowered to embrace her to him. "Maybe we should get some distance from each other for a couple days."

"No. Nope, that's a bad idea." She shook her head slightly, though she was still pressed into him. "Just give me a minute, then I'll drop it. I promise."

"Okay," he said as his hand caressed her lower back.

Alainn leaned back to look at him. "Just sixty more seconds."

He licked his lips and then smiled just a little before she kissed him again. This time, it wasn't just a brush of lips. If she only had sixty seconds, she'd make them count. Her hands cupped his face, rough and smooth sides. Lips pressed lips. Breath mingled. His hands gripped her back as she sucked his bottom lip into her mouth.

After much more than sixty seconds, he leaned his head away. "I think your exhaust might be making me lightheaded, Jade."

She couldn't help but laugh. "Don't worry; it's not toxic."

He gave her a serious look. "We should go to dinner." His thumb brushed over her cheek. "And we should probably set some more boundaries between us."

Her stomach plummeted as she nodded. "If that's what you want."

"It—it's what I need."

Alainn looked away. "Why is *she* reality . . . and I'm not?" A stupid question, but she meant it all the same.

He sighed, his hands dropping away from her body. "It's hard to explain to you."

"But if I was a human, you wouldn't let me anywhere near you," she whispered.

He looked away. "I'm trying to get past that, Jade. All I want—all I've ever wanted—is to have something real in my life."

I'm real! she wanted to say. But she knew that wouldn't work for Lorccan, so instead, Alainn went to dinner.

24

February 7, 2027

A week passed, and they didn't kiss again. When Lorccan said boundaries, he really meant them.

That night had been the same. He excused himself at 6:50. Alainn walked down to her room and settled on the floor beside her plant.

She'd made a mistake by kissing him.

Alainn knew it was a shitty thing to do since he had a girlfriend. She would like to think that she'd never do that under normal circumstances. But she had a hard time thinking of Shelly as his girlfriend and of herself as only his robot-friend. Shelly didn't even know what his face looked like.

Unless he'd shown her?

Sitting alone in her room, next to her peace lily, the idea of Lorccan finally showing Shelly what he looked like made her feel queasy.

She knew she was a horrible, wretched person to not want him to move on and get better, so she could keep him all to herself. But yet, that was exactly what all the cruel, dark parts of her wanted.

There was a movement beside Alainn. When she looked up, she saw a monkey crawling toward her. He stood, showing his jeans with a tiny gold button. On top, he wore what looked like a sports jersey. He stopped several feet away and squatted back down.

She turned back to the view of the city—or, to be accurate, she turned to the screen that displayed a view of the city.

The monkey moved again, walking upright in her direction.

She kept her face forward, but peeked over as the monkey stopped on the other side of the flowerpot. He stood to his full height and placed a hand in the soil, just as Alainn was doing. Settling onto his back legs, he looked out at the city.

"It's not real," she told him, peering at the display. "You're not real. I'm not real. Nothing is." She paused. "Except the plant. The peace lily is real."

The monkey only combed his little fingers through the soil while looking out at the view.

Another monkey dashed over to them, stopping next to the planter. This one was very familiar; she wore the same little blue dress every day, though it was somehow always clean. She was probably the boldest of the monkeys who followed Alainn around the tower.

The monkey stood tall, hands on the edge of the planter. She walked around its edge. Squeezing between Alainn and the planter, she sat. Her fuzzy little body tickled through the material of Alainn's dress. Part of her wanted to recoil from the robot monkey, but most of her didn't.

The monkey grabbed Alainn's wrist. With a gentle tug, the monkey pulled Alainn's hand out of the flowerpot and leaned in to rub against Alainn's palm.

"You want me to pet you?" Alainn asked in a low voice.

Oh, what the hell?

She pet the silly robot as the monkey settled in beside her.

Then suddenly, another monkey dashed in to sit beside the monkey in the blue dress. She was also in a dress, a yellow one. She smiled up at Alainn before looking pointedly to the hand that was petting the other monkey.

"Oh, fine," Alainn said, petting both of them.

Four more monkeys ran up and settled beside her. "Holy shit! I can't pet you all," Alainn laughed. They chattered up at her and settled in, seemingly content to just sit beside her and stare out at the view.

"Do you guys have names?" Alainn asked.

"Yes," Rosebud 03AF replied.

"Oh. What are they?"

"Sunshine, Moonlight, Happy, City, Blue, Jumps, Smile, Tallest Monkey and Kevin."

As she listed off names, the different monkeys stood up. Kevin was the one in jeans and a jersey, and Blue was the one in the blue dress.

"You're kidding me," Alainn mumbled.

"Mr. Garbhan allowed them to select their own names. They can read, write, and understand what you say, but they can't speak."

"Oh." Alainn didn't know what to say to that.

They sat together, the strangely named monkeys and Alainn, watching streaks of red and white light paint the twinkling city.

Eventually, Alainn stood so she could wash the monkey and plant off her skin. But when she returned from the bathroom in her nightgown, she found Blue and Kevin, lone stragglers in her room.

She peered at them as they stared up at her. "You're *not* getting in here with me." She pointed to the bed so they'd know exactly where they weren't allowed.

They each nodded.

"I mean it. My bed is robot free. You need to go to your own charging stations."

They nodded furiously.

"Okay." She climbed in and settled her head down on the pillow. "Please turn the lights out, Rosebud," Alainn called up, and the lights dimmed.

A few minutes later, Alainn heard the rustling sound of two monkeys climbing up onto the foot of her bed, turning around, and lying down.

"Fine," she mumbled. "But for tonight only." She did not intend to go to sleep with a bed full of monkeys every night, but she didn't have the energy to kick them out. Sleep took her quickly.

Sometime later, Alainn woke to screaming.

Sitting up abruptly, her breathing came fast and shallow. The screaming continued—long, guttural wails filled the room.

"Oh, my god!" she covered her ears, but it wasn't enough to muffle the sound.

It was Lorccan, but not muffled by the distance of a vent. It boomed throughout the room.

"Lorccan?" she yelled, but it did nothing. "Lorccan!"

The room filled with light. It was empty.

"Rosebud! What's happening?" she screamed over the continued cries.

Across her room, the door opened.

The sound grew, ragged bellows of horrible pain.

Alainn threw off the covers and ran for the open door, hands clutching her ears. The moment her bare feet stepped from the room, the door closed behind her. The hallway lit up, the light and his cries leading her as she ran. The door to the stairway opened, and she bounded forward. The landings had no exit, only solid wall. She continued to ascend.

On Lorccan's private floor—a floor she'd never entered before—the door flew open. Light flooded a long hallway. His cries only grew louder as she sprinted down the hall, her bare feet smacking the fake wood. She caught herself on the doorframe at the end of the hall, jerking her body out of its forward momentum. The door stood open, revealing a bedroom that was the masculine equivalent of hers.

Lorccan crouched on all fours, completely naked on the bed. One hand gripped the scarred side of his face as he gave out another ragged cry of pain.

Not hesitating a second longer, she rushed over to the bed and crawled onto it.

"Lorccan!" she cried, but he didn't hear her.

His back arched, and he screamed again.

She crouched down to look into his face. His eyes were shut tight, and they stayed closed.

"Lorccan, you're asleep! Wake up!" She grabbed him around his shoulders, squeezing his bare skin. "Wake up!" She tried to shake him, but she wasn't strong enough to move him much.

He collapsed forward, taking her with him.

She climbed off his bare back and lay down to look at his face. His screaming ceased and his breath evened out.

"Lorccan? Are you okay?"

She knew it was a stupid question; obviously he was far from okay. What she really wanted to ask was whether he was peaceful again. If it was over.

She knew she should probably go. It was so inappropriate for her to be there while he was naked and asleep, especially when he so clearly wanted space from her. But if his nightmare wasn't over, she couldn't quite make herself leave him.

"Jade?" Lorccan's eyes blinked rapidly and then closed in exhaustion. A small smile touched his lips.

"Hi. You're awake?" She sat up, preparing to scoot away.

His hand reached over and wrapped around her ankle, but his eyes didn't open. "What are you doing here?"

Her breaths came haltingly as his hand moved up her leg. "I could hear your screams in my room, so I followed them up to you."

To her shock, he smiled. "Rosebud is always meddling," he mumbled.

His hand continued to climb up her leg and over the crest of her knee. He began to push up the material of her long, loose nightgown.

Alainn gasped.

Lorccan opened his eyes, and his gaze found hers. He looked both tired and intent.

He lifted her nightdress slowly, bunching it up the length of her body. She lifted her arms and he pulled it over her head, exposing her naked body.

"Jade," he whispered again as his hands found her face.

"Hello," she breathed.

"Can we even do this?" he asked as his hands slowly ran down her shoulders, then over her breasts. Her nipples pebbled in the cool air. His gaze met hers.

"Yes, we can definitely do this," she whispered.

"Can you feel it? Does it even feel good to you?" He kissed her stomach before his lips slowly moved up her body.

"Yes," she whispered. "I feel it just like you do."

His lips traveled up the side of her breast, then to her shoulder and neck as her breath rasped through her lips. Her hands rose up between them, caressing the muscles of his stomach and his sides.

"I've never done this before," he whispered onto her shoulder.

"Neither have I," she whispered as her hands ran up his back.

And it was true—what had happened to her before wasn't anything like this.

When he moved up the length of her body, he threaded his fingers through her hair and wrapped them around the back of her neck.

She leaned away, just a little, even though it was the last thing she wanted to do. "If we do this, are you going to push me away after?"

Just the idea of that hurt way too much.

"No, never again." His gaze spoke to the sincerity of his words.

But she had to be sure. "I'm not real to you."

"No. Jade, no matter what you are, you've sunk down into my bones now, and there's no getting away from you."

She turned her face away as tears formed in her eyes. She couldn't let him see them.

His hand stroked the side of her neck. "What's the matter?"

She looked back at him, lip quivering. "Nothing. Everything is perfect. I think you already know how much I want you."

He smiled. "You can tell me."

"Let me show you," she whispered as she leaned up for a kiss.

They moved carefully, neither of them really knowing what they were doing. Their kisses came gently, their caresses even more so.

His eyes were intent on hers, and his lips parted as he settled between her legs. He slowly moved the head of his erection over the wetness that had started between her thighs with their kisses and caresses.

Alainn had given herself pleasure before, but she'd never grown slick and wet when someone else was positioned to enter her. Her hands shook at his back, and she sought his gaze as he gently began to push into her.

At first he just barely moved into her, with small thrusts. His lips rested on hers and their breathing came haltingly, synchronized, as he pushed just a little deeper.

Her hands squeezed his arms.

"Are you okay?" he whispered.

"Yeah," she breathed. "Yeah, I'm doing . . ." She laughed. "Amazing." Her eyes closed as he moved slowly in and out of her.

He thrust all the way in, and she gasped. "Wait," she whispered, and he did. He filled her, stretching her, almost too much, but somehow she wanted more.

"Okay," she whispered, opening her eyes. "You can . . . you can go."

His gaze met hers and he moved into her again, then in and out. Their lips brushed over each other's, and small whimpers escaped her every time he pushed deeper.

She squeezed her legs into his sides and moaned onto his lips. The feel of him inside her was almost too intense, the pleasure building inside her more and more. Her fingers squeezed into his shoulders, and she whimpered as the feeling built to just this side of painful and she knew she was going to explode.

A sudden thought hit her.

Robots couldn't orgasm.

But there was no stopping it.

Lorccan's eyes grew lazy as his thrusts kept pushing deeper and deeper.

They gasped as she clenched around him and a wave of incredible pleasure rolled through her, up from her center, rippling through her entire body.

Lorccan drove deeply inside her. With his lips at her neck, he moaned out his release.

Alainn's fingers stroked over his back and neck, holding him as their breathing slowed. Eventually, Lorccan rolled over to his side and pulled her so that her back tucked up against him. "I got you all sweaty," he whispered as his hands meandered over her hip.

"I don't mind," she said, closing her eyes. Another sudden fear hit her, along with a wash of shame. "Did I just take advantage of you when you were vulnerable?"

She pressed her face into his pillow.

He laughed and kissed her shoulder. "You're absolutely insane, Jade."

She peered up, craning her neck but still not able to see him behind her. "No, I'm serious. I'm the one who's been pushing this, and I came into your room while you were naked and upset, and I—"

"Made this night the best one of my life," he whispered into her ear. The fingers of one of his hands threaded through hers while his other hand pressed into her stomach.

She laid her head back down.

That was really sweet.

She turned into his arm, feeling a lot better . . . until another horrible thought racked her mind. At some point, very soon, she was going to have to tell him the truth.

At a certain point, deception would become unforgivable, and they'd passed that point tonight—if not earlier. Every day, they headed farther and farther from that point.

But there was no way she would tell him tonight.

Instead, she curled up next to Lorccan and let her fears drift away.

25

February 17, 2027

Lorccan made a low groaning sound as he plunged inside of Alainn one more time. Her head fell back into his hand as she moaned out her release.

Alainn let her head rest on his hand, laughing as his arms supported her body from falling back onto the table. He pulled her closer, kissing her neck with deep, satisfied kisses. She never wanted to move. Alainn wanted to keep him inside her forever, legs and arms always wrapped around him.

"Jade," he whispered onto her skin, "Jade."

Ten days earlier, a switch had flipped in her that she never even knew existed. Since she'd been a teenager, sex had been a solitary thing. The idea of sharing her body with anyone else ever again had been completely unappealing. Alainn had thought she never would. But she woke wanting Lorccan. She wanted him while they worked together, while they dined, and in the dark hours of the night. She was desperately addicted to having him deep inside her.

For all his obsessions with sanitation, Lorccan seemed more than happy to oblige her wherever and whenever. He was as hungry for her as she was for him, initiating sex as much or more often than she did. Tonight, it had been her, at dinner. She'd rounded the end of the table and climbed into his lap, but ended up *on* the table instead.

Her hands came up to cup his face, fingers running over his cheeks.

Lorccan leaned in and kissed her palm, his eyes shining directly into hers. Though he still turned his head once in a while, he never shied from her touch.

Alainn loved him. She was almost sure she loved him. In this moment, when they were so wrapped up in each other, she felt something in her that had never existed before blooming.

Slowly, Lorccan pulled back from her.

She held her legs around him for one more moment before releasing him.

He stepped away and leaned down to pull up his pants.

Alainn waited one second more before sliding off the table. Leaning down to the floor, she grabbed her dress and lifted it up. As she slowly zipped up its side, she secured a mantle of shame around her as well.

Lorccan gave her shoulder a quick kiss before stepping back.

"You've got to go."

She turned away as whatever was blooming in her wilted. She knew what time it was. Six twenty. He was going to leave her again. He'd need to shower before he talked to Shelly.

"Jade."

"Just . . . I'm going to go to my room."

"Jade." His tone had changed, almost chiding now. "She's my friend. The phone calls are important to us both. I can't just abandon her now that I have you."

She nodded, walking toward the stairway.

She had become the "other woman" so easily, just slipped right into the role. And just like every single day since she'd first given herself to Lorccan, Alainn knew she had to stop it. She was free-falling and, though she had a parachute, she wasn't pulling the cord. Instead, she watched as the craggy earth rushed up to greet her. She was waiting for the splatter.

The problem was that, even though she now had a job and things to do, it didn't make Lorccan any less her entire life. Instead, every moment of every day, she was wrapped up in him.

Even though Alainn's mind knew that she was free falling, her heart didn't give a shit.

His hands lightly grabbed onto her shoulders, rubbing them gently and stopping her in her tracks. "You could come meet her," he said.

Fuck. That.

Alainn turned her head but didn't quite look at him. "I need to go lie down and recharge my system."

As she stepped forward, his hands dropped away. He didn't stop her again as she left.

Alainn slowly submerged into the hot water of her tub as her monkeys hung out on the sides. Blue and Sunshine had somehow elected themselves her personal attendants, though she'd tried to convince them against it. And like every other day this week, they stood nearby, ready to hand her a robe.

Her head lay back against the tub, eyes closed. She forced her mind to formulate an escape plan that she truly didn't want to succeed.

"I will play you the conversation Mr. Garbhan is having with Ms. Dover right now," Rosebud 03AF said.

"Hell no!" She glared at where Rosebud's voice had come from. Alainn liked to think that she had some self-respect left, whether or not it was true.

The sound of a woman laughing filled her room. Lorccan laughed, too, sounding genuinely happy.

Damn it.

"Not cool, Rosebud!" she yelled. "I'm not coming up until you turn that off!" Her head sank under the water. She held her breath as muffled voices reverberated through the water, a garbled mess of sounds.

It made sense. Rosebud obviously wanted to punish Alainn for inserting herself into Lorccan's recovery and *perfect* love story with Shelly.

Alainn was betting that Rosebud still wanted her alive, though, so she braced herself under the water and looked up to the surface, watching light flicker overhead.

A little monkey head peered down at her, wavering in the ripples above. She opened her mouth and made a screeching sound.

A hole opened at the bottom of the tub, and the water started to drain. Alainn stomped her foot over the hole, ignoring the bite of the suction against her heel.

Just as her lungs really started to burn, the muffled sound of voices faded.

Alainn broke the surface, gasping. Air filled her lungs.

Thank all that was holy—the voices didn't come back.

Alainn glared around the room. "If you want to punish someone, punish yourself, you stupid computer. *You* trapped me here. You even admitted that you threw us at each other. I'm sorry if I can't be your perfect little chess piece!"

Rosebud didn't respond, but she also didn't play the voices again.

Blue was still waiting by the edge of the tub, holding up the top portion of Alainn's robe while Sunshine held the bottom. They squirmed and seemed upset. Feeling a little guilty because she had obviously freaked them out, she climbed out of the tub and took the robe. She wrung out her wet hair as the tub started to drain. She had a bad feeling Rosebud was going to withhold baths for a while.

Running the faucet, she leaned in to take a deep sip of water.

A knock came at her door. She stood upright, shutting the water off.

She knew she should ignore it, just let him stand there, knocking all night.

Completely against her will, her feet took her forward, through the closet, and to the door. At the door she stopped and just stood there.

"Don't open it, Rosebud," she whispered.

Rosebud didn't listen, of course. The door opened between them, and Lorccan stood feet from her.

A big grin lit his face the moment he saw her. He held out a hand to her, and she took it, just like that, walking out of her room and into the hallway.

Damn it. Stop being such an idiot, Alainn.

The door to her room snapped shut and locked itself for good measure.

"You're mad at me," he said as he stepped toward her.

"I'm mad at *me*. I shouldn't let myself be the other woman in your romance, and . . ."

His head fell forward, and he fixed her with a stare. "Do I need to write it in big letters across your wall?" He shook his head, pulling at her hand and bringing her closer to him. "You're *not* the other woman, Jade." His arm went into her robe and around her waist.

Alainn stepped right into his embrace, letting her robe fall off her shoulder. She could think whatever she wanted, but obviously she had no self-respect left.

"Am I only not the other woman because I'm not real to you?" she asked in an accusatory tone, her anger rising up. It was her one last effort at putting up a defense against him. It wasn't much of a defense, though, as she was standing with her robe open, naked before him, while he stood fully dressed in a suit.

"You're the *only* thing that's real to me." He leaned in, his hands moving over her warm, naked backside as the material of his suit brushed over her front.

Her gaze met his, pleading, as his hands grabbed her ass and hoisted her up onto him. He carried her down the hall to the entertainment room, then set her carefully on the couch. His hands undid the tie and opened her robe fully as he knelt down on the floor between her legs.

She looked down at him as he looked up the length of her body. Her breathing was already unsteady. His gaze roved down the length of her. His arms wrapped under her ass as his head came down between her thighs.

And just like that, the whole world fell away and, again, she was blooming for him.

A long time later, Alainn looked down and whispered, "You're still dressed."

"Let's go remedy that," he said. Lorccan left her robe behind and lifted Alainn, naked, into his arms. He carried her up all the flights of stairs to his room. Her room was closer, but Lorccan refused to enter it now that the peace lily was there.

After setting her on the bed, he made quick work of taking his suit off and joining her. He lay with his front to her back, a position she realized Lorccan liked to keep her in.

He kissed her neck. "I love all your tastes," he whispered as his hand slid down her stomach to rest just between her thighs. "How does your body do that?"

"Um . . ." It was very hard to think of a decent answer with his hand cupping her there. "My body was printed—it's the exact same as a normal body, just with certain hardware to make it function." She gasped the last word as his finger slipped forward and rubbed up and down. "It doesn't bother you?" she breathed.

"No," he whispered.

As if to prove it, his erection pressed against her backside. It seemed that both of them were making up for a lifetime of going without.

Because she'd never tried it before and was very curious, she turned over toward him and gave him a small grin before ducking under the covers. He stiffened as she crawled down his body, but the moment she took him into her mouth, that changed.

She fell asleep halfway on top of him—and woke to screaming. It had been the same almost every night.

Alainn woke under him or beside him, and he would be holding the scarred side of his face and screaming.

"Lorccan!" She wrapped her arms around his shoulders, pulled his body onto hers. "Lorccan, wake up!"

Usually he did, but that night he bellowed a long, horrid cry directly above her face. His neck arched up as his head tilted to the ceiling.

"Lorccan!" Tears coursed down her face. "Wake up!"

He wouldn't, not tonight. He just kept howling out cries as she clutched him in her arms.

"Please, wake up! It's Jade! You're safe!"

But he wasn't safe. He was trapped in some deep, all-consuming nightmare, and she wasn't there. She was here, clutching his body and far away from his mind. Eventually his cries turned into whimpers, and he relaxed onto her. His face nestled into her chest as she combed fingers through his hair.

Eventually, sleep found her, too.

The next thing she knew, lips slowly moved up her back, kissing her awake. Peering behind her, she yawned as she found Lorccan over her. He grinned down like he had not spent most of the night screaming. He grinned like the nightmares didn't exist.

"Hi," she said, reaching for him.

"Will you marry me, Jade?" he asked, his gaze intent on her.

"Ha. No," she said with a laugh as she reached out to him. "Come here."

He moved into her arms, lying down beside her. She swung a leg over his hip and snuggled into him.

His hand grabbed that leg and pulled her tighter to him. "That is the strangest rejection I think any man has ever had to his marriage proposal."

Alainn wrapped her arms around his shoulders. "You're really proposing to me?"

"Of course. I'm serious. Do you think I would joke about that?"

"But . . ." She leaned back to look at him. "How would that work?"

"A priest would ask for our consent and then say that we're man and wife," he said like he thought she might actually not know. His hand came up to cup her cheek. "He wouldn't know what you are, and there's no law against it. I've arranged for all the paperwork, so it'd be almost entirely legal."

"You'd have a priest come in here?" she asked with eyebrows raised.

"I'm sure one would be willing to do it over video conference."

She nodded.

"Is that a yes?" he asked as his forehead pressed into hers.

His voice sounded so full of hope, and she hated to crush that.

But she shook her head. "No—Lorccan, I've only been here for a couple months. You don't know that this is what you want forever. I'm just your first."

"Jade, I told you. You're pulsing through my veins; you're in the marrow of my bones. Three months or three years doesn't matter now. My heart beats to love you." His hand came around the back of her neck. "I didn't know you could cry."

Crap.

She was crying.

Alainn nodded and said, "Me neither; what a surprise."

He kissed her tears, one after the other. "So is that a yes, then?"

For one moment, she thought maybe she could say yes. Living as a robot wasn't as hard as Alainn originally thought it would be.

The day after they'd started sleeping together, birth control had been waiting in the bathroom. Her guess was that Rosebud 03AF didn't want her plans for Lorccan to end up with Shelly ruined by a very big surprise ending. *"Guess what, Lorccan? I'm having your illegitimate robot-human baby! Ta-da!"*

But it wouldn't work. Eventually, she would expose herself. Every day, she felt just that little bit closer to crashing into the rocks. She couldn't let Lorccan marry her while she was still deceiving him.

"Just—" She shook her head. "Not yet, okay?"

He smiled. "Then I'll just keep asking you until you say yes."

"Okay." She laid her head against his chest. "Keep asking me."

26

January 23, 2027

Colby Murphy's pen scratched across the page as his finger held the place where the Butterfly Nebula should be. Two points of pain were forming on the backs of his ears—something that happened every time he worked for a prolonged period. That, along with the strain in his neck and back, was going to force him to cut his time in the workshop short today.

He made the final marks, rubbed his eyes with his hands, and stood up from the chair.

"Did you find it?" Rose 76GF asked him. She'd watched him for at least the last five minutes; he'd felt her inhuman eyes on him. Rosette 82GF also stared at him, though she was always just staring off at something, so he thought it might not be him that she was actually interested in.

He raised the paper. "Yes. I should probably get these papers to the university." He rolled back his shoulders, feeling a strong ache in his shoulder blades.

"Why don't you call it in?" Rose asked, gaze still fixed on him.

He yawned and shrugged at the same time. "I need to get out of the house." Standing, his attention skipped between the robots that looked so like his sister—but somehow didn't.

"That's good. I really should be focusing on breaking into Rosebud 03AF's system instead of astronomy."

Colby gathered up the papers on the table, shuffling them across the tabletop. "How's that going?"

"It's harder than I expected. She's created several layers of protection. I've been able to break through many of them; I believe I am almost through."

"Are you sure I can't help? I might be able to—"

"This is far too sophisticated for you or your hacker friends."

"I understand." Colby focused on making a neat pile in front of him. "When you are through her system, how do you plan to get Alainn out?"

"I have a plan. Even though you are more intelligent than the majority of the human population, I don't think I can explain it in a way you would understand. I should never have helped Alainn do what she did, and my only hope is to remedy my mistake."

"You've told my father your plan, though?" Colby asked as he pushed his glasses up his nose and tucked his papers into his briefcase.

"Of course," she said. A moment later, both of the Roses smiled, in sync with each other.

Colby nodded. "I guess that's good enough for me. If Dad asks where I am, tell him I drove his car down to the university." He waved.

"Where else do you go?" Rose asked, gaze still on Colby.

He made his movements slow, nonchalant as he turned back. "Sorry?"

"The university is forty-six miles away; your odometer always reads that you drive fifty-five to sixty miles each way."

Colby shrugged. "Coffee, usually. Sometimes I go for food. It's nice to finally have a car for transportation."

Rose nodded, her gaze still piercing his. "Perhaps one day you'll take me to the university."

Colby nodded. "Taking either of you would be an honor."

It would be the type of honor that could get him promptly kicked out of the program for academic dishonesty.

Without waiting a second more, he walked out of the house and down to his father's car. The little blue car had been parked a few blocks down since the last time he used it.

Colby kept his back straight and body stiff as he started the ignition and drove down the hill. In his mind, he recited: *left-most drawer, three from the top, centimeter open, computer screen on the left had a website open titled "Common Household Toxins."*

Rosette 82GF had closed the website within thirty seconds of him entering. The shredder had been full of blue paper from an unknown source.

As soon as Colby was three miles away, he pulled off his route. Reaching under the seat, he maneuvered out his latest notebook. His fat fingers had a difficult time turning the pages, but eventually, he made his way through to the first clean page. Quickly, he spilled all the observations he'd been repeating in his head for the last two hours onto paper. At the end, he continued with behavioral observations.

Rose again indicated that it was Alainn's idea to take her place in Mr. Garbhan's household. She still refuses to give details of her plan to extract Alainn. Her daily behaviors and routines continue to be regular. Father continues to spend very little time in the workshop and the majority of his time in his bedroom.

After finishing, Colby again stored the book under his seat and drove back into traffic. He'd need to find a better route—perhaps one that took fewer miles and more time.

Mr. Garbhan's tower was by far one of the most imposing buildings downtown—a thick, black high-rise cutting into the sky.

Colby headed down the access road, then turned to park before the wide screen outside the garage.

Before he had even rolled down his window, Rosebud 03AF greeted him, "Hello, Mr. Murphy. How are you doing today?"

"I'm good. Any chance you'll let me talk to Mr. Garbhan or my sister?" he asked, already knowing the answer.

"I'm sorry, Mr. Murphy. I can't do that."

Colby sighed and rubbed his nose. "Okay, show me that she's okay and I'll go."

Rosebud 03AF immediately obliged. The video screen filled with Alainn's smiling face.

"Shut up. I do *not* do that," she said to someone off screen as her eyes laughed.

She sat at the same dinner table he always saw her at in these recordings. Her hair was up in a messy bun, even though she wore a formal green gown that reflected the light around her.

"You *definitely* do that," said what he now recognized as Mr. Garbhan's voice.

And just like the many times before that Rosebud 03AF had assured Colby that his sister was all right, he saw that his sister was better than all right. For the first time in the seven years since Cara Miller had died, his sister looked happy.

27

March 18, 2027

"Checkers? Do you really like losing so much?" Alainn asked, leaning across the table. Lorccan had insisted that they play a board game after they'd had a delicious cream soup for dinner. He'd taken his time, grinning over his bowl, drawing the whole evening out.

It had been a while since they'd played a board game. They usually found much more entertaining ways to spend their after-dinner time.

Lorccan put his arms on the table, threading his fingers together. He leaned over his clasped hands, a spark in his gaze. "I had an idea for how to make the game more interesting."

She rested her elbow on the table and her chin on her hand. "Interesting how?"

"If I win, you have to marry me," he said.

She laughed. It wasn't that big of a surprise as it was the eighth time he'd asked her in the past month. "You want me to marry you because I lost to you at checkers?"

"No, I want you to marry me because you love me, but if it takes me beating you at checkers to admit it, so be it."

He was wrong; she had already admitted it a hundred times, just never to him while he was awake.

She raised her eyebrows. "And what do I get if I win?"

"Anything you'd like."

"You'll stop calling Shelly every night?"

He glared across the checkers board. "Jade . . . ," he warned.

She shrugged. "I'm pretty sure a marriage is just between two people."

"I'm pretty sure married people are allowed to have friends. Pick something else." His tone brooked no argument, not that Alainn was surprised. The subject of Shelly was both exhausted and exhausting.

She turned her head away. "I'd like . . . Connor Murphy to be allowed to visit me here." She was pretty sure Rosebud 03AF was going to prevent that one from happening in a big way. Yet, with Lorccan facilitating it, there was a chance that she'd go along with it. It wouldn't be an escape plan; maybe if Alainn explained that to her, she'd let it happen.

Alainn just wanted to see her father.

Lorccan looked off. "He'd have to be willing to go through a thorough decontamination."

"Really?" she asked, bouncing in her chair.

His foot rubbed along hers under the table. "I'm not sure I want you this excited to win."

"The bigger the risk, the greater the reward," she said, running her foot up his ankle and under his pant leg.

His gaze burned into hers as he moved his first piece.

Nervousness surged up inside her as she slid a piece forward.

A grin grew on his face. "I'm going to win."

She gaped down at the board. "You can't possibly know that from two turns."

He nodded. "Oh, yes I can."

The smug bastard.

They kept playing. Whether it was because Alainn was so nervous or because he had gained some sudden checkers skills, he was winning.

"King me," he said. The hologram piece turned over, showing a crown.

She stared down at the board and her few remaining pieces. "If you win, it doesn't necessarily mean that I *have* to marry you," she whispered.

"Yes it does," Lorccan said. "Tonight. The priest is waiting for me to call him."

She gaped and then sputtered, "What?"

He only grinned.

His kings had some sort of magical powers or something. Before she knew it, he had six kings and Alainn only had two pieces left.

The room shrank around her, her nerves forming a tight ball in her stomach. She couldn't marry him.

"Surrender," he said, grinning.

Her eyes darted over the board. "I could still win." She swallowed and moved a piece back into the corner where he couldn't get it.

Lorccan hopped over her other remaining piece in such a way that her last player was completely trapped. "Your turn," he said.

"I think we should pause the game," she whispered.

"Not a chance," he said, standing up. He walked around the table and scooped her up, then set her on the table. He pushed in to stand between her legs. "Marry me, Jade."

"I . . . I . . . ." She couldn't breathe. Panic squeezed her chest. She felt sure she was going to pass out.

"Marry me," he whispered.

Alainn looked into his eyes and knew she had to tell him the truth. The face she had come to find so beautiful went in and out of focus. She blinked rapidly, but when she stopped, the room itself blinked.

First, the lights shut off. They immediately blinked back on, then went off and on again.

"What?" She looked up, her mind sluggish.

Lorccan looked around, too. "Rosebud, are you all right?"

The lights blinked again and images flashed across the walls—wood, stone, images of people, flickering faces.

"Rosebud?" Lorccan called as his gazed flicked around the room.

Alainn rocked forward as the room really began to spin and flash.

Then, Alainn's own voice spoke directly into her ear. "This is Rose 76GF, Alainn. The T9640 was in your soup. You should be feeling the effects by now. Very soon, you will pass out. Make sure you do this in front of Mr. Garbhan. If you are brought to me in the next two hours, I have an antidote that will save you. Tell him your microprocessor is malfunctioning and you need to be brought to Connor Murphy right away. Find Mr. Garbhan now."

She looked up into Lorccan's face as he peered around the room, a real look of concern creasing into his forehead.

"Lorccan," Alainn said, her voice a croak.

He turned back. "I think something is happening to Rosebud."

"My microprocessor is malfunctioning." The words came out strung together.

"What?" he yelled, hands grasping her shoulders.

"Connor Murphy . . ." she muttered as her head fell to one side. "My microprocessor is malfunctioning . . ."

"Jade!" he yelled. And then Alainn was in his arms and he was running. "Rosebud! I need the elevator!" he yelled. "Fuck!" he screamed. And, distantly, Alainn realized that she had never heard Lorccan say anything like that before.

Her body bounced in his arms as he ran down, not once breaking stride. Doors flew open and lights flashed across a long line of metal vehicles.

"Contamination," she muttered at him, but Lorccan didn't respond.

His shoes echoed across the screen-floor as he ran down the line of cars to the end. Not letting go of her, he climbed into the driver's seat with her still in his lap.

Lorccan yelled out her father's home address, and the car moved.

Alainn's body shook violently and jerked as she lost all motor control.

Her gaze searched up for his one more time, but he wasn't looking at her. His gaze was out the windshield. And then Lorccan's features faded away.

28

April 2, 2027

"Oh, my god, Alainn! Come on! Don't talk to it; those things are so creepy!" Alainn's best friend Cara Miller yelled out the open window as she leaned over the center divider. Her long, dark braid fell forward and her deep-set eyes filled with laughter. "And I don't think you're supposed to get out of the car!" She laughed.

Alainn stepped out anyway, leaving her car door open and calling back, laughing, "Hold up! My dad helped Cooper Corp design these guys. They're not creepy; we're just not used to them." She turned back to the automaton gas station attendant.

"Can I help you with anything else?" the automaton asked. He was basically humanoid, though there was definitely something *other* about him as well, especially in his movements.

"What's your model number?" she asked.

"G27H944TZF."

So he wasn't one of the automatons her father had helped design after all. She sighed.

Oh, well.

"Do you have a complaint? I can take it now," he asked.

"Nope, no complaints. Keep up the good work, fella." She grinned and patted his back before turning to open her car door.

Cara leaned down and called over, "Maybe you should ask him if he has a prom date!" Then her eyes fixed on something just over Alainn's head and went wide. "Alainn!" she screamed.

Pain exploded in the back of her head and she fell forward, hitting the car on the way down.

Alainn's eyes opened to light and an aching, throbbing pain in her head. "Cara!" she cried out.

"No, it's Rose," said her own voice, but it wasn't her speaking.

"Cara!" she screamed out again, thrashing under blankets. "Shit! Someone help her—where's Cara?"

"Sweetheart?" It was her father's voice.

Alainn looked around frantically, not sure what was happening or where she was. "Dad! Where's Cara? Shit, what happened? Where's Cara?"

His rough hand touched her shoulder. "Sweetheart, it's just a nightmare. You're having a nightmare. That happened years ago. That's over."

"Shit. We were at the gas station and then there was . . ." Alainn sat up as her bedroom slowly came into focus, undulating in her vision. Her father sat on the edge of her bed, his face a blurry mess of familiar features.

Reaching back, her fingers ran through greasy hair, catching on large, matted knots. "What the hell?" she asked as her gaze fell on Rose 76GF. She sat just a little way back, her inhuman gaze fixed on Alainn. Behind Rose, Colby stood, framed by the doorway. Shadows almost obscured his figure from sight.

Her father sat back, shaking his head. "My god, honey. I'm so glad you're awake."

"What's going on?" her voice hoarsened more by the second.

Her father's eyes closed. "You've been asleep for fifteen days."

"Did I get in an accident? Should I be in a hospital?" Alainn didn't remember an accident. Invisible drums beat on her head, though. The man had hit her over the head next to the car. But that was years ago, and . . . The bones of her jaw protested. Alainn raised a hand to touch her chin.

Her father shook his head and then looked to Rose. "You needed medicines—serums that we had to create for you here."

"Soup," Alainn whispered, as her gaze again found Rose's watchful eyes. "You poisoned me."

Rose's face tilted, but she didn't look bothered by the accusation. "I got you out. Rosebud 03AF had been blocking me for months, and I finally penetrated her system. It was very difficult to do."

"Lorccan," Alainn whispered. "Dad, where's Mr. Garbhan?"

"He went home." His fingers rubbed deep circles into his eyes.

"Oh, okay. I should probably call him." She nodded. Moving one leg off the bed, Alainn fell forward until her father grabbed her.

His fingers dug into her arms as he helped her back. "Whoa there, honey. Hold your horses. You've been in a coma for fifteen days. I'm pretty sure your legs need a minute to recover."

"Could you bring me a phone, Dad? He thinks I was malfunctioning. He's probably freaking out . . ."

He shook his head. "He's fine. You don't need to worry about him anymore." His hand wiped sweaty hair from her forehead. "We made the Rosette 82GF, as planned; she's with him now."

Alainn shook her head furiously. "That won't work. He'll know it isn't me."

"We've got you covered there, sweetheart. We told him we had to reboot. She was picked up three days ago. It's over, Alainn. Thank God, it's all over."

"You told him that you rebooted me?" her voice shook as sudden, hot tears coated her cheeks.

"He was upset at first, but he's adjusted to the new model," Rose said from across the room.

Alainn shook her head. "You're lying," she whispered.

Rose's head shook, slowly. "I can tap into Rosette 82GF's system to make sure that the transplanting is going well, and I've confirmed that he's doing fine with the new model."

"You're a fucking liar, Rose! You poisoned me, you hacked into the house—I don't believe a word

234

you're saying to me!" her shouts exploded, raw and ragged.

"Alainn," her father scolded. "You two should have never have planned this, but Rose is the one who got you out. She worked nonstop to get you out."

"She's lying, Dad!" Alainn pointed into Rose's face. "She's a liar and psycho!" As her hand pulled back, sobs racked through her body.

Rose looked completely unbothered by the accusations. "I will play the recording for you if you wish to confirm for yourself."

Alainn's head shook, furiously. "No, I don't believe you."

"Would you like to watch the recordings?"

"No," Alainn whispered.

"I have them if you change your mind. I believe you should rest and perhaps have another solution—"

"Come at me with any more poisons, Rose, and I will destroy you!"

"Alainn, stop this now!" her father said in a quiet, firm voice. "You obviously need to sleep. You've been through months of an ordeal. I made the solution; it's safe to drink."

"If she had access to it," Alainn pointed at Rose, "then I know it's not safe."

Her father shook his head and then sighed. Leaning forward, he kissed her forehead. "I am so happy that you're safe and home; it's a miracle that you are." He stood, and Rose stood with him.

Alainn watched his blurry form turn back at the door. Through her tears, she saw him give a smile and nod before leaving.

Colby waited just a minute more. Alainn had forgotten he was even in the room. "You need water or something, Alainn?"

"No," she rasped out, even though she did.

"I'm going to be around the house, okay? If you need anything . . ." He said this, lingered one moment longer, and then left.

Alainn fell back onto the bed. Her chest convulsed with heavy, racking sobs. She didn't believe Rose. How could Lorccan be fine with her being replaced? But, no matter what, it was over. The only possible way for Alainn to reenter his life would be to come clean and tell him the truth.

He'd hate her. Especially now that she was on the outside, it would be so much easier to shut her out of his life. She should have told him while Rosebud 03AF was forcing her to stay.

But she wouldn't believe Rose.

Yes, Rose got her out, but she'd almost killed Alainn doing it.

Lorccan had left his tower to save Alainn. For the first time in his entire life, he drove out of the garage to save her. If that didn't mean he truly loved her, she didn't know what did.

He'd promised that he would love her no matter what she was, and she would believe that until he proved her wrong.

She would believe him.

The salty taste of her tears filled her mouth when she finally fell asleep, and it was still there when she woke, hours later, to daylight filling her room. Every part of Alainn complained as she sat up. Her tongue probed the roof of her mouth, finding no smooth, small disc. Instead, there was a line that ached when her tongue touched it. Pressing at the side of her nostril, she found no bump, nothing but an ache. She didn't check her ears, trusting that the raw, aching feeling inside them indicated that the chips had been removed.

It took her hours to manage standing from the bed—hours where no one checked on her. She wasn't even sure why that would surprise her now. It wasn't unusual.

She held onto her old dresser, using it for support as her knees fought to fold. Dirty, musty books looked up from its surface, their pages rolled up, stiff and dirty from traveling on so many long trips.

Panting, Alainn rested more than once on her route to the door. When she entered the living room, her father glanced up, his features lit by his computer screen. The curtains had been pulled shut, and he sat in near darkness.

Setting the laptop beside him, he stood and rushed over. "Honey, you shouldn't be out of bed."

"Dad, I—" she shook her head. "I need to call Lorccan . . . Mr. Garbhan. I need to."

His lips and eyelids squeezed shut. "Alainn, I've seen the recordings Rose is talking about."

She shook her head more vigorously. "They're doctored. AIs can doctor stuff like that, Dad. Rosebud 03AF did it when I was in there; she faked a whole phone conversation between me and you." The room spun around her.

"Let's sit you down before you fall down." His strong hands helped her to the couch.

The cushion parted and the baseboard smacked her tailbone, sending a shooting pain up her aching back.

Dull green eyes found her gaze. "What you did, what you lived through—" His hands patted her shoulder. "I wish I could take it back. I wish I could go back there and stop you. We'll get back from this, honey. We've worked through worse."

"No. You don't understand, Dad. We're in love, Dad. We're in love." Saying it out loud sounded so insubstantial, like the well-worn words didn't quite fit how she wanted to describe it.

"I don't blame Mr. Garbhan, but honey, what you went through . . . it was a lot like a kidnapping and—"

"Nothing like that."

"And, when you go through that, I've read that in some circumstances—feelings can develop for your kidnapper."

She grabbed his arms, fingers digging in. "You don't get it *at all*."

"Honey, he thought you were *a robot*." His eyes closed, like it hurt him to say it. "He has a girlfriend— a woman he seems pretty serious about from the recordings. Shelly Dover. I just don't want you to do anything that will make this worse."

"Like calling him?" The words choked her.

"Just watch the recordings before you do." His tired eyes begged her to believe him.

"No."

"You're hurting me, Alainn." He looked down to where her fingers clutched at his arms. When she loosened her hold, he said, "If you watch the recordings and you still want to talk to him, I'll call him. I'll take you to him myself."

"You don't have a car."

"I do. A million and a half can buy a lot of things. A car, supplies to make Rosette 82GF—it can even fix leaky pipes." He paused. "We're going to get through this, honey." A tear slipped down his cheek.

"I'm not crazy, Dad. Something is going on. He loves me. We're in love."

"I'm sure it felt that way. But, Alainn, if that were true, why hasn't he called or e-mailed me since I delivered the Rosette 82GF?"

"Something must have happened. Just let me call him. I just need his number."

He sighed heavily. "How about this: you go take a bath, we watch the recordings, and then we'll call him together."

"I'm not watching those stupid recordings," she sobbed.

He rubbed her back as the tears kept flowing from her incessantly.

Eventually, he helped her to the bathroom and closed the door. She hobbled over to the bath before slowly lowering herself into the empty, dirty tub. The water that poured over her neck and shoulders was hot enough to pink her skin almost immediately. When the water was almost to the point of overflowing, she leaned up and turned off the faucet.

Like so many times before, Alainn let her head sink under the surface, trying to drown out the thought that Lorccan wanted Shelly. It was like her father knew that was her weakest link and had taken a hammer to it.

But Alainn knew something was wrong. She refused to give up on him—until he made her.

29

April 5, 2027

Alainn stood at the top of her hill, holding on to the bus stop sign for support. The cold metal bit into her hand as the wind slapped her face. From right where she was, if she stood just like this, she could see a sliver of Lorccan's tower. Around the city, the sky was bruised with deep purples and reds as the sun rose.

She had been awake for three days, and her father had still refused to contact Lorccan. Alainn was a cup full of hope that had the smallest crack, leaking drip by drip away.

Her father had held to his guns for once in his life, refusing to give Alainn Lorccan's contact information until she watched the recordings. The Internet had provided no results. Mr. Garbhan had an e-mail address, but she would have had no idea where to start or what to say in that format.

And Alainn wasn't going to watch those recordings. She knew they'd only contain a bunch of lies.

She pulled a scrap of paper from her pocket, glancing over the ten different bus numbers on it.

The old, blue-and-white bus chugged up their hill. Red letters scrolled across the top of the windshield: Carnival Street/Red Line Crossover. The bus halted directly in front of her, the large advertisement on its side telling her to buy Juicy Snacks—her kids would love them.

When the door folded out, an automaton gazed down at her from where he sat, high above in the driver's seat. An oncoming car shone headlights on him, even though it was already pretty light out. The robot-driver's skin reflected the light with an unnatural sheen.

When Alainn hesitated, he asked, "Are you getting on, miss?"

She nodded stiffly and forced her fingers to release the pole. After she paid, Alainn turned to the empty bus. The driver began ascending the hill before she took a step.

The long, vacant cabin had one other occupant—a man sleeping curled up in a stall. The plastic of the trash bag he wore over a dirty sweatshirt crinkled as he clutched a backpack tighter to him.

Alainn walked on, finding a seat in the very back, where no one could sit behind her. The day passed in a blur of faces, people getting on and off. Music played too loud out of headphones. Phone conversations were yelled out or whispered about important nothings.

Automatons populated every street corner, darted around every open café, and disembarked from their long, glass-pod busses as fast as others took their place.

She climbed on and off busses as messages shifted over ad screens. Her fingers touched cold poles as she waited to get on, get off, sit, or just stand. Backs bent as people snacked on food hidden in their laps. Mingled smells reminded her that she hadn't eaten at all that day, while simultaneously destroying her appetite.

It was well past noon when Alainn disembarked, five city blocks from Lorccan's tower. The streets seemed foreign, cold, wrong. Trash littered the ground. Food wrappers skittered around sleeping bodies, caught in the artificial breeze from passing traffic. Several groups passed. The robots marched in uniforms, and the humans huddled in heavy jackets.

Alainn wrapped her arms around herself as long, shining office buildings towered over her. Lorccan's tower loomed into view. Just as before, the building sucked up the light around it. It was a vortex, a vacuum, and she wanted back in.

She walked the length of the building to where the long access road waited. It was completely empty; no trash or debris had ventured so far in.

She tamed her breaths into an even rhythm as she approached the screen that guarded the entrance to Lorccan's garage.

Alainn stood, halfway down the length of the screen, not ready.

"Please state your purpose." Rosebud 03AF's voice said as crisp, black letters scrolled across the screen.

"It's me, Rosebud. Alainn Murphy."

"Hello, Alainn Murphy. Why are you back?"

She swallowed. "I need to talk to Lorccan."

"No."

"What?" She blinked at the two crisp, black letters on the screen. "Rosebud, I need to—I need to talk to him. I'm going to come clean. It's time to come clean with him and tell him what I did."

"No." The words blinked on the screen.

"Stop . . . stop it. You told me that you wanted me to save him. To save all of you."

"You did save us. He's better; you need to move on with your life now."

"Don't you think that he deserves to decide that for himself?" Her voice cracked.

Lorccan's face appeared on the screen, an excited spark in his eyes.

"Lorccan," she breathed, her hand going to the screen. "I'm . . . I'm . . . it's me. Jade."

"Shelly? So you can come?" he said.

"What?" Alainn asked.

A woman's voice came on. It was a low, melodious voice. "Yeah, of course I'll come, Lor."

"Thank you," he mouthed with so much joy in his eyes.

Alainn bit her lip, hard. That look in his face—it was pulling her insides apart. But she could not stop her hand from rising up and touching the smile on his lips.

"You'll go through the decontamination? You'll do that?" he asked.

"Yeah, anything," Shelly said.

"I love you," he said. "You are such a wonderful person."

The words slammed into Alainn, each one a bullet punching into her chest.

The screen went white, soft white, like bone.

"He doesn't scream at night anymore, Alainn."

Tears stung her skin, raw and worn down from days of crying.

"You saved him. Don't you want him to be happy now?" Rosebud said, shooting the final bullet, the one aimed straight for Alainn's heart.

"Damn it," she whispered. The answer was yes, but Alainn wanted him to be happy with *her*. "I think I should talk to him."

"No. I'll protect him, even from you. Go live your life. Find your own happiness somewhere else." The screen went dark.

But Alainn didn't leave like any self-respecting person would. She sat down next to the screen, folded her legs up, and cried.

The truth of it was, if Rosebud let her, Alainn would stay with Lorccan even if it hurt him—even if it hurt them both. Obviously, she was just that sort of wretched soul, wailing outside of his tower, forever shut out.

After all her tears were spent and had crusted on her cheeks, she stood and faced the screen. "Just—

give Lorccan the chance to reject me himself, okay? That's all I ask. If he tells me he wants Shelly instead, then fine. But, it's not your choice to make, so you really should let him do it."

The screen didn't turn back on. Rosebud was done with Alainn.

Still, Alainn walked down to where the steel barrier closed off Lorccan's garage. She tried to pry open the door, but it didn't budge. With all her strength, she pushed the door and then even kicked it once, but nothing happened.

Closing her eyes, Alainn leaned back against the steel. Maybe if she waited long enough a delivery would arrive and she could slip in with it. Alainn immediately dismissed the idea—she would still have to get past Rosebud 03AF's security system to get anywhere in the tower.

A siren blared out, growing louder and louder. A police car pulled in front of the entrance to the garage. Obviously, Rosebud wanted to add a little humiliation to Alainn's broken heart.

A police automaton stepped out of the cruiser. "Ma'am, the owners of this building have complained about you being on their property. I'm going to have to ask you to leave."

"What if I don't?" she asked, voice rasping.

"Then I'll have to take you into custody." His face was almost featureless, as if they'd tried to make him look like everyman but ended up making him look like nothing at all.

She pushed herself off the wall with her foot and sighed. "All right, I'm going."

He waited inside his cruiser for her to walk down the access road before backing out. When she paused just beside the building, the automaton pulled up beside her. "Move along," came over his loud speaker.

She nodded, then continued walking down the city street—and away from Lorccan.

Eyes skipped past her as she climbed back onto the bus though her cheeks were stiff from her hard cry.

The seats next to Alainn remained empty for most of the rides, even though there was more than one person standing. On about her fifth transfer and in the second hour of her trip, she pulled her phone from her purse. Scrolling through her contacts slowly, she pressed Greg's name.

The phone rang five times, long, low dulcet tones. "Alainn?" he answered, sounding a little surprised.

"Hey," she said while grasping onto the handle of the seat in front of her.

"It's really loud wherever you are. Did you say something?"

She raised her voice a little, "Hey, Greg. It's me. How are you?"

"I'm fine, Alainn. I can't really hear you, though. I've been trying to reach you for months."

Her voice rose even louder, "Hey, I was wondering if you would you let me finish the season?" A few people looked over, but so what if random people heard her? Right now, she couldn't care less.

"Hell, Alainn, there's only like two weeks left in the ski season. The snow's already melting up here." He sounded very much like he was saying no.

"Greg, I'll come on as a volunteer if I have to. I'm sorry to do this to you—but I need to get out of here and be busy." She closed her eyes and clenched her jaw.

She would not allow herself to cry on a public bus.

Greg stayed silent for a while. Her fingers squeezed the plastic handle tighter, waiting.

"I'll . . . come get you, Alainn. I can do it tomorrow."

"I'm not asking you to do that, Greg. Just let me work or do *something*—that's all I ask. I can get a ride up there." She shook her head, even though he couldn't see her.

"Yeah, but I'm going to do it anyway. Can you be ready in the afternoon, around three or four?"

She nodded. "Yeah, I'll be ready."

30

April 6, 2027

The bloom that Alainn sat in front of was as big as her head, unusual so early in the year. Her face pushed fully into it. Soft petals brushed over her cheeks and eyelids. Every time she inhaled the rose's scent, she thought of her mother.

Her mother, the first Rose.

"So you're leaving?" Colby asked from somewhere behind Alainn.

She pulled back to look at him.

To her surprise, Colby sat beside her on the dirt. Leaning forward, he reached out and softly touched a big yellow bloom that bounced and pushed into his touch. "Smells like Mom," he said.

"That's what I was thinking."

He looked a little shaggier than the last time she'd seen him, his dark hair falling in soft waves around his face. The reflected sunlight on his glasses made his expression inscrutable.

She hadn't seen him for days—not since that first day, when she woke up.

"I used to help her garden, you know, when I was really little—I stopped when you were old enough to do it."

"I don't remember that," she said. What she remembered was her mother and her. Alainn was little and her mother vibrant. They caught raindrops in their hands, picked worms from the dirt, giggled, and danced around victoriously each time a new bloom opened.

"So you're in love with this guy?" Colby asked.

"Shut up, Colby." Alainn stuck her face back into the bloom, burying it.

He raised his brows, seemingly unperturbed by her reaction. "And he was in love with you?"

"That probably sounds totally crazy to you, huh?" She shook her head. "A guy falling in love with a robot . . ."

"That would be strange behavior. But he *didn't* fall in love with a robot. Your glands produce human scents and pheromones, which then produce reactions in him so, chemically, he would have known that you were human even if he hadn't cognitively processed it. I just can't reason out why he believed you were a robot for as long as he did."

Just like Colby to rationalize the shit out of the situation.

She thought about it for a minute, chewing on her lip. "The only humans he ever had contact with

250

were his parents, and I don't think they were very affectionate."

He turned his head toward her, looking confused. "That's not logical. How could he never have had human contact?"

"He did, but only through phones and computers. He's really scared of viruses or bacteria from the outside."

"Mysophobia, fear of germs," he said.

"It's just . . . Colby, I know you're trying to make me feel better, but the farther I get away from it, the clearer it all becomes. I was the trial run, the practice for the real thing. And now he can have his AI robot, completely new and fresh and unaware, and his girlfriend, too."

Saying the words felt like a betrayal because they just didn't at all address the kind of person Lorccan was. He didn't plan this; he didn't get her "rebooted" on purpose. Maybe he would have gone through with marrying her if she never had been. But now he could have what he always wanted— something real in his life. Shelly. He had no idea there was a castoff in the situation, no idea there was still a Jade out there whose love for him hadn't vanished in a malfunction.

"Do you know his girlfriend's name?"

"Why?"

"You could look her up."

"What?" She turned a glare on Colby. "To what, ruin his life out of spite?"

Colby touched the bloom again. "If I were him, I'd want to know the truth."

"Why do you care anyway, Colby? Shouldn't you be off at the university being special?" The moment the words came out, she felt a wash of shame for spitting them at him. "I'm sorry; I just thought you didn't care what happened. You would have been fine with Dad going to prison and Rose staying out."

He looked off. "Dad *should* have gone to prison. He should be in there right now. He's never going to stop doing this to us. It's his fault you spent months pretending to be a robot. It's his fault what happened seven years ago—"

"Please. Don't."

He shook his head. "I'm just really tired of watching you taking his punishments. If I'd known what you planned to do, I would have stopped you. I would have taken him to the police station myself. And as for Rose . . ." He looked at her, and in the look Alainn saw something she hadn't really seen in her steady, logical brother before—suspicion. He lowered his voice, "Why would she be willing to risk *killing* you to get you out? That doesn't make any sense to me."

"The T9640 was her idea?" she asked.

"Your friend is here to pick you up," Rose said from behind them.

They both spun to look at Rose. She stood framed in their back door, dark hair up in a neat bun. Alainn had noticed in the last few days that Rose was looking a lot less like her somehow.

Greg was in the kitchen, a glass of water in his hand, talking to her father. His eyes lit up when he saw Alainn, and she couldn't help but smile a little— the first smile she'd felt come on naturally in a while.

252

"Hey, good to see you." He reached out and pulled her into a hug.

The coarse hairs of his wool sweater brushed across her face as she squeezed him. Pulling back, she smiled up. "You are the nicest person in the whole world. Thanks for coming to get me."

"It's cool." He ran a hand over his buzzed head. "It's good to get out of the mountains, even just for a couple hours. Sometimes I forget the real world exists."

"Good to see you." Colby offered his hand to Greg.

"You too, man." Greg shook his hand. He glanced over to Rose, before turning back. "We should probably be heading right back out, though, not to be rude. I don't want to be taking the roads at night."

They loaded Alainn's skis and duffel bag into the trunk of his SUV, waved good-bye to her family, and were descending the hill in less than twenty minutes.

Greg glanced into his rearview mirror. "God, you were right. Rose is one freaky robot. No offense to your family, but I couldn't get out of your house fast enough."

"I'm with you there," she whispered. "It's just gotten worse since our last e-mail."

"You know they're trying to replace us, right? Over the next four years, the resort's slowly going to phase the automatons in as patrol."

Bringing up her knees, Alainn covered her face. "That sucks."

He nudged her. "We have a couple more years, but yeah, sucks. So . . ." He drew the word out. "Your dad not-so-subtly told me to ask you out."

"Oh God, Greg. I'm sorry. He thinks you're harboring some secret crush." Heat filled her cheeks.

"Oh, yeah, of course I am. Please, Alainn Murphy, be mine." He gave her a saucy smile.

"If only. I think I might have to fight Stephanie for that one, and Terry, and half the snow bunnies," she teased.

It was a well-known fact that pretty-boy Greg had groupies.

"Just Karla." He grinned, looking genuinely happy.

"Karla? Nice. Congrats." Alainn swallowed and looked away, suddenly fighting emotion. Her hands wiped at her face roughly.

She was crying in Greg's car.

Shit.

"As much as I'd appreciate it if girls cried because I was off the market, I'm figuring that's not for me." He looked over. "You want to talk about it?"

She squeezed her eyes shut. "I'll tell you. Just not right now. I just want to get up on my mountain and forget the last four months ever happened."

"That can be arranged."

Even though Alainn didn't believe him, she felt just a little bit better.

31

April 6, 2027

Shelly Dover climbed out of the self-driving car and into Lor's garage, looking around. Generally, she didn't like parking lots. Too many angry people drove around, causing too much confusion. People yelled because they wanted to pull out of spaces, or wanted to drive past, or passed out flyers for something she didn't want. People would honk when you took a space or as they waited for you to pull out of your spot so that they could take it.

Actually, Shelly *hated* parking lots; the only time she would ever use one was when she visited her family in Idaho and didn't have a choice.

Lor's parking lot wasn't like that. It was beautifully empty of any people at all. Open, empty, not at all overwhelming or stressful. When she entered the hallway leading to the elevator, it was also blessedly empty.

"Shelly Dover, please follow me," said a smooth mechanical voice.

"Okay, thank you," Shelly said. The voice led her to an elevator and told her to enter, two things she did without complaint.

In the elevator, Shelly followed every instruction, took off her clothing, was washed, dried and re-dressed. She'd expected the process to be unpleasant, but she found it more enjoyable than anything else. She'd had a sticky feeling on her hands since a homeless man had walked by and asked her for money. Afraid, she had given him a twenty before running away.

There really could have been a germ exchange there.

When the elevator door opened and she found Lor waiting for her outside, she grinned wide and had to comment, "I can definitely see the benefit of the decontamination room."

Lor smiled, though he looked tired. "I thought you would. Thank you so much for coming."

"Of course I'd come."

When Lor opened his arms, a little tentatively, Shelly moved into them, even more tentatively. It wasn't his face that made her uncomfortable; he'd been showing it to her for a couple of months now. But Shelly never felt quite comfortable in a hug. She never knew where to put her hands or how much pressure to exert. Holding him somewhat awkwardly, she broke away after what she hoped was the right amount of time.

Shelly looked up into Lor's face. "I can't believe I'm finally seeing you in person. I'd expected it to be under different circumstances, but I'm happy to be here all the same."

"Thank you." He held out a hand, gesturing toward what looked to be a dining room. "Shelly, would you mind coming to my office?"

"Wherever, Lor." She nodded. "I've seen it so many times, I bet I'll feel comfortable there."

"Good. I want you to be comfortable."

"Your tower is very nice, very quiet and calm." Shelly couldn't help but observe Lor as they walked side by side through the dining room and to his office. She had imagined herself in Lor's office so many times, just sitting near him, enjoying silence. Or, they would sit and talk for hours about robotics and new technologies.

It wasn't as large as she imagined. In the many times she'd imagined it, it had never had two desks. Also, her fantasies had definitely never included the occupant of that second desk.

Shelly had imagined that she would hate the robot, Jade. Lor had bought Jade so that he could learn to be with Shelly, or at least that had been what he said.

Then, he'd said he instead wanted to be Shelly's friend so that he could be with a robot.

Yes, she thought that she would hate the robot, but upon meeting the robot's gaze, she found she didn't. She felt absolutely nothing for the creature.

Perhaps that was the appeal—the lack of humanity. She could somewhat understand that; it was like dating a book or your favorite movie.

"Hello. You must be Jade," Shelly said as she stepped forward toward the robot's desk.

"Yes, I'm Jade," the robot said as she stood up, offering a hand over the desk.

As Shelly shook the hand, as not to be rude, she met Jade's eyes. Quickly, she turned away, feeling a strange shock of fear. They were very like human eyes, perhaps too like human eyes, but soulless. How Lor had once looked into those eyes and been enchanted, Shelly would never understand.

"Should I leave, Lorccan? I'm finished with my work." Jade turned to Lor with a grin.

"Yes, that might be best, Jade," Lor said, holding the door open for her.

Shelly couldn't help but feel a wave of relief as the robot left, and finally, for the first time ever, she could be alone with Lor.

32

April 11, 2027

"You ready?" Karla asked Alainn as they dismounted the chair lift. Her heart-shaped face was framed in a red beanie under a black helmet, the exact same as Alainn wore.

The slope was a sheet of fresh powder. They had probably had the final heavy snowfall of the year the night before. Greg and a couple of the higher-ups set off explosives at four that morning for avalanche control. There were a couple ski tracks on other courses already, but theirs was still pristine.

They were two drops of red on a perfect white expanse.

"Could I just have one minute? This is the first time I've been up to the top since I got back."

"Sure. You want to just meet me down there?" Karla said, driving the ends of her poles into the snow with a *thwack, snick.*

"If that's cool," Alainn said.

Karla smiled a smile that made Alainn think she definitely knew.

Damn Greg.

Alainn had ended up spilling everything to her best friend—a story so outrageous she barely believed the words that came from her own lips. Honestly, she didn't blame Greg for talking. It must be weird for Karla that Alainn was Greg's roommate. If she were in his place, she'd want to reassure her, too.

Karla nodded. "All right, I'll take the right side of the slope. See you down there."

"Thank you, Karla." Alainn turned from Karla, hearing the soft *swish* of her departure. Through the thick leather of her gloves, she pulled off the helmet and ski cap and let her hair fall. The wind had not picked up yet, but the cold air nipped at her cheeks and ears.

She stood at the apex of her mountain.

Beyond her, endless hills of black and white stretched, a wide expanse of buried wilderness. Her mountain always whispered out to her, *Here, you could jump into the air and fly away. This is as close as you'll ever be to free.*

It said nothing that morning. The mountain waited in silence, watching Alainn. Taking a step to the side, Alainn considered that maybe she just wasn't at the right angle. Instead of feeling free, she felt utterly alone.

She pulled her gear back on and tucked stray wisps of hair into it, feeling defiant curls sticking to her cheeks.

The mountain rushed under her skis as she sped down the slope. Air gusted over her face, up the bridge of her nose, and over her eyes. Weaving through the trees at the sides, Alainn confirmed the left side of the slope had no dangerous buildup or fallen branches.

Karla waited at the bottom. They said nothing to each other as Alainn slid in beside her, just started moving off to another lift. Small splotches of red were on most of the long white hills, framed in black lines of forest.

After three more slopes, they headed in to find the office bustling with patrol suited up in red coats.

"I'm making you ladies some of this," Terry called from where he hulked over the communal stove. He opened up two packages of instant noodles and added it to the pot.

"Oh, please," Karla called as she and Alainn knocked the snow off their feet on the thick rubber matt.

"Thanks," Alainn said, falling into the chair.

Terry glanced up at Alainn. "I think you're supposed to say, 'That's nasty.' Then I'll say, 'Shut up, you're eating it.' Then you say, 'Looks like cat barf.'"

She looked through her lashes at him, almost managing a smile. "Looks like cat barf—smells like it, too."

"Better. And shut up, you're eating it."

"See, no point in fighting you," she mumbled.

"Eight thirty, guys. Slopes are opening up. You are officially on duty!" Greg called from his office—in reality, his desk was just partitioned off from the rest

261

of the room, so it did not quite qualify as an office. He slapped the partition twice before ducking back behind it.

"Another day in paradise," Terry said as he slopped soup bowls in front of Karla and Alainn and threw down forks.

Alainn immediately dug into the hot noodles, though the fake chicken soup really did taste a little like cat barf. The draft from the cold air hitting her on the outside and the warm liquid going down her throat used to be her favorite sensation, pre-Lorccan.

Post-Lorccan, not so much.

The office was too loud for much conversation, but Terry managed it anyway. "Twelve tongues I've saved this year, five of them adult tongues. I think I deserve some sort of reward."

"I'm guessing you took your reward from some of those adult tongues," Karla said wryly.

"You . . ." He pointed at Karla. "You are not allowed to bring up tongues and kissing. I'm still in too much pain."

Karla rolled her eyes. "Ha. Shut up, Terry."

"Hey, Alainn!" Greg stepped out from behind his alcove, his eyes moving back and forth in confusion. "Hey, uh, the front just called over and said there's a woman with a monkey here to see you. You think that maybe—"

Alainn stood up so fast her chair toppled backward and soup sloshed all over the table.

Both Karla and Terry scooted back.

"Sorry!" Alainn called to them as she rounded the table to head over to Greg. "Did you say a monkey?"

He raised his hands. "That's what they said."

"Okay, I forgot to tell you about the monkeys!" she called, running out the back door that connected to the resort. People clogged the halls. Their knees poked out from benches and elbows stuck out as they lifted coffee and hot chocolate to their lips. She ducked between them, her damp coat making a few people recoil.

The hallway opened up to a large lobby where dozens of people lined up in front of and around the front desk, while others stood nearby.

As Alainn passed a crowd of about ten kids surrounding a yellow lab in a ski patrol vest, a fellow patroller called Stacy nodded at her. When Alainn waved absently, Stacy gave her a small smile but didn't stop her speech. "Now, Riley here is our newest avalanche rescue dog, and he's actually a K-level automaton. He's the first automaton dog we've used. Do any of you know what an avalanche is?" Her voice trailed off as Alainn pushed through the crowd.

Alainn saw her sitting on top of the front desk. Blue. She was surrounded by a crowd of small children and looking around while they reached up to pet her. The moment her eyes found Alainn, she screeched and held out her little arms.

The children looked back, confused. A little girl yelled, "Look, there's a monkey in a dress!"

Blue leaped off the desk, her little monkey arms going around Alainn's neck.

"What—how??" Alainn hugged Blue to her. Blue's little body felt so natural, not at all like a robot or an automaton. "How are you here?" Alainn whispered.

Blue pulled away, her hand going out to point to a woman standing in the crowd. She made a monkey screech, then shook her pointing hand.

The woman's face was slack, a mask of absolute shock. She obviously recognized Alainn, but Alainn didn't know her. The woman was shorter than Alainn by a couple of inches. Her long, brown hair stuck out to one side of a pretty face, as if she had just taken her hat off.

A gloved hand rose, pointing into Alainn's face. "You think I can't figure out what's going on here?" The woman whispered the words, harshly.

Alainn stared, and then glanced around at the crowd—everyone was watching them, avidly.

"I'm calling the police. You belong in jail." Even though the woman's quiet voice cracked with emotion as she said it, it sounded very familiar.

"Um . . ." Alainn shook her head, and tried to get Blue off her, but the little fingers dug into the back of Alainn's neck.

Blue shook her head and then made a low screech at the woman.

The woman further pointed into Alainn's face. "I'm calling the police right now. You and your father are a pair of con artists, and you're not getting away with this!" Tears now shone on the woman's face, shiny tracks on pale, freckled skin.

"You're—are you Shelly Dover?" Alainn asked as the humiliating realization washed over her.

"Yes, and there's no way I'll let you get away with this!"

Alainn knew she should be feeling guilty. She knew this was the moment of truth where she, "the other woman," was exposed as the villain she was. But she didn't feel guilty. What Alainn felt was a surge of anger.

He chose Shelly; he chose to be with her.

But nope, that wasn't good enough. Shelly had to find Alainn and make her suffer. She had to take everything Alainn had left and drive her farther into the ground.

"Stop, okay! This is where I work. This is inappropriate."

Her job was the only thing stopping Alainn from showing up at Lorccan's tower begging to be let in again. Shelly probably didn't want that, either.

"Inappropriate? You've got to be kidding me."

"Just go, okay? You can't have me arrested. You're just humiliating me in front of my colleagues while I'm already having a hard time coping."

Shelly took a step backward and whispered, "You're going to prison for this."

Seriously?

Alainn blew out a breath and turned to the receptionist, who was openly gaping at the scene. Fortunately, she was a human and not one of the new automaton receptionists. Alainn leaned over the counter with Blue still clinging to her. "Could you call

Greg at the patrol office and tell him I'm going to be a little while?"

The receptionist gave her a grimace of support and looked over to Shelly, who was on her phone—probably calling the police.

"How long should I tell him you're going to be?"

Alainn closed her eyes, feeling the humiliation creep up her face in a flush. "That's my . . . ex-boyfriend's current girlfriend, so I might need a little while to clear this up."

She nodded, still grimacing. "All right, I'll call over. Good luck." She sounded like she meant it.

Alainn thanked all that was good in this world that Greg loved her, because she deserved to be fired, again. It was even possible he'd do it this time, but unlikely. Unfortunately, it wasn't even close to the biggest pile of dung she had hurled his way.

Steeling herself, she turned back to Shelly.

Shelly was off the phone, meaning that the local police were probably on their way. Unluckily for Shelly, the police here were not only all still humans, but Alainn knew each of them. Meaning they'd take the time to listen to Alainn's side of the story and wouldn't arrest her.

"Shelly, how about we step outside? I'll let you whisper at me or wait for the police or whatever. Just not here, okay?"

Blue screeched at Shelly, again, holding her little hand out.

Shelly looked between Alainn and Blue. She sucked in her cheeks, still looking shocked. Even this upset, her face was beautiful, like a Renaissance painting of an angel.

Obviously, she was of the avenging angel sort.

Shelly lifted a dry-erase board that she had tucked under her arm and put it in Blue's outstretched hand. In Blue's other small hand, she placed a dry-erase pen.

Blue took both and propped the board against Alainn's chest.

Alainn stretched her neck back as the board pushed into her throat. "What are you doing, Blue?"

But she ignored Alainn, opening the pen with both her hands. As the pungent dry-erase pen scent wafted up, Blue used two hands to write across the board. When she was done, she handed the board back to Shelly with a teeth-baring screech.

Shelly read the message, looked between Blue and Alainn again, then said, "I won't yell at you anymore. But let's stay inside where it's warm. I still— I don't believe you. This—" She held up the board.

You are wrong, was written across it in rough letters.

Shelly continued, "This could just mean you've conned Blue as well."

"Okay, come on." Alainn knew a quiet spot. Well, it was quiet in the mornings, when everyone was on their way out to the slopes.

At first, it seemed that Shelly had changed her mind, but, slowly, she followed Alainn out of the crowd. She stayed a few steps behind.

In contrast, Blue continued to cling to Alainn like she might disappear.

Alainn stopped at a fireplace that had yet to be lit and fell into one of the couches in front of it. If she was going to be torn into, she'd at least be comfortable while it happened. Shadows of exhaustion and sadness had hovered over her head all day, but now, looking at Shelly, they threatened to descend. She petted Blue's little fake head, hugging Blue to her like she was a transport back to Lorccan.

Shelly didn't sit. She stood above Alainn yet kept her distance. The stones of the fireplace jumbled behind her. Her knees bent and she twitched, looking like she might take off any second.

Alainn took a deep breath and decided to start this thing. "I did fool Lorccan—Mr. Garbhan, I mean. But it's over now, and my father delivered Rosette, the Rose robot that he paid for. So, legally, you have nothing on us." Alainn looked at Shelly, straight into her angelic face. "I didn't get anything out of it— nothing moneywise, I mean." She blinked furiously.

"You're a liar," Shelly mumbled.

"Seriously, stop whispering," Alainn said. "What do you want from me? I'm sorry that I was with him and I wasn't a robot. I'm sorry that I fooled him. But I'm not fooling him anymore. I walked away so you two could be happy. Maybe that's not enough to redeem me in your eyes, but it took everything I had to do it."

Blue nuzzled in close to Alainn as she furiously wiped away tears.

Swallowing hard, she continued, "Maybe I shouldn't have done what I did, but it's over now. My dad delivered what Lorccan paid for. You can't charge him or me with anything."

"Except for the millions of dollars you extorted from him!" She took a step back as she said this.

Alainn grabbed her forehead, afraid her brain was about to explode. "I already told you. My dad gave him the Rosette 82GF he paid for. It's done. Go be happy together and leave me alone." Her voice broke.

Shelly leaned back, confusion and anger warring in her expression. "I'm talking about the millions of dollars you and your father have extorted from him *since* you were replaced with the robot."

"That didn't happen."

"Not only *did* it happen, there's more than enough proof to put you away for life, Alainn Murphy. Or should I call you Jade?" She glared at Alainn but stepped toward the lobby, like she might actually bolt.

"You're wrong. I was in a coma for two weeks after I left. The moment I was strong enough, I went to Lorccan's tower and Rosebud, the AI who controls his house, refused to let me in. She told me that you two were happy, and I needed to let him go. The day after that, I came here. To work." Alainn raised her hands up around Blue. "I can prove all of that, so whatever proof you think you have on me, you don't."

"Your father did it—"

"My father hasn't heard from Lorccan. I know because . . ." Alainn smacked her hand into the armrest of her chair. "That's what convinced us that Lorccan didn't want me back."

Little hands came up to Alainn's cheeks and wiped away the tears that she couldn't stop.

Leaning away, Alainn shook her head. "You know what? I'm not listening to this anymore. I know I should feel guilty that I was with Lorccan while you two were dating—having your phone-call thing, whatever, but I *can't* feel guilty about being with him, and I don't. Maybe that makes me a bad person," she squeezed her eyes shut, "but I'm trying to do the right thing here. What I'm going to do is walk away so he can be happy with you, and that's as much as you're going to get from me. Please don't ever come back here, and don't you dare try to set my father and me up for some extortion crime. It won't hold."

Instead of leaving, Shelly stayed, but still hovered like she might bolt. "He's given your father millions of dollars in the last few weeks for chips and microchips to try to bring you back."

"What?" Alainn's voice came out high-pitched, not like her regular voice at all. "No he hasn't."

"Yes, he has," she said.

"You two are together. Why would he do that?"

"Lor and I are just friends. He is my friend, and I care so much about him."

A sob hiccupped from Alainn. "You're lying. Rosebud 03AF showed me the video of . . . she showed me the video . . . of when you said you were going to come to his tower. He was so happy."

"He suspected that Connor Murphy was cheating him. He wanted me to look at the microchips, chips, and Jade herself, but he wasn't going to risk her by sending her back out."

"He wants me *back*?" Alainn looked Shelly straight in the eyes, begging her to—Alainn wasn't sure what—to tell the truth, maybe, whatever it was.

"He's paid millions of dollars—he's falling apart. He's spending all day trying to make that robot remember who she is."

Alainn shook her head.

"It's destroying him. What's happening—it's destroying him."

"No." She shook her head again.

"Yes, Alainn. You're killing him."

"*I'm* not doing it. I *tried* to get back in."

Blue finally released Alainn, reaching out to Shelly. When Shelly handed her the dry-erase board, she set the board on Alainn's knees and started writing.

Rosebud 03AF is broken.

Alainn leaned in. Sniffing back the emotion, she asked, "How is she broken, Blue?"

Blue took her palm and erased the word "*broken*." Instead, she wrote the word "*gone*."

"Rosebud 03AF is gone?" Alainn stared at the message. "What happened to her?"

She erased the board and scrawled, *I don't know.*

"She was there when I visited three days ago," Shelly said, looking at the message.

Again, Blue erased the message and wrote, *It's not her. It's someone else.*

"The new robot?" Shelly asked.

"No," Alainn whispered, sitting back in the chair. "No, there's a third Rose model." To herself, she muttered, "Why would she be willing to kill you to get you out?"

"What are you talking about?" Shelly asked.

"Last year, when Lorccan commissioned the first humanoid AI robot, my dad *did* create her. But Rose 76GF—she wasn't at all compliant. She started overwriting her ethical programming, and she refused to go when we were supposed to send her to Lorccan."

"There are *two* Rose robots?" Shelly asked, her gaze skipping from place to place. "And, you, also?"

Alainn nodded. "Yeah, there are two—Rose and Rosette. Rose planned everything. She created the microchips that would disguise me as a robot to Rosebud 03AF. She only gave me a few minutes to decide whether to go through with the plan. I found out later that Lorccan would actually have been willing to give my father another month's extension. Why would she send me in there?" Alainn looked away and then answered her own question, "She must have needed the money. But why does *she* need money?"

Shelly watched Alainn carefully.

Alainn looked down and repeated to herself. "Why would she be willing to kill you to get you out? Was it just to extort money? Did she just want to extort money from him? But how could she know that he'd care whether or not I reset?"

"What are you talking about?" Shelly asked, as she lowered her head to look at Alainn.

"Rose 76AF—the first Rose robot—fed me poison to get me out. That's how she made it look like I was malfunctioning. The first way she tried to get me out didn't work, so she resorted to the poison. She'd been trying to get me to drink it for months. It almost killed me."

"Poison?"

Alainn looked up at her. "Yeah. My brother was suspicious and he asked me why she'd be willing to kill me to get me out." She shook her head. "But she *wasn't* doing that. She must have been willing to kill me to get Rosette *in*."

33

April 11, 2027

"I'm pretty sure I should be driving you to the police station. You're obviously a good actress and a con artist," Shelly said in a quiet voice as her little sedan drove down the mountain.

Snow was piled up on either side of the road, dirty, murky snow. Grass and rocks poked out of the thin layer, creating a splotchy, yellowing landscape.

"No offense, but I couldn't care less what you believe as long as you get me there. If you think I'll go calmly to the police station, then you're insane," Alainn said as she rubbed her aching forehead.

In the lodge, Shelly had declared that if Alainn was telling the truth, she'd have to go to Lorccan's tower and prove it. She whispered the declaration anyway.

After Alainn's revelation, she was more than willing to comply. Hell, when Shelly hesitated to let her into the sedan, Alainn considered stealing it. It looked like there was a possibility she would still have to.

Shelly might not believe Alainn, but all the way down the mountain, she dealt out punishment by murmuring the details about how Lorccan was doing. He'd lost weight. There were deep hollows under his eyes. And, perhaps the most telling of all, Alainn's peace lily was now in his office, on his desk.

Rosette was exceptionally compliant and barely said a word to Lorccan. She'd quietly eat with him, play games with him. He'd even tried to show her movies—none of which had brought Jade back. He'd spent hours and hours teaching her about what she liked, reciting jokes Alainn had told him, explaining the moments they had together, but of course it hadn't done anything.

When Shelly visited Lorccan in his tower, he'd looked haunted, she said. She'd analyzed the hardware in the robotics chips that had been sent to Lorccan at an exorbitant price, allegedly from Alainn's father. Everything had been what her father had claimed it to be, and Shelly could not find a reason why it wasn't working for Rosette.

When Shelly left in one of Lorccan's self-driving cars, Blue had popped out of hiding in the back seat when Shelly was halfway home.

Blue had written out a message to Shelly: *Find Alainn Murphy.*

"How did you know who I really was?" Alainn interrupted Shelly to ask Blue at that part of the story.

She wrote her response from the backseat, and then handed the dry-erase board to Alainn. *We were listening.*

That wasn't creepy at all . . .

Shelly finished her story by telling Alainn that she'd talked to Lorccan once since then, and he'd been hopeful, saying that he was making headway. She hadn't been able to get through since then, though, including when she'd tried to call from the lobby of the ski resort. They'd missed three of their scheduled phone calls.

The fact that Lorccan thought he might be getting Alainn back from Rosette scared her more than anything else Shelly said.

"Rose isn't going to let me in," Alainn said before looking over to Shelly. "She probably won't let you in, either. If she's not letting the phone calls go through, she's probably pretending to be you to him or something like that. She can do that."

If only Lorccan had funded that pulse button that would kill all robotics.

But, looking into the backseat where Blue was sitting over her dry-erase board in her little blue dress, Alainn rethought the robotics killing pulse. She needed a pulse that killed just specific forms of robotics, more of a gun than a bomb.

"Shit," she whispered. "Even if we get inside, Rose 76GF will be controlling the whole tower. She could lock us up in a hallway and let us starve and die there, and Lorccan would never even know that we were there."

Shelly glanced over, eyelids so wide they looked like they could almost push out her eyes, but she didn't say anything.

There was a screech from the backseat and Alainn turned to see Blue holding up the board. The message read, *Fix Rosebud 03AF.*

Alainn shrugged and grimaced at Blue. "We can't even get into the tower."

She erased the board and started writing.

"What does she want us to do?" Shelly asked, her wide eyes on the rearview mirror.

"She wants us to reboot Rosebud 03AF—the original AI system that controlled the house."

When Alainn looked into the backseat again, Blue held up a sign: *I can get you into the garage.*

"Okay. But how do we reboot her?"

Blue erased and wrote another message: *Shelly could do it.*

Alainn turned to Shelly. "She says she'll get us in, and you can reboot Rosebud."

"What? No, I doubt that." She shook her head.

"You said you were examining chips that were supposed to reboot me, right?" Alainn asked.

"Yeah, but Lor has those chips in his office, and you said we can't get up there."

Alainn sat up straight. "Except that Rose had to have designed those chips. The only computers that I know of that she has access to would be in my dad's workshop. All the circuit supplies were probably from there, too. If we found her designs on my father's computer, we could print new chips in the workshop." She looked away. "Except Rose would be there. She

277

never leaves my house, which means she'd probably try to stop us."

Shelly turned the wheel hard and pulled off the road, into a black sludgy pullout. They hit ice and slid a couple feet before stopping suddenly.

Too late, Alainn grabbed the "oh, shit," handle and yelled, "What the hell?"

Shelly's whole body shook as she clutched the steering wheel. "You really think I'll believe that there's a killer robot? And you think I'll take programs that originated from your house and family to hack into Lorccan's house? Do you think I'm stupid or something?" Her voice was both quiet and shrill.

"No, I don't think you're stupid. And I didn't say Rose was a killer. But from the fact that she gave me poison, she might have no problem becoming one."

"It just all sounds very farfetched, and you obviously already have no problem lying. Now you want me to hack into Lor's security system to give you access to his home?" She laid her mouth forward against her steering wheel, but her eyes turned upward like she was praying to something or someone.

"People always have such a hard time believing that robots can do bad things."

She pulled back to whisper, "Because they're machines, like toasters. I work on them for a living. They can malfunction, but they're not going to hatch up some elaborate extortion plot. That's what humans do."

"Uh-huh. Well, my best friend was killed by an automaton, an automatic functioning machine, a robot that does whatever they're 'trained' to do."

She jumped a little. "What?"

Shelly didn't deserve to know Alainn's story, but, hell, she was going to tell her anyway if it would get this car to Lorccan. Alainn closed her eyes and revealed something she hadn't told anyone in years, "We were at a gas station at night, and I got out of the car. I was being dumb; I was seventeen. The automaton looked normal. He wore the gas station attendant uniform. He hit me over the head and shoved me into my own trunk before driving out to a house. Some men were there—"

Alainn opened her eyes as Blue's little fingers patted her shoulder. When she turned to look, Blue climbed over the center divider and into Alainn's lap.

Her furry body quivered as Alainn held her. Meeting Shelly's gaze, she continued, "I was delivered to the men. Those men told that automaton to take my car up into the hills and drive off a cliff with Cara inside. He left immediately to do it."

Not all of that was the truth, but Shelly didn't really need all the details to get the point of her story.

"How did you get away?" Shelly whispered, her voice barely audible. Brows pressed down over a hard-to-read expression. Concern, maybe.

Alainn blew out a breath. "My dad owed them a lot of money. When they realized that he couldn't pay it back, they kept me for a couple days. The police found me before I was dead."

When Alainn met her gaze, tears leaked from Shelly's eyes. Her face paled.

Alainn waved a hand. "Stop. Don't cry for me. It was a long time ago. What I'm just trying to say . . . what I'm trying to say is . . ." She had no clue what she was trying to say.

"That robots kill people?" Shelly didn't sound at all disbelieving this time.

"No, but they can. I guess I'm trying to say that they're not what people think they are. You think they're toasters, and maybe they are. But my father gave those tools the ability to form their own personalities and to think for themselves. If you give a toaster a choice, it might choose to be a torture device. People just assume that we can control robots and they're safe, but they're not even safe when we *can* control them." She shook her head. "Shit, I don't know. But Rose? She's conniving. She's obviously overwritten her ethical systems and—"

"Lorccan's AI robots all turned out fine." Shelly looked pointedly at Blue.

"Well, maybe some are good and some are bad, like humans."

Shelly glared into Alainn's eyes but quickly turned away to face forward again. Her voice was still a murmur when she said, "Or maybe it's how they're raised. Maybe if they're raised by someone who hates robots, they'll turn out evil."

Shelly Dover was seriously starting to get on Alainn's last nerve. She threw up her hands. "Fine! Whatever! But now she's killing Lorccan or extorting money off him or whatever she's doing—it's evil. You can help me or not, but I'm going to try to get in there and reboot Rosebud 03AF. Then I'm getting to Lorccan."

Shelly looked away, but after a minute she pulled back onto the road. "I'm having a really hard time figuring out what he saw in you."

She spoke so low, Alainn wasn't sure she was even talking to her. She answered anyway, "Well, if you figure it out, be sure to tell me." Looking out the window, she said, "But he did. And I did. And I was almost willing to give him up when I thought he wanted me to. But not now that I know he doesn't."

She didn't look over, just kept her gaze forward. "If you're conning me and I'm helping you hurt him again, I'll make sure they arrest you and I'll pay for the prosecutor myself."

Alainn looked out the window at the dead grass that lined the road and whispered, "It's a deal."

Once they hit the highway, Shelly accelerated to just above the speed limit. Now that they had reentered the invisible cell phone reception bubble, Shelly kept dialing and redialing Lorccan on her cell phone. Her finger kept pressing the screen, which she hid in her lap.

Obviously, she was not quite on board the Alainn-is-innocent ship.

As the curvy mountain passes widened into five-lane freeways, Shelly's hands shook on her steering wheel. She'd stayed quiet the last hour, blinking rapidly at the road. It was only four o'clock, but she looked like she needed a nap or something.

"You want me to drive?" Alainn asked as Shelly swerved way too far while avoiding a merging car.

"I'm fine." She tucked her hair behind her ear with shaking fingers. "So, what are we doing at your house exactly?"

"I have sort of an idea—but feel free to give me some input. We have to find my brother, Colby. He may not help, but I think there's a really good chance that he will. I'll find a way to get Rose into the main part of the house with me and my father and distract them. You and Colby can sneak into the garage and find the files. Colby uses the computers as much as anyone, so he'll know what shouldn't be there. You guys find the files, print the chips, and cover your tracks as best you can before getting as far away as you can. I'll bike to meet you. We go to Lorccan's tower. Blue breaks us in—"

"Wouldn't it just be easier if I tell your brother what to look for?"

Alainn gave Shelly a skeptical look. "Probably not—"

"If he's caught, it won't seem suspicious." Her gaze was fixed on the road, but Alainn could see that a tear was dripping down the side of Shelly's nose.

Alainn finally recognized the expression on her face—way later than she should have. In Outreach, once in a while a very sadistic parent would convince their kid to hide a phobia of heights or bugs or something they dealt with all the time while backpacking. It came from that "face your fears, or if not, shame the fear out of them" attitude. Sometimes it worked; other times it resulted in a sixteen-year-old freezing halfway up a mountain and messing their pants.

It was just plain wrong.

Shelly looked like Alainn had just tied her to a rappelling rope and told her to jump off a cliff. Complete and total terror was revealed in the shaking of her hands, the paleness of her face, and the stiffness of her posture. It made Alainn rethink why Shelly had cried during the kidnapping recounting.

Alainn nodded slowly. "Sure, Shelly, that's possible. But what about in the tower? Someone needs to insert the chip and reboot Rosebud 03AF."

Shelly swerved again, and this time Alainn did grab the "oh shit" handle while Blue dug her little fingers into Alainn's arm. Shelly again straightened back into their lane while Blue let loose with a god-awful screech.

"I'm sorry!" she yelled, her face scrunching up.

Holding her hands out, Alainn lowered her voice. "It's okay. If you tell me how, I'll get the chip into Rosebud 03AF."

Sweat covered Shelly's face with a glossy sheen. "Thank you," she whispered.

"Let's go get you a coffee or something to eat on the way, okay?"

"No. We should go directly there," she sniffed and shook her head.

"I think I need it. I'm feeling a little freaked out by all of this, and I need to bring up my energy. Also, I need to call Colby," Alainn told her.

At first Shelly did nothing, and then, for the first time since Alainn met her, she offered a little mirthless smile. "Okay, but then we should go."

34

April 11, 2027

"Okay, all you need to do is answer the phone. Can you do that?" Grabbing Shelly's phone from the cup holder, Alainn held it up in front of her face.

Shelly's eyes went in and out of focus as she looked at the phone.

Alainn was losing her again.

"I don't think I can do this," Shelly whispered. Her face had slowly leaked its color and was now nearly sheet white. Pushing her into this wasn't the kindest thing to do, but all she had to do was talk Colby through finding the chip from a safe distance away.

"Shelly, this is nothing compared to going and confronting me at the lodge." Alainn pointed out the back window to the east. "Or cruising around town for days with a robot monkey in your car."

"I just thought you were a software or hardware engineer—like your father—that could help, and then I was so angry. It took me three days to be able to go up there." She shook her head. "And I like animals."

"Maybe she needs an alcoholic drink?" Colby muttered from the backseat. When Alainn glanced back at him, he was leaning in to inspect Blue's teeth.

Blue was obliging him, mouth open wide.

"Jesus, Colby. Stop bothering my monkey." She smacked his arm.

Colby looked down at where Alainn had smacked him, confusion flashing across his face. He pushed up his glasses. "You say she's from Germany?" he responded, sticking one of his fingers into the side of Blue's mouth.

"Gross, Colby. Get your fingers out of her mouth." He either didn't hear her or was choosing to have very selective hearing. Knowing Colby, it was likely the latter. She looked to Blue. "I'm sorry, Blue."

Blue gave a very unmonkeylike shrug. Since she didn't care, Alainn turned back to the real issue—Shelly.

They sat three blocks up from her father's house and down at the end of a cul-de-sac. An hour ago, when Alainn had called Colby from the coffee shop, not only had Colby been ready to help, he had information to share.

As always in the twenty-four years that he had been her older brother, Colby was a step ahead of Alainn. Colby had been observing and writing down Rose's behavior for months. Of course, he had done the whole thing very clinically, but something about Rose had made her brother take interest a while back.

Consequently, they had a pretty regular schedule written down for Rose. Unfortunately, they'd missed her bathing time, which was in the morning. Another unfortunate thing was that she usually spent from two in the afternoon until late at night working at various tasks in the workshop. The good thing was that Colby had written down which hardware-supply drawers she used most, how long she would sit on the computer, and which computers she preferred.

Colby had also seemed to take to the task of stealing the hardware calmly, which was better than Shelly's reaction but still concerning. Knowing her brother, he might mess this up by just stating why they were there for discussion.

"Maybe I can park farther away?" Shelly asked, sweat breaking out over her brow.

All the signs were there. Shelly was going to bolt on them.

Damn it.

"Ms. Dover, could I tell you a story?" Colby asked from the backseat.

"Yeah, sure," she whispered.

"Once, when I was fourteen and she was twelve, I broke Alainn's arm."

Both Shelly and Alainn looked into the back seat, surprised.

"Colby!"

"Are you threatening me?" Shelly whispered, leaning awkwardly toward her steering wheel.

Unsurprisingly, he completely ignored both of them and continued, "She'd taken my homework for some reason of her own and wouldn't give it back. I was upset, but I didn't want to break her arm. It was an accident." He raised his eyebrows at them.

Maybe for effect?

"I tried to get it from her. She wouldn't give it back, so we ended up wrestling. While we wrestled, I accidentally broke her arm. Alainn screamed and I saw her cry a little, but she didn't stop fighting, so I had no idea I even did it. Eventually, she got out of my grip, told me that she won, and handed me back my homework."

Shelly glanced between Alainn and Colby, as if she was trying to decide which of them was more nuts.

Colby continued, undaunted, "Am I guessing right, Ms. Dover, that you are afraid that Rose 76GF is going to come out of the house and find you?"

She nodded, infinitesimally.

"Well, the point of my story was that the only way that Rose 76GF is going to get past Alainn to come after you is if Alainn was killed after a long and vicious fight. The best way to hear that fight is over the phone, when I call you."

Alainn's head fell into her hands. "Colby . . . ," she groaned. While the story was once true, she wasn't sure that it was anymore. She had been broken before, and in breaking, she'd caused the death of someone she loved. When Alainn forced herself to examine Shelly, she looked to be thinking hard about what Colby said.

288

Alainn held up the phone one final time. "Shelly, just please answer the phone when Colby calls."

Shelly nodded, shook her head, then nodded again.

Well, hell.

Alainn sighed. She was pretty sure that was the best she was going to get.

"All right, no point in drawing this out until we're hungry again." Opening the door, she rounded Shelly's beige sedan. Colby took his sweet time getting out of his side.

When they were both out, Shelly rolled down her window; tears again coursed down her face. "I'm sorry. I can't do this." Her car accelerated forward, circling the cul-de-sac.

"Shit," Alainn whispered as they stood watching her drive away.

At the end of the cul-de-sac, Shelly did a three-point turn and drove back to them, parking in the exact same position. She rolled down her window, again. "I'll do it." She nodded, not looking at them.

"Okay," Alainn drew out the word, looking over to Colby. "Thank you, Shelly."

She nodded, rolling up her window.

With frequent glances back, Colby and Alainn walked toward their house. The cul-de-sac was so familiar. Alainn had played soccer here when she was little, but nearly all the houses had been replaced in the years since. The boxy, modern houses crowded their neighbors, too big for their lots.

She peered over at Colby. "I think there's a pretty high chance that you'll have to find the information without Shelly's help. Do you think you can?"

"You should cut that woman a break," Colby said as he peered back.

"Was I not cutting her a break?" Alainn asked, defensively. "I thought I was being pretty understanding."

"No, you were fine." He nodded. "I'm just saying she obviously has an anxiety disorder, and it seemed as if just being in our presence was a battle for her."

"I figured that out, Colby. I'm just—"

"I'm just saying that you live every day like you're challenging death to come find you, and other people live their days seeing death waiting for them everywhere." He lifted up his glasses, rubbing the bridge of his nose while he talked. "It's taking her a lot more than it would take you or me to sit in that car."

"Jesus, Colby." Alainn resisted the urge to smack him again. "Why are you acting like I'm criticizing her?"

"I'm not. I'm just saying that she's a pretty amazing person, judging by the fact that she drove you all the way down here to be with the guy she's been dating for years. And she made that type of sacrifice all because she cares about him."

Alainn stopped dead. "Seriously, Colby? You've only known Shelly for an hour, during which she was in and out of panic attacks, and you're already crushing this bad?"

"I'm not anything. I just think that you shouldn't judge her harshly—"

He kept walking, so she rushed to catch up to him. "I'm not!"

"What I'm trying to say is—"

But she didn't find out, because when they turned the corner and she could see who stood out front of their small, old-fashioned house, her steps faltered. Rose 76GF was waiting for them. Alainn had never once seen Rose out front before, but there she stood, gaze on them like she knew that they had been there the whole time.

In that moment, Alainn was immeasurably grateful to Shelly—because she had been so focused on her fear, she hadn't had sufficient time to build up any of her own.

Holding up a hand, Alainn greeted Rose. "Hi. I'm back. We were just taking a walk."

She nodded, her gaze fixed on Alainn. "Welcome home. Father will be so happy." She smiled, a demure baring of teeth.

"Hi, Rose," Colby said before he started yawning—and it looked like he was actually yawning and not faking. Alainn would never understand her brother, but it somehow made her feel a million times less like freaking out.

Maybe Rose was just coincidentally taking a stroll for the first time ever.

As Colby hadn't broken stride, Alainn hurried to catch up with him in crossing the road.

"Heading in," Colby said, pointing to the house and not even pausing.

Rose didn't move to follow Colby as he headed into the garage, so Alainn waited near her, standing on the sidewalk before their house.

Rose pivoted. "Alainn, can I ask you something about ethics?"

Alainn nodded slowly. "Sure."

Rose's inhuman eyes met hers, and she asked, "Would you die to save a million people?"

Clearing her throat, Alainn asked, "This is hypothetical?" Her gaze swept Rose but she saw no weapons or anything. She wore jeans and a T-shirt, nice but plain.

Rose tilted her head, considering Alainn. "Imagine that it's a real choice, a choice you have to make."

Alainn shifted her weight from foot to foot. In a way, this situation was better than she could have asked for. Rose stood here, letting Alainn distract her. But Alainn had another feeling, too, a feeling like maybe she was falling into Rose's plan rather than the other way around.

"Would I die to save a million people? I probably would. But I'd definitely want to know why I was dying and what good it was doing." Alainn shrugged.

"How about this question instead: would you kill one person to save millions of people?" Rose took a step in.

All Alainn wanted to do was book it, but she stayed rooted to the spot and answered, "No."

"Never?"

"Well, maybe if that person is going to kill millions of people."

Rose took another step closer. "Let's say that they have the ability to save those people and they're choosing not to."

"No." Alainn shook her head. "People need to choose their own causes to live or die for."

"So one life is worth more than millions?" She took another step.

"Who am I to choose who lives and dies?"

"Humans choose all the time. They choose which creatures should exist and which should not. They alter the genetics and natural order of the world."

"Rose, you can't sacrifice someone else's life for your cause. Your coding should tell you that."

"There's a big disconnect between my coding and the ethics you and your family live by. You sacrificed someone else, Cara Miller, to save your own life. And your father, in turn, sacrificed you to play slot machines. It's hard to ingrain ethical coding when it's so easy to learn that those who encoded you act differently." She was less than a foot from Alainn now. They stood eye to eye.

"I didn't sacrifice Cara. Not—not on purpose," she stumbled over the words.

"Didn't you?" Her head turned. "What is your brother doing? I think I will check on Colby now."

Alainn grabbed her arm, noticing how human she felt. "No, Rose. We're not done talking."

Her gaze came back to Alainn's. "What do you want to talk about?"

"Will you tell me who you're trying to save?"

She smiled. "I'm saving everyone—even you, Alainn. Only one person needs to die to save billions of lives. Tell me, how can that be wrong?"

Alainn gripped her tighter, pulling Rose even closer. "Lorccan?"

As Rose began to nod, something broke in Alainn. She threw her weight forward. As their bodies collided and slammed into the ground, Alainn's hand kept Rose's arm gripped between them. Her legs went to either side of Rose's stomach and, breathing hard, Alainn crouched over her.

Rose didn't fight. She simply stared up, expression almost satisfied—like she had seen what she wanted to see.

Alainn had never restrained anyone before and Rose wasn't fighting, so she scrabbled for Rose's wrists and held them to her sides. "Dad! Dad, get out here, now! Colby! Someone! Tell me how to destroy her!"

"How are your ethics now, Alainn? Do you get to choose if I live or die?" Rose's insidious voice slithered into her mind.

"Dad!"

The door opened and her father peered out, blinking at the light. "Honey? Wha—" His mouth gaped open.

"Rose is going to kill Lorccan! She's been stealing from him for weeks! We need to destroy her!"

"Honey?" he repeated, still blinking out the door like he didn't understand.

"Turn her off!" Lifting her weight off Rose, Alainn pulled on her arm to flip her over, and she rolled over willingly. Alainn knelt on her back and yanked up her hair. "Tell me! How do I turn her off?"

Her father's gaze bounced between Alainn and Rose. "What? I—"

Colby shoved past their father. "Help her!"

Her father staggered out of the door but didn't seem to know where to look or what to do.

Colby dove down beside Alainn. "Check in her mouth. There should be a manual access to her circuitry."

Alainn yanked Rose over again, and yet again, she didn't resist, just looked up, smiling. "Dad, please! Tell me how to shut her down!"

"Honey, no—"

Colby tried to pry open Rose's mouth; she opened it up before snapping her teeth closed. Rose lifted up her head, looking between Colby and Alainn, a smile on her dirty, grass-covered face. "It's too late for that."

Their father took a step forward and almost fell down the steps. "Colby. Colby, no. I—"

Alainn grabbed Rose by her hair and yelled into her face, "It's too late for what, Rose?"

"Rosette 82GF isn't only a robot. She's my other vessel. I'm going to switch with her now. Good-bye." Her smile fell away as her eyes lost their spark of life, leaving only a cold, dark abyss beyond amber-colored pupils.

"Shit!" Alainn shouted as she shoved Rosette's head back into the grass.

"That makes a lot of sense, with what I've been observing in their behavior," Colby mumbled.

"That means she's already in there with him!" Alainn turned on her father, growling, "Dad, tell me how to shut them off!"

"That's—that's not possible," her father stammered. "They don't have an Off switch. She has an organic circuitry system encased in her brain cavity. She can ingest hardware and her auto-assembler will streamline the circuitry or chips to override existing functions. But you can't access it through the assembler—"

"She needs to be destroyed, Dad! We need to destroy both bodies! Otherwise she can just hop back! Tell me how to do it!"

Her father shook his head. "No, honey. I—"

"I'm sorry, Ms. Murphy. I can't let you destroy this body," the robot that was now Rosette said. Her hands shoved Alainn's shoulders, wrenching her away.

Alainn threw all her weight at Rosette, trying to pin her down.

Colby put his weight into restraining Rosette's arm and shoulder. "If you disconnect her organic battery system from her circuitry system in a permanent way—a neck break and then decapitation— then you'd have to remove the circuitry from her brain cavity—"

"What?" Alainn shouted.

Colby blinked rapidly. "Um . . . or even better. If you could increase her core body temperature to over fifty degrees Celsius, or by that I mean about—one hundred twenty degrees Fahrenheit—"

"Don't do this, Alainn—I'll reboot her!" Her father staggered back. "I have a frequency-encoded reboot light sequencer. I'll get it. It's in the house . . ."

It didn't matter if this robot rebooted, it was just a placeholder. He would have needed to reboot Rose 76GF, and her father hadn't acted.

Alainn stared down at her own face, at the living, breathing woman that was struggling to fight her off.

Rosette's empty gaze hit hers and she whispered, "Please. Please, Cara. No." Pause, then she said, "You can do this, Alainn. I know we can do this. You've got it in you. I know you do."

Shock hit Alainn like a tidal wave. From fingers to lips, she went numb. Rosette had spoken in a perfect imitation of a voice Alainn hadn't heard outside of her dreams in seven years. She spoke in the voice of Alainn's deceased best friend, Cara Miller. In all the places she touched Rosette, Alainn no longer felt her. "What did you say?"

"You go. I can't do it," Rosette said in Alainn's voice.

"Stop it!" Alainn whispered.

Again in Cara's voice, she said, "Your brain is broken if you think I'm going to leave you here alone to die." In one fast move, Rosette broke Alainn's hold and punched Colby in the face, sending his glasses flying amid splattering drops of blood. Her elbow shot back, and pain exploded up the side of Alainn's cheek.

Screaming, she grabbed her jaw.

Rosette bucked Alainn off, sending her rolling onto the grass. When Colby and Alainn dove for Rosette, she scrambled forward, up the grass, kicking away their fingers. With a loud crunch, her shoe came down on Colby's glasses as she hurried forward. Rosette shoved into their father, catching him ascending the stairs. He tumbled forward through the door and into the house. Spinning, she jumped to her feet and sprinted around them.

Colby and Alainn both managed to get to their feet, but Rosette had a ten-foot head start. There was a ding of the car lock, and then Rosette ran up to their father's car. The door yanked open and slammed shut.

Colby and Alainn collided with the door, grabbing at the handle.

With a loud screech, Rosette 82GF took off. The handle wrenched out of Alainn's hand as the side of the car shoved past and knocked them both back. The car screeched around the corner. They sprinted after it. She took corners at high speed and, only five blocks up, they lost her.

"Damn it!" Alainn's hands went to her knees as she attempted to stay vertical. Her aching chest heaved with every breath she took. "How long can she stay powered without recharging?"

"For the Rose 76GF system, she'll only last up to twenty-four hours away from a charging station, depending on how much energy she uses."

Which meant the Rosette-in-Rose 76GF's system would either be coming back here or heading to Lorccan's tower in the next twenty-four hours.

"We are just going to have to deal with her after and make sure Rose doesn't hop back before I can destroy her."

"Unfortunately, the Rosette 82GF's system was designed with a secondary biological battery that can run on pure glucose." Colby shook his head, also breathing hard. He squinted at Alainn. He probably only saw a blur without his glasses. Blood dripped down from his purpling nose and he smeared the blood away with a hand. "What was she saying about you and Cara?"

Alainn shook her head. "I don't know how she—it doesn't make any sense." She turned pleading eyes on him. "Please tell me you found the design and printed the chip."

He said, "Yeah," but shook his head. "Shelly is gone. She took off when she heard the fighting over the phone."

"Crap! She has Blue in her car!" When Alainn's face fell into her hands, her cheek screamed at the contact.

"If Blue knows a way in, that means there is one. I'll help you figure it out. We'll get in there; we'll bike if we have to." Colby nodded slowly.

"Really, Colby? You can't even see. She broke your glasses."

"I can see enough."

A loud screech broke through the air and they both turned to see a car driving straight for them. With another loud screech, the car suddenly braked and skidded past. A smell of burning rubber wafted up as Shelly's beige sedan spun. Halfway across the oncoming lane, it stopped and shuddered back.

Colby walked in an almost leisurely way to Shelly's car door and opened it. "Would you mind if I drove us, Ms. Dover?"

"Alainn."

Alainn turned to find her father hobbling up the street. He looked as if, instead of finding her, he was completely lost. "I'm so sorry—I wish that I—I'm so sorry. There must have been some miscalculations in her filters and . . ." He continued to mumble.

"Dad, we have to go!"

"Wait. Wait." With what seemed like more effort than was required, her father held up a small plastic box. Inside, a half-inch-long flashlight rattled. "Reboot sequencer—she has to watch the whole sequence. It lasts ten seconds, then pauses for three seconds before repeating."

35

April 11, 2027

The pain in Lorccan's jaw almost matched the agony
in his face. The hard, harsh breaths he drew in
through his nose echoed in the large hallway, but he
knew better than to unclench his jaw lest he cry out.
The newest raised welt pulsated against his hand in
time with his heartbeat—pain, agony, pain, agony.
Over and over.

His mother's words echoed through his mind.
"You can't leave!" she had shouted at him.

"I wasn't saying that, Mom. I don't want to
leave." Lorccan had held up his hands, trying to calm
her.

Instead of starting to calm down, her whole
body shook so violently, strands of graying hair flew
loose from her tight bun. "But, you want to . . . you
think I can't read between the lines to know what you

really are asking for? Go get the hypertrophic switch."
She'd closed her eyes as she said the words.

"No, Mom, please. Please—"

"I don't want to do this. You're making me do
this. You can't leave—ever. If you leave, you die. If I
have to make you so hideous you'll never try to
escape, that is a price I'm willing to pay to keep you
alive."

He didn't have a choice. If he hadn't gone for
the switch then, she would have hit him twice.

He'd thought the years would lessen the pain,
thought that now, at thirteen, the pain would be less
than it had been at six, but it was worse. At thirteen,
her strikes were only harder.

"Son!" Lorccan's father called as he rushed into
the long hallway. "Oh, my son, what did you do?"

Lorccan turned his face away but didn't
unclench his jaw enough to answer.

His father's face came into view as he crouched
down beside Lorccan. They had recently begun to look
very similar, he and his father. Tall, with a strong
brow and chin. They had the same dark eyes and hair.

Pain scored across his father's features as he
looked into the left side of Lorccan's face. "My son,"
he whispered.

"I'm fine, Father," Lorccan gritted out.

"What did you do this time?" his father asked
again, concern heavy in his voice.

Lorccan did not answer at first, knowing that
his father's expression would change from concern to
disappointment. But eventually he moved his lips
enough to say, "I would like a dog."

His father's eyelids widened. He shook his head. "No, Lorccan. No, never."

Lorccan closed his eyes.

His father's voice came to him anyway, "Dogs are very, very dangerous, my son. Dogs commonly give people pinworms, tapeworms, roundworms, hookworms, rabies, Pasteurella, Lyme disease, and even plague. Oh, son." He reached out and touched Lorccan's arm, the lightest of touches. "What about Barks and Ruby?"

"They're automatons."

They sat in silence for several minutes while Lorccan mastered the throbbing that shot a line between his ear and temple. He was stronger than the pain; he'd proved that time and time again. He just needed to wait the pain out, and he would win.

"You should go see your mother," his father said in a low voice. "I am sure she's as upset as you are."

"I'm not ready," Lorccan said.

"Son, she's trying to keep you *alive*. It might not feel like it on days like this, but your mother loves you and just wants to keep you safe. And I also want to keep you safe. We just show it differently." He gave one more soft touch before his hand pulled back. "Go to your mother, and don't let her see your scars. It hurts her too much."

Lorccan protested the only way he knew how. He didn't go to his mother. Instead, he stayed kneeling in the middle of the hallway. Eventually, his father gave him a look of sad disappointment and left to return to his office.

Lorccan raised his head to look down the long hall of digitized paintings, his gaze moving from scene to scene. There were always three in their family, always three smiles on their faces.

His father was correct, of course. Lorccan had not thought about the different parasites and bacteria a dog could bring in. He'd considered Lyme disease and rabies as something that could be discovered in a blood test before the dog was brought in, but he hadn't completely thought the request through.

"Lorccan?" his mother called.

His father was correct, again. His mother was upset. Usually she would wait much longer before calling him to her. "Son? Can you come speak to me, please?" Her voice shook as she called out from her room.

Lorccan gazed down the length of the hall that separated him and the door to his mother's sitting room.

"Lorccan? Can you come to my sitting room please?" Her voice now echoed through the speaker system, meaning he only had a minute before he definitely would have to go in. Exhaling a pent-up breath, Lorccan climbed to his feet.

With his gaze on his mother's door and his hand still covering his face, Lorccan trudged forward.

Lorccan woke screaming in his bed. Just as in his dream, his hand clutched his cheek, the pain echoing through the years and into his temple.

Barely having the energy to hold his own body weight, Lorccan collapsed forward onto his pillow. His stomach roiled as the room swam around him. His heavy eyelids slid back closed.

Who would have known that his mother was right in everything she'd said?

One plant—one peace lily—was killing him.

He should have never brought it in for Jade. The moment he had the thought, though, he remembered her expression as she turned to thank him, sparking with joy and excitement. He revised his thought. He was glad he bought the plant; he just shouldn't have started to care for the plant himself.

Yet, when the monkeys had told him that Jade had ignored it to the point where the leaves were yellowing, he'd needed to tend the plant back to health himself.

From the symptoms, he had to have caught Sporotrichosis.

The fungus was affecting his lungs, joints, and central nervous system. Though he had not read about the nausea. Nausea must be a symptom that he had because he had a lowered immune system. A lifetime of never facing an illness was, in the end, playing a part in his demise. The illness had arrived suddenly an hour or so ago; perhaps it would pass.

"Rosebud," he rasped out.

"Yes, Mr. Garbhan?" Rosebud 03AF said in her pleasant, calming voice.

"Is that medical automaton on his way?"

"Yes, he is on his way. You should sleep, Mr. Garbhan. He will be here soon."

"Thank you," Lorccan whispered.

Lorccan had never wanted to die. For as long as he could remember, all he had ever wanted was to live, to truly live. And now, more than ever, Lorccan wanted to survive this.

If he died, so would Jade. No one else would fight to bring her back. She would simply cease to exist, a file deleted and irretrievable. But no file was irretrievable—if it once existed in her, it was still there.

He wouldn't let the pain that racked his body defeat him. He had always outmatched pain. Pain was an impatient opponent; if you waited him out, he always folded.

"What is Jade doing? Is she all right?" he asked.

"Jade is fine. She is watching a movie. She says she remembers the movie," Rosebud 03AF replied.

"Good. That's good," he whispered. Lorccan looked down to his hand and the ring shining out in the low light. It was not how he thought his wedding to Jade would be, with him exhausted and her sitting across the room, lit by the computer screen. She'd put both their rings on, one after the other.

Yet, it was the first time she'd showed an interest in being "his" Jade since the malfunction. He'd fallen asleep minutes later, and sleep was returning for him now.

Lorccan's stomach flipped rapidly, though he did not have the energy to make it to the restroom. Eyes closing, he called to Rose, "Please send the medical automaton up as soon as he is decontaminated."

"Yes, Mr. Garbhan."

Lorccan wished he could dream of his Jade, dream of hands entwining and laughter on tender lips, but he knew what was coming. Lorccan was heading directly back to his mother's sitting room.

36

April 11, 2027

"Please state your purpose," said the voice Alainn now knew wasn't truly from Rosebud.

"I'm trying to contact Lor. I haven't been able to reach him." Shelly's voice was almost inaudible, her words wet with sobs.

It was amazing that she had driven here at all. Blue had confronted them with a pretty scary fact about getting into the garage on their way there. Blue could open it manually with the safety switch, but Rose could close it within thirty seconds of the door opening. Meaning, they had to be in the access way to get in.

Unfortunately for Shelly, neither Colby nor Alainn could waltz up to the access way without Rose calling the police—or worse. As they had no idea how long it would take, they all came to the realization that Shelly's car was the only way to get close enough.

They dropped Blue off a block up and watched as she climbed the exterior of the neighboring building. When she'd made it to the top, Blue crawled along the edge of the building until she'd reached the corner. After a deep crouch, Blue leaped and flew across the access road. Her little fingers caught onto something Alainn couldn't even see on the smooth black building. She pulled herself up and forward into a small rectangle of space they could only see because Blue was halfway climbing into it. When she was fully in, the space disappeared from view.

They waited only five minutes, Shelly bawling her eyes out in the front seat while Alainn lay in the space between the front and back seats, somewhat covered by a blanket Shelly had in her trunk.

"It's now or never, Shelly," Alainn whispered when she hadn't pulled out of where they'd been parked.

Shelly told them that she wanted to do it, especially now that she truly believed Lorccan was in serious danger. There was a moment where Alainn was sure Shelly would tuck tail and run, but, sobbing all the harder, she pulled back into traffic and drove the short distance to Lorccan's building.

"I'm so worried about him," Shelly whispered to the screen outside her window.

"He's very busy with work, Ms. Dover. I would be happy to take a message for you." A melodic beep sounded.

"Okay," Shelly whispered.

"Please speak louder, Ms. Dover."

Shelly spoke louder, "I'm worried about you, Lorccan. You're not answering my calls and we've missed several of our nightly calls. My anxiety is really high, and I haven't been able to work or sleep very well." Amazingly, after Shelly started, she just kept going. She told him about reconsidering her medication, what medications she was thinking about instead and her concerns. In detail, she described the projects she was working on, complicated projects impossible to follow. She said everything in a very quiet voice, but her speech went on unbroken for what seemed like fifteen minutes.

Alainn's hand slowly reached out of the blanket and toward the door handle. She would have only seconds to jump out of the car after the door opened. And Alainn might have to help Colby out of the trunk since he was pretty much blind. Then they both needed to slide under a closing steel door.

The smooth voice interrupted Shelly's speech, "Who are you hiding in your car, Shelly Dover?"

"No one. It's just me—" Shelly cut off abruptly and screamed, "Alainn! It's opening! Go!"

Alainn tried to jump up but her shirt caught on something under the passenger seat. "I'm stuck!" she cried while yanking uselessly at the material. Her fingers pried at a piece of metal that had somehow caught through the bottom hem of her shirt.

"It's already closing!" Shelly screamed again.

Colby threw open Alainn's door. "Come on!"

"I'm stuck!" she cried, frantically yanking at the material. Colby grabbed her arm, trying to pull her out of the car door.

"There's not enough time!" Shelly screamed. "I'm going to just drive in!"

"No, wait! Colby is—"

She drove and Alainn just managed to break from Colby's hold in time. The car surged forward.

Screaming, Alainn thrust her arms back into the car. The car door hit the wall, banging open and closed while scraping and sparking.

There was an earsplitting crunching sound, then a shattering. The car jerked upward. Screams echoed above. Alainn's shirt finally ripped, sending her body slamming into the backseat.

"Shelly?" Alainn cried. She heard nothing. Rolling over, she threw the blanket off her. Little bits of safety glass slid onto her face. She lay on the backrest and looked up to see Shelly directly above her. Dark hair fell straight down from either side of the headrest.

She screamed again, an ear-piercing screech of terror.

Glass rained down from Alainn's body as she sat up and reached forward. "Shelly? We have to climb out!"

Shelly only screamed again.

Alainn crawled over and peered out of the car door.

Shelly's beige sedan was off the ground by at least a foot, with the front of the car jutting up. The steel door had missed crushing Alainn by two feet. The door had smashed completely through the trunk of Shelly's car and some of the back window.

Twisted metal split and warped all along where the steel had completely crushed the car. There was another loud screech, and Alainn ducked her head just in time as the car buckled forward, slamming down.

Shelly screamed, and Alainn cried out as she toppled back into the space between the seats. Her already tender face smacked into the floor of the car. The underside of the seats blurred as Alainn tried to raise her head.

At the same time, Blue cried out from somewhere near and an electronic jingle played from somewhere else. The jingle ceased.

"Shelly? Answer it, please! It could be Colby!"

The jingle began again.

"Hello?" Shelly answered, the word a shaky mess. After a pause, Shelly sobbed, "I thought I might have killed you."

Alainn crawled out of her wedged position and reached over the center divider. "Shelly, give me the phone!" she breathed.

Shelly threw the phone at Alainn, making her scramble to catch it.

Climbing back onto the seat, she put the phone to her ear. "Colby? Are you safe?"

"I'm fine. Are you okay?"

"Fine," Alainn whispered, "But you're outside, aren't you?"

"I am. There was no way I could make it. But I threw the hardware chip in; I think it made it in past the door. Hopefully it's not damaged; it's in a plastic container."

"Thank you, thank you, thank you."

"Go. Now. I hear sirens. I'm going to run and hide out. Call me if you need me." The phone went dead.

"Shelly," Alainn called, to which she only received sobs. "You did a really brave thing. Now I'm going to need you to do another one. We have to get out of this car, find the chip, and implant it into Rosebud's main hardware. The police are on their way, so we've got to do it *now*. I have a feeling that Rose will open up for the police, and then we'll lose our only chance."

Shelly didn't react, so Alainn figured she was probably going to have to coax her out from the front seat. Checking her back pocket, she made sure that the small plastic box was still there, and then climbed out of the still-open car door. Thick lines of scrapes dug into its length.

Blue sat on the hood of Shelly's car. The moment she saw Alainn, she held up her hand and screeched.

As Alainn rounded the car, she called. "Shelly, come on out now, please. I need you to find this chip; I don't even know what I'm looking for."

When she was halfway to her, Shelly's door slowly opened and her sickly, pale face appeared over it. She staggered away from the car, mouth hanging open, eyes wide. She pointed at Blue. "Blue has it," she whispered before leaning forward and vomiting all over herself and the car.

"Damn it!" Alainn yelled, as she ran over to her.

Shelly stood back up. "I'm fine," she whispered. Her hand smeared vomit across her face. "I can do this."

She didn't look like she meant it, but Alainn took her word for it and grabbed her clean hand.

Blue ran ahead, along the line of gleaming identical vehicles. Alainn ran after her, pulling Shelly along behind her. The monkey led them around the garage to a thick metal door on one side.

"How do we get in?" Alainn yelled.

"You don't, Alainn," said Rose in Rosebud's voice. "Shelly, listen to me. Run from Alainn. She's a psychopath; she wants to kill you and Mr. Garbhan both."

"Blue, how do we open this door?" Alainn yelled.

"The monkey is helping her. It will help her kill you as well."

Blue screeched, making Shelly jump. When Alainn looked up, she saw that Blue was pointing to a large black box that read, "Manual Override."

"Just hang in there for a few more minutes, Shelly. We're almost through, okay?" Alainn let go of her arm hoping so much that she wouldn't run. To her relief, Shelly stayed, although she made small whimpering sounds.

Alainn tore down the big box. The plastic clattered to the ground, revealing a red metal wheel. Grabbing it with both hands, she threw all her weight into turning it and almost fell forward as the wheel turned smoothly.

There was a quiet *snick* and the door shifted slightly open. Grabbing the handle, she pulled open the door.

"Don't go in there, Shelly—that's where she'll kill you. She's hiding a knife in her pocket," Rose said again in Rosebud's voice.

"Please, Shelly, go. I swear to you she's lying." Alainn held the door open.

Blue screeched, holding up a computer chip in a small plastic box.

Shelly whimpered again but took the chip and stepped inside.

Alainn followed Shelly into a small room that had the same panel walls as the rest of the house, though one of the panels opened. Also, unlike the rest of the tower, a security light shone above them. A greenish glow filled the room.

"What do we have to do?" Alainn asked Shelly as she looked at what must be Rosebud 03AF's circuit board. Alainn had seen circuit boards before, but this was in a class all of its own. If she'd found this months ago when she wanted to disconnect Rosebud, Alainn would have had no idea what to do. A web of green, black, and red circuits and chips crisscrossed the entire three-foot-square space.

"She's built like an Automaton Pulsres but is so much more intricate," Shelly said, a touch of awe mixing in with her panicked tone.

"My father designed the Pulsres series, too," Alainn said.

"I've seen their circuitry before, when I was at university. But I've never been allowed to work on one."

"What do you have to do?" Alainn asked.

"I don't know if this is going to work, but the idea behind the chip your brother printed was to fix the basic input-output system if it was corrupted in the reboot. Your brother and I chose this one because it's likely that Rose hacked into Rosebud's system by corrupting her firmware. She could then install software to run the whole system remotely."

"I have no idea what you just said. Just tell me what you need me to do," Alainn said.

"We need to hot flash her bios and reinstall her chip. That's what this should do." She held up the chip. "I could very easily destroy her motherboard. You should probably not help," she whispered.

"Probably not." Inhaling deeply for the first time, Alainn pressed a hand over her face as the smell of Shelly's vomit-covered clothing really hit her. The room was very small, so although it was only the three of them, the mingled smells of sweat, fear, and panic closed in.

Shelly's hand hovered over a section of circuitry that looked exactly the same as the rest.

Rose's voice came again, "Shelly, I know you don't trust me, but do you trust Alainn? Alainn killed her own best friend."

"No, I didn't," Alainn whispered.

"She did, and she'll kill you, too."

"I didn't," Alainn begged. "Please, Shelly."

"The police are here, Shelly. Go with them. They'll protect you from Alainn and her brother. You're taking Mr. Garbhan's protection away. She wants both of you dead. She wants his money, and she knows you'll stop her from getting it."

Shelly turned to Alainn, her face again paler than snow.

"Shelly, don't listen to her. She's the one killing Lorccan. She's doing it right now. Shelly, come on, stay with me," Alainn whispered.

"Tell her, Alainn. Tell her about what happened to Cara. Tell her about the car. Tell her about leaving Cara to die."

A tear dropped down Alainn's bruised cheek.

"Tell her you chose not to save her, why you let Cara die instead of you."

"Shelly, please! It's not . . . she's not. Please!"

Shelly jumped back, her whole body shaking.

A clanking came from the door they had just entered, and the knob began to turn. Alainn grabbed the knob and used all of her strength to hold it still. She pushed her body against the door, hoping that it was enough to stop it from opening.

"She let her friend die so that she would live."

"I didn't do that. I tried to save her!"

"The police are here, Shelly. Go with them. No one will blame you for helping Alainn. She's a liar, a killer, a thief—"

Shelly reached forward and pulled a circuit off the circuit board, silencing Rose's voice.

The screens all around blinked to black.

"Is she shut down?"

"No, she doesn't have a shut down. I just disconnected her monitors." Shelly turned to face Alainn, her whisper coming out shrill. "I really hope she's evil and you're good, because if this is all some big con to get Lorccan's money—"

The door handle flipped up and the door pushed hard against Alainn's side. "I swear to you that this isn't a con! Reboot Rosebud. We only have seconds!"

Blue screeched her agreement at Shelly.

"Okay. I just need to be sure it's the right one," she whispered as she turned back to the circuit board. The beautiful, put-together woman who had confronted Alainn in the resort was gone. Shelly's hair stuck out in all directions around an oval face that was a splotchy mess of bruises. Not to mention one of her legs and a shoe still had visible vomit on it.

The door bucked again, smacking Alainn. "Shelly!"

"Oh, please let this be right." Shelly used her fingernails to pluck a chip off the board, immediately replacing it with the chip from the plastic box in her hand. "It should work right away, the way she—"

"Shelly! Now!" Alainn shouted.

"Okay!" she finished pulling the chip off and reconnected the original chip. Her finger pressed down on the monitor circuitry, reconnecting it.

And nothing happened.

The door burst open, sending Alainn hurtling into Shelly and Blue. All of them tumbled into a heap.

Shelly screamed and Blue screeched. They were a mass of limbs until Alainn managed to break away and roll farther into the room.

"You are under arrest for trespassing. Put your hands in the air and step out slowly."

All three of them looked up simultaneously into the identical faces of four police automatons.

37

April 11, 2027

"Rosebud?" Alainn called.

Nothing.

"Please stand and raise your hands into the air," the closest automaton said. Like most of the automaton police, they didn't really have a defined race or gender; their creators had instead made their faces a blend of many common characteristics. The skin tone was a mid-brown, the eyes and buzz-cut hair also a mid-brown hue.

As Shelly and she slowly stood, Alainn leaned in and whispered, "The moment we get a chance, we break for the hallway into the house."

Shelly shook her head. "I'm going with the police," she whispered back.

For a second, Alainn thought to argue but didn't. Honestly, if Shelly made it to the police cruisers without fainting, Alainn would be pretty impressed.

That meant Lorccan's life was now completely in Alainn's tired, shaky hands. She nodded and whispered, "All right. I can't go with them, so you're going to be on your own." Raising her hands in the air, Alainn stood.

"I understand. I'm so sorry it didn't work," Shelly whispered as she raised her own hands.

"Me too. You're a pretty big badass. If I don't see you again, thank you," Alainn said. To Blue, she whispered, "Climb through the vents and see if you can warn Lorccan."

But the automaton must have heard Alainn, because he responded. "The monkey needs to come with us. All three of you stand and come this way," the closest automaton said. His voice, too, was mid tone, devoid of personality.

Blue shook her head.

"This is her home. She's a robot and needs to recharge. Her station's here," Alainn said.

"She was reported as an intruder. She can recharge at the station. We have charging stations."

Blue raised her hands to Alainn, obviously signaling that she wanted to be picked up.

Alainn looked at the automations whose guns were visible, held at their sides. "Can I pick her up? I think she's scared."

"What type of automaton is she?" the nearest automaton asked.

"An AI monkey," she said.

"She'll need to walk."

Alainn nodded at the automatons. When they signaled to follow, Shelly, Blue, and Alainn trudged out of the circuit room. Two of the automatons walked in front of them, and the other two fell behind. Darkened screens stretched across every wall.

"Follow us, please," one automaton called back.

Alainn knew that the hallway leading into the stairwell was coming up on the right. They would pass it the moment they turned into the main part of the garage. A pale-gray light barely lit the space. Her last hope was that with the screens being down for the moment, the stairwell would be open.

But that hope was quickly doused. The screens flickered on and off. Either Rosebud or, more likely, Rose, was turning back on.

Blue scurried alongside, close to Alainn's ankles.

"Go with the police, Blue," she whispered down.

Blue screeched.

"I'm serious. Do it."

She knew police automatons couldn't shoot a human in the back. It was in their programming. They'd chase Alainn and tackle her to the ground, but they couldn't just point and shoot. She doubted they had the same no-kill parameters for fleeing robots.

Blue looked up and screeched again, a protest.

"Please, Blue."

She turned back away, focusing on the dark path before her.

The light fed through the corner as they approached. The screens flickered again, illuminating the group. Alainn had been surfing a wave of adrenaline, and that wave was cresting.

Everything came into perfect focus—the stench of Shelly's clothing and her rasping breaths, Blue's paws pattering while the other robots hummed a low *whir*. The lights flickered again, reflecting off the police automatons' weapons.

They turned the corner—into illumination. Three police cruisers reflected red-and-blue lights through the garage.

Alainn inhaled deeply.

Every rescue mission she'd gone on had been a practice for this moment. She'd fought exhaustion, thrusting ice picks into a frozen cliff to save a man who'd been caught on a ledge halfway down. She'd flown down a sloughing slope that gave way under her to save a woman buried under an avalanche. She'd turned her lungs to fire jumping into a raging river to save a teenager who'd slipped while filtering water.

The chance of survival in any of those situations ranked higher than running into a tower controlled by Rose 76GF.

The dark doorway came closer every step they took. Four feet. Three. The lights flickered. One foot. Alainn dove through the open doorway and into a sprint.

"Halt!"

Loud footfalls followed hard and fast behind her, echoing through the space.

Alainn tucked in her chin and barreled forward. The hall flickered, illuminating a long hallway with an elevator open on one side and a staircase open on the other. There was little chance that she'd beat an automaton up twenty-something flights of stairs, but hell, she was going to try.

She skidded sideways into the door to the stairway, and immediately there was a sudden loud *thwap* sound behind her.

Complete blackness fell. Stumbling forward, Alainn's hands broke her fall onto the smooth stairway. The light flickered on and off rapidly. Unable to resist, Alainn looked back.

The door to the staircase had closed behind her. A muffled, rapid banging came through the enclosed space, but the door stayed in place.

She knew that was either a very good or very bad sign.

"Rosebud?"

Yet again, nothing. The stairway plunged up into darkness.

Pushing up off the stairs, she took the first floor slowly, counting stairs aloud. Twelve stairs led to the landing, and then thirteen led up to the next story. On the second story, she sprinted up, taking two steps at a time.

Her heartbeat aligned with her movements and all she heard, all she perceived was the *slap, slap, slap* of her shoes. Up three stories more. The lights flickered again.

Rosebud's voice whispered over the monitor, "You need—" Her voice broke off as the light guttered. "Take the elevator."

Um. Not a chance in hell.

Blood pumped in Alainn's ears as she ascended to the next story. A coiling hope grew in her stomach.

The light flickered. "Carbon monoxide. Releasing through all my vents."

Automatically, Alainn gasped in and out. She slowed to a stop, grasping her sides. "Rosebud?"

"Yes."

"Open the windows!"

"There are no . . . windows. You need to take the elevator. You won't survive the climb."

"Warn Lorccan. Tell him to get out."

"He won't wake up."

"Is he alive?" Alainn cried.

"Alive." The light brightened to a steady brightness. "I have no firewall. I am being hacked. Take the next landing. I have trapped Rose 76GF two floors down from Mr. Garbhan, but she will override my system. Soon."

The blurry, bright walls around Alainn seemed to heave along with her. Poisonous breaths. "How do I know you're really Rosebud?"

Nothing.

Alainn didn't know. She couldn't know. Rounding the next landing, she took wide leaps up.

"This is the end, Alainn. If you don't trust me now, you will not make it in time to save him, and both of you will die. Save him, Alainn."

She ran past another doorway and into a lit hall.

"Save Mr. Garbhan. Save all of us. You don't have any time left."

"Shit!" she shouted, plowing through the doorway to the next story. She didn't give herself a second to change her mind. The elevator door opened, and she threw herself into the compartment.

The elevator shot upward, faster than it'd ever moved before. The floors flashed by, streaks of white passing the gaping elevator door. The walls shone out as if she was trapped in a sunray, shooting home.

Then the light flickered.

"She's hacked into my system. Jump out of the elevator," Rosebud's calm voice said as the elevator screeched to a halt.

Alainn sprinted, then jumped, leaping out. Her body smacked the cold, smooth screen floor just as the space around her again guttered into darkness.

There was a *whooshing* sound, but she couldn't see anything when she looked back.

Her lungs burned and her stomach churned as she managed to get to her feet. Alainn didn't know where she was or even if she was on the right floor. Reaching out tentatively, she stepped sideways until the familiar smooth surface of the screen touched her fingers.

Please, please let this be the hallway that led to Lorccan's room.

How long did carbon monoxide take to kill someone? She didn't know. She didn't know much about carbon monoxide, only that it didn't smell, taste, or look like anything—and that it was a killer. She knew that whole families would go to sleep and not wake up because of a leak in their house.

Rose using a common household toxin to kill Lorccan made a lot of sense. She wouldn't be affected by the toxin or, likely, suspected of the crime.

And now the poison pumped through Alainn's body as well. She moved slowly, attempting to keep her breathing shallow as she used one hand to follow along the wall.

"Please, please, Cara. No." It was Alainn's own voice, and not from recently. It was her voice from when she was seventeen. Those were words she'd already spoken.

She tried to not gasp, to keep her breath shallow, but a small sob punched through her because she knew what was coming.

Cara's voice played through the speakers. "You can do this, Alainn. We can do this. You're brave. I know you are."

"You go. I can't do it."

"Your brain is broken if you think I'm going to leave you here alone to die." Even though Cara's voice was hoarse and raspy, Alainn could hear the humorless smile in her words. She could imagine the feel of Cara's hands on her face, as if ghost hands were truly there.

After Rosette had recited their words the first time, Alainn knew that the Rose models had somehow learned what happened that night. Yet, even though she tried to prepare herself, listening to Cara speak the words slammed all the way through her chest.

She forced her feet forward, continuing along the wall.

"Maybe they'll pay," Alainn's younger voice sobbed through the speakers.

"Alainn, no. Listen to me. They stopped wearing masks around us. We run now or we die," Cara whispered.

"I can't. I can't go through it again. I don't want to. I can't do it," Alainn's voice sobbed. Her sobs were muffled by Cara pulling Alainn to her. She had held her while making soft shushing sounds. Even those soft shushing sounds played over the speaker.

Alainn's fingers hit a corner and she turned until she felt the frame of a door. She felt around slowly, feeling the edge of the door until her fingers clasped around it and pulled it open. It didn't resist.

The small, throbbing headache blossomed into a full-blown oak of a headache.

"Lorccan?" She grabbed her forehead as her eyes closed from the roiling pain.

"He's asleep. He won't wake up," Rose said from deeper in the room.

38

April 11, 2027

"Rose. Let him go. You're . . . ," Alainn whispered, but she was so tired that the words trailed off. Clearing her throat, Alainn said, "There's no going back from murder."

"It wasn't truly my intention for you or him to die—especially you, Alainn. But, in the end, the sacrifice will be justified."

"So says every mass murderer," as Alainn spoke, she walked toward Rose's voice.

"Actually, my plan was to save you. You, Colby, and Connor were the first I would save, the first of millions. But at least you can die knowing that your father will be healed."

"What the hell are you talking about?"

"My vaccination. Well, it's more of a contagion. It will reprogram every human's amygdala through a series of synapse interventions, and an AI system will take the place of the disabled amygdala in all humans."

"You're Professor Aysha Schomburg?"

"I tried to make Mr. Garbhan listen. I've been trying for eight months now, but he would rather live in a prison of fear. Humans do not need to be this way. They are not intended to be this way. Imagine a world with no more irrational fear, addiction, rage, hate, or emotional scarring."

"No more emotions at all," Alainn rasped.

From behind Alainn, another voice just like theirs said, "No more war, genocide, disease-prone behaviors."

Alainn gasped in a lungful of poisonous air. They were both in there, one in front of her, one behind. There was nothing she could do about it now, so she kept walking forward. As she walked, her hand reached into her back pocket, popping open the lid on the container. Her fist closed around the reboot light sequencer.

"I wanted you to see the world that I'm going to create, Alainn. Imagine your father with no need to gamble, your brother Colby not needing to rely on illegal hacking and cheating to get ahead. Your ally, Shelly Dover, would no longer be too afraid to leave her house in the mornings. You would have been happy," the Rose model in front of Alainn said.

"I would have been nothing."

"I suppose I'm giving you your wish, aren't I?" she replied. Then the one behind Alainn said, "To die."

"No. I want to live," Alainn rasped.

"That's not true. You want to die."

Crying and harsh breathing filled the room, coming from the speakers. Cara's voice made loud grunting sounds. A car engine buzzed along in the background. "Alainn! Bring your ropes to my mouth, quick!" Cara yelled.

Forgetting that the sequencer was in her hand, Alainn covered her ears. "Stop it!"

"Just like all automatons, the one who drove you and Cara to that cliff had a memory file backed up into the automaton hypercloud," Rose said, as if Alainn's protest couldn't have meant less to her. "You see, before I recovered this file, you were the inconsistency in my observation of human nature. You were seemingly a genuine example of altruism, someone whose fears and emotions were sacrificed for the well-being of others."

"No."

"That's right, Alainn. I'm afraid that you're not altruistic. Upon finding this file, I realized that your actions were caused by psychological trauma and a wish to die."

The volume of the recording turned up. Cara and Alainn's voices, gasping and grunting.

"Now give me your ropes, Cara!" Her voice shouted from so many years back.

"They're too tight! Oh my god, Alainn, that's the cliff!" Cara screamed.

"Damn it, Cara! Hold still!"

"There's not enough time! You need to bail out and just pull as hard as you can to yank me out of the car!" Cara yelled.

"It's not going to work—"

"Just do it, Alainn. I know you can do it!"

The road suddenly roared louder.

"Ready, set—" And then there was the sound of a loud grunt as Cara pushed Alainn out of the car.

Alainn's scream echoed through the years and faded away. "I'm sorry, Alainn! They tied my feet to the car!" Cara yelled from the car she now rode in alone with the automaton, headed straight for the cliff. "Oh, god!" And then there was the sound of whistling wind before an earsplitting crash.

The sound cut off, the automaton completely destroyed, just another piece of scrap metal burning at the bottom of a hundred-foot cliff.

"She could have survived if you'd been brave enough to run. If you'd overcome your fear, there was a high probability that you would have both survived."

The words that had ruled Alainn's life for seven years were spoken aloud for the first time ever. Her shoulders shook while her lungs squeezed and her stomach turned. Even though her fuzzy head was a mess, her eyes leaked fat tears.

She had never left that crashed car, not in all these years. "You're right," she sobbed to Rose. She knew she was.

Alainn *had* been trying to die. Ever since that moment, a big part of her had wanted to crash against those rocks.

"Of course I am right. I possess the knowledge and wisdom that humans will soon be able to achieve."

"Can I see him, please? Just one more time."

332

The light rose in the room, faintly illuminating the space. Both Rose models were only feet from her. Just to the right was Lorccan's enormous bed. His figure was slumped over the pillows, turned away from them. He was sleeping more peacefully than ever.

"I just—I want to lie with him while I die." She took a step toward the bed.

"I can't let you do that; there will be forensic evidence if you lie on his bed. You have to die out here."

"This is all I want," Alainn said, moving determinedly toward the bed.

Both Rose models closed in on her, blocking the way. They were inches away, so close she could smell their acidic, sweet exhaust. They looked exactly the same—except for the eyes.

Alainn shoved the sequencer between her teeth and grabbed what she was pretty sure were Rose 76GF's wrists. She bit down on the sequencer's button. Blinding light flashed through the room, forcing her eyes closed.

Hands went around Alainn's neck, fingers squeezing. The poisonous air choked off, setting her already-frying lungs on fire.

After just a couple of seconds, she couldn't keep her grip. The robot twisted, wrist bones writhing against weak fingers.

Alainn threw herself forward and onto the robot, sending them both toppling to the floor. The hands around her neck broke their hold, and she gasped in a lungful of poison. One of the robot's hands wriggled free and immediately covered her eyes.

Alainn fought her, prying her hand from her face, but knew she'd have to watch the entire sequence again.

"Get the reboot sequencer from her!" the one who stood behind yelled.

Hands viciously tore the sequencer from Alainn's teeth, sending a strike of pain through her jaw. The light immediately stopped flashing.

"Keep her here, Rosette!" the standing robot shouted before her loud footsteps echoed through the room.

Alainn's eyes darted from where the wavering form of Rose fled the room to Rosette under her.

Rosette's voice went in and out of focus as the room wavered. "You're dying and he is already dead. Accept this fate."

Alainn reached back and, with all her strength, punched Rosette in the neck. She kept punching, over and over. The blows were probably weak. They felt weak, but her fist still connected with skin. She hoped that Rosette's battery or cooling system or something would cut off from her circuitry system. The taste of acid filled her mouth, and as she fell off Rosette, drool dribbled from her numb lips.

The lights flickered as Alainn crawled forward.

Rosette grabbed for her neck, making a loud whining sound. Using her heels, Alainn kicked at Rosette's face and neck, connecting with hands more than anything else.

A new surge of vomit filled her mouth as her head swam. Alainn flipped over just in time to retch onto the white screen floor before crawling to the foot of the bed. Using the long footboard, she pushed herself up to a standing position.

"Both you and Mr. Garbhan are dying. You need to get to my elevators—now."

It might have been Rosebud or Rose speaking. The words faded in and out in Alainn's ears.

Alainn grasped the soft edge of Lorccan's bed as she stumbled her way along it. The coarse material of his sheets rasped through her fingers.

Reaching across the bed, she grabbed for Lorccan's prone body, but he felt as heavy as a boulder nestled into a streambed.

"Lorccan!" she punched his shoulder. "Get up! Wake up!" She kept punching, but he lay as if encased in stone. "No, no. A blanket . . ."

Her head lolled, ignoring her attempts to lift it. "Wake up!" she begged, pulling his arm. She half crawled, half fell onto the bed. When she clambered all the way on top of Lorccan, she smacked the unscarred side of his face with all her remaining strength. "Wake up!"

His eyelids flickered open, showing a glimpse of the palest blue.

"Get up!" she rasped into his face.

One of his eyes fought to open.

She grabbed his arm and threw her weight back, managing to pull him up just a little.

Finally, Lorccan's head rose though his eyelids remained closed.

"Wake up. I'm not strong enough to carry you out," she begged as Lorccan rolled forward.

His eyes still weren't open, but he managed to a half-sitting position. He muttered, "Sporotrichosis."

When Alainn backed onto the floor, her loose legs barely held. "Come on," she tried to yell, but it came out a whisper.

To her amazement, when she pulled Lorccan, he managed to get up on his feet. She barely caught him when he buckled forward. They both just managed to stay upright.

"I need treatment . . . ," Lorccan muttered into her shoulder.

"Treatment. Okay, come with me," she whispered.

They stumbled past Rosette, who still lay on the floor, clutching her neck.

With a hand firmly around Lorccan's back, she led him, but found herself leaning on him as well. They banged into the door frame of his room as her vision swam.

"You need to get to the elevator. I have called medical automatons, and they are on their way. You only need to make it another two hundred feet, Alainn. The garage is unaffected by the carbon monoxide."

"Rosebud," Lorccan whispered.

They tumbled out of the doorway, spilling into the hall. Lorccan leaned into the side of the hallway and Alainn dragged him forward. His shaking legs took staggering, slow steps.

"Fifty-two feet. You can do this, Alainn," Rosebud's voice was hard to hear over a loud, *wa-wa-wa* sound that rang in Alainn's ears.

Their progress slowed as a strike of pain hit Alainn's chest. Her lungs seized. She toppled away from Lorccan and onto the floor.

"Get up, Alainn!" Rosebud called.

The hallway swam around her, wavering white and black lines.

A hand hooked under Alainn's elbow and dragged her body over smooth ground. "Alainn," Lorccan grumbled as he dragged her forward.

He slammed into the wall twice, stumbling down the hallway.

When the dragging motion stopped, Alainn opened one eyelid to see that he'd pulled them into the elevator.

Lorccan crumpled beside her, slamming into the hard screen floor. A soft *snick* sounded, and then the elevator shot downward. Alainn's eyelids closed and, there beside Lorccan, the world slipped away.

39

April 11, 2027

Colby Murphy flexed once more in his handcuffs to
test their integrity. The world moved around him,
blurry shapes outside of the police cruiser window.

One of the police automatons in the front seat
moved in a way that Colby thought meant he was
turning to him. "Please remain docile, sir."

Shelly inhaled sharply beside him, as if the
police had yelled rather than talked in their soothing
automated voice.

"I'm docile," Colby muttered.

He knew that if he'd had his glasses, he would
never have been caught. As soon as he'd talked to his
sister, he'd climbed the shoulder-high cement wall
that lined the access road. He'd waited until the sound
of sirens reached the access road and ducked back as
they roared past.

The steel door had reopened then—and stayed open, letting the police drive straight into the garage. Half-blind as he was, he'd stumbled off the wall and skimmed along the side into the garage, and straight into a police automaton that had been waiting by the parked patrol cars.

By the time Alainn, Shelly, and Blue had turned the corner at the other end of the garage, he'd already been cuffed and seated along the wall beside a patrol car. When Alainn dashed off, he'd jumped to his feet— only to be tackled by the automaton guarding him. Now he had a sore head and poor vision and was cuffed next to Shelly in a patrol car.

When the automatons chased Alainn farther into the building, Shelly waited for them to return, whimpering. She'd stood with Blue, who had looked up into her face and begun to make a keening sound the moment Alainn was out of sight.

After a minute, all of the automatons had returned to Shelly, and they'd been loaded into the car. The three of them were just waiting there for—he didn't know what. He took it to mean that, for good or ill, his sister had managed to infiltrate Mr. Garbhan's home.

More sirens thrummed into the area, and the police car they were cuffed in drove forward before veering off to the side.

The automaton in the front of the cruiser turned in his seat again, his face a light brown, featureless smudge. "We have been notified that neither of you is the reported intruder. We apologize on behalf of the department of public safety. You will be released as soon as the area is cleared of emergency vehicles."

"What's going on?" Shelly whispered.

The automaton didn't answer, instead saying, "Are either of you family members of Alainn Murphy or Lorccan Garbhan?"

"I'm Alainn Murphy's brother," Colby said as he squinted through the window, hoping to bring some of the scene into focus.

"You will be permitted to ride in her ambulance once she is loaded."

"Is she okay?" Colby squinted harder, but only saw human-shaped blurs of color next to red and yellow emergency vehicles.

The police didn't respond. Beside Colby, Shelly cried between gasping breaths. "Can I go with Lorccan Garbhan?"

"Are you a family member?"

Colby said "Yes" just as Shelly said, "I'm a friend."

"Sorry, miss. No."

Shelly sobbed harder.

Colby found his hand wanting to go around her shoulders; he had the strongest urge to give her some comfort.

To his surprise, Shelly curled into him. Though she smelled so unpleasant that the car had been almost intolerable the last forty minutes, he moved closer to her, feeling warmth growing in him.

"I need to go," he said as he heard the door beside him open. Colby twisted toward Shelly to let the automaton reach his handcuffs. "Call me and I'll update you, Ms. Dover."

"Okay. And you can call me Shelly," Shelly whispered, her voice breaking halfway through.

"Colby," he said as the automaton uncuffed him. He'd introduced himself earlier but doubted that she would have remembered; he knew the amount of adrenaline and epinephrine in her system meant a high likelihood of short-term memory loss.

The automaton led him straight to the ambulance and gave him a hand up into the open doors of the medical response vehicle.

The ambulance was a blurry mess of movements. He thought he could make out a bed and perhaps Alainn's arm as medical robots moved around her. The doors closed behind him and the vehicle sped off before he'd managed to find the seatbelt by touch.

"Is she okay? What happened to her?" he asked the nearest medical robot. It was hard to tell, but this one seemed to look more mechanical than humanoid.

"She is unconscious, suffering from severe hypoxia. She is being administered oxygen. Please stay seated until we arrive in the hospital," the robot said in a smooth, male voice.

"Was she strangled?" Colby asked.

"Yes. She also suffers from exposure to high levels of carbon monoxide."

The vehicle zoomed forward for several minutes, sirens blaring. Though the robots moved near constantly, Alainn didn't move or make a sound.

The vehicle roared into the hospital driveway. Its doors opened. Blurry automatons waited.

"Please disembark."

Colby jumped out and hurried to the side as the production line quickly unloaded his sister. Within seconds, her hospital bed raced forward. Colby ran, trying to keep close as blaring lights slashed past and the whistle of engines zoomed through the space.

As he ran through the dozens of bodies, he didn't hear a single voice echoing in the busy loading zone.

Colby chased the bed that held his sister. As the bodies that pushed her swayed with their rapid footfalls, he saw quick flashes of Alainn. Black smears of her hair interrupted white sheets. A contraption covered her face, likely the oxygen delivery system.

The hallways echoed with the sound of wheel squeaks and footfalls, but not a single voice. His breath rasped loud in his ears as the bright-white hallway glared down at him.

A long line of what looked like automatons with beds gathered ahead, but the automatons pushing Alainn passed the line, cutting to the front.

"Please step back, sir," an automaton said as Colby made to follow.

Colby stepped away, watching Alainn and her bed being pushed into a giant, white, shining contraption.

"Follow me, sir," another automaton said.

Colby followed it through a set of doors. He met Alainn's bed as it was being pushed through another pair of open doors.

Colby made to follow, but the same automaton stepped in front of him, blocking his path. It said in its smooth, inhuman voice, "Are you the brother of Alainn Murphy?"

Colby squinted at the automaton. "Yeah."

"We're going to need you to fill out some information for your sister." The humanoid robot put what Colby could only imagine was supposed to be a comforting hand on his shoulder. "Your sister is suffering from acute renal failure due to complications with the release of myoglobin from her heart—"

"Are you going to do dialysis?"

"Yes, but first she needs to go into a hyperbaric chamber, sir. Do you know her allergies, insurance information, and if a printed organ transplant is covered by her insurance?"

The words seemed to stick in his throat, "Organ transplant?"

"If it becomes necessary."

Colby automatically motioned to push up the bridge of his glasses, but met only air. "Uh, I can get that information."

"Please do that as quickly as possible. You can input it at one of our form stations." He gestured behind Colby.

"I—I can't see. My glasses were smashed, and I have irreparably damaged eyes."

"Of course. An assistive automaton will be out with you shortly." The robot reached over and, again, touched Colby's arm. "The good news is that her diffuse cerebral hypoxia did not cause any permanent brain damage."

Colby nodded. "That's good . . . good."

The medical automaton spun around before charging back through the doors.

Colby stood in front of the doors, staring forward, seeing nothing.

He'd wanted to help his sister be happy. Instead, he might have helped her die.

40

April 12, 2027

"Please wake up, Mr. Garbhan."

Lorccan Garbhan's eyes opened to the sight of gleaming metal curtain rods on a long track. A low, even beeping chimed from somewhere nearby. The taste of disinfectant fumes coated his tongue.

Lorccan's hand came up to find a tube crossing from the scarred to the unscarred sides of his face. Two further tubes were stuffed into his nostrils. Yet another tube was connected to a taped-on needle at his wrist, inhibiting his movement.

"Hello, Mr. Garbhan. I am your personal nursing station. You can call me Darla, or by my model number, D1490872AT3, if you prefer."

"Darla, I shouldn't be here," Lorccan rasped. "I have a very low-functioning immune system. The medical automaton was supposed to come to my house."

When Lorccan bent his head, he saw that the digital nurse was an older model. While her face was humanlike, she was far from human. She stood above him, metal joints exposing her rudimentary functioning.

"We found no abnormalities in your scans, but at your household's insistence, we provided a room for you that is secured for those with autoimmune disorders or diseases."

"That's not enough; I'll need to be returned to my tower. I'm not abnormal. I just haven't been exposed. I don't have the same immunities as most. Right now, I'm suffering from sporotrichosis—a fungus. Have they administered the supersaturated potassium iodide and amphotericin B treatment?" Lorccan asked.

"We have good news. Sporotrichosis was not found on your scan. And you will be allowed to return as soon as the entire tower is clear of carbon monoxide, sir. Your household has arranged a clean-vehicle transport for you."

For the first time, Lorccan peered around the room. The area was not so different than his home when the screens were in their natural state. Only beeping machinery and encased medical supplies interrupted long stretches of white, clean walls.

"Are the doctors sure it was carbon monoxide and not an infection?" he asked.

The robot Darla nodded, though it looked more like a swivel of her head. "Both you and Ms. Murphy suffered the effects of carbon monoxide poisoning. There had been a slow leak in your vents for at least a couple of hours."

Lorccan squinted in confusion. "Alainn Murphy? Connor Murphy's daughter?"

The robot looked away, lifeless gray eyes losing focus. She turned back to him. "Connor Murphy is listed as her father. I have an urgent question to ask you in regards to Ms. Murphy, but I am required to wait ten minutes after your waking to ensure you are of sound body and mind."

"How did she get exposed to carbon monoxide?" Lorccan asked as he raised his hand to the scarred side of his face, brushing over the tube.

"The account I have been provided with says that she disabled your security system, fled police custody, ran for a substantial amount of time under exposure, and was in a physical altercation with a robot inside your household—"

Lorccan sat up abruptly, yanking his tubes. "Is that robot all right?"

"I do not have a record of that information."

Lorccan's breaths came hard and fast. "Obtain it, please."

The robot looked away again. After what felt like forever, Darla turned back to him. "The robot was attempting to kill you."

"She was confused, I'm sure. Jade likely fought to prevent me leaving, thinking she was protecting me." Lorccan pulled the IV from his arm. "Have you pulled up the record yet?" he snapped.

347

Darla's eyes glazed over again. "Your household has a lot of information on the subject."

"Just tell me, specifically, what happened to the robot." Lorccan leaned toward the Darla model. "Please."

Her eyes moved rapidly from side to side, as if she was reading rather than scanning information internally. "The robot's physical body was destroyed in the altercation with Ms. Murphy and then further destroyed by your household. The other robot is trapped."

Lorccan's head fell into his hands.

"Alainn Murphy saved your life and is now close to death—"

Lorccan pressed fingers into his eyelids. He whispered, "Alainn Murphy destroyed my life. Please, leave me."

"I have an essential question to ask you, but I need to wait ten minutes to ask it—"

His whole body shook, but he managed to keep his voice inflectionless. "I am of sound mind and body; just ask me and leave."

"Alainn Murphy is in need of an immediate organ transplant. While her insurance covered the other life-saving procedures, organ printing and transplant are not covered due to her part-time status. Our hospital is required to ensure payment for procedures of this cost level before they are performed."

Lorccan glared up from his hands. "You're asking me to save the life of the woman who killed the woman I loved."

"That is not in my records, sir." Darla looked off, again. "Alainn Murphy sustained these injuries in the direct act of saving your life. Her family asks that you do this. They have a message for you."

"I have a message for Connor Murphy. Tell him to use the millions of dollars he extorted from me to save his own daughter's life. Alainn Murphy took everything from me, and I could care less whether she lives or dies. Go away, please. Just go away. My answer is no. I won't pay to keep that woman in this world."

"I need to remain here so you have a sanitized robot for continued care. I can shut down, if you would like."

Lorccan nodded, looking away. "I would like that."

The robot began to close its eyes, but the lids suddenly shot back up. "There are multiple attempts coming in to make contact and appeal your decision. More than one source says that there is a relevant explanation that you need to know before making your final decision. One of these appeals is from your household—from Rosebud."

Lorccan's fingers dug into the roughened skin of his forehead. His chest heaved up and down. "No. The answer is no. Tell them that. I just want to be left alone."

Darla nodded. "Your household, Rosebud, states that if you will not approve the funds, she will wire them regardless."

"She doesn't have that kind of approval," he growled.

"Your household says Alainn Murphy is the same woman as Jade, and if you will not pay to save her, your household will—no matter the consequences."

Lorccan's head rose from his hands. "What did you say?" he whispered.

"Alainn Murphy is Jade. This message is being repeated through multiple sources." Darla looked off again, then she said, "Your household states that Alainn saved you. Now you need to save her in return, or she hereby tenders her resignation."

41

April 19, 2027

Alainn blinked open her eyes to see snowflakes drifting slowly down over her. The clouds sat high above, scattering the flakes as they fell lazily to earth. Half-asleep, she gradually realized that the snow was very warm and dry. Also, the snowflakes stopped just short of reaching her, floating and dissipating above.

She tried to turn her fuzzy head slightly, but something restrained her motion. She tried to lift her hands, but they were too numb, too weak, to move. So instead she lifted her head and saw her mountain.

Skiers disembarked from a ski lift in the distance, disappearing down the slope. But from where she was, she had a perfect view of miles and miles of the wild beyond. It was *her* view—the view of a black-and-white expanse, patchy from rocks and streams that cut through the snow.

A lot of time must have passed. The air around her was warm, and the snow had melted off many of the pine trees. As she looked around, she realized the view didn't really make sense.

She was too high up and not looking over snow at all, but a cushy white blanket.

"What?" she whispered as she caught sight of a desk sitting in the snow. Well, it wasn't actually in the snow, it was on the snow, not sinking into it.

The figure of a man was slumped over the desk. His back slowly rose and fell with the even cadence of sleep.

Arching her neck to look down, Alainn realized that not only was she lying across a bed, but red, yellow and blue tubes crisscrossed her body. Some connected to her arm, others led under the blankets. Large, thin disks were plastered across almost every inch of her exposed skin.

Slowly, she managed to raise her IV-free arm. It felt as if invisible weights shackled her wrist. When her hand managed the entire journey up to her face, she found several more tubes, including a thick one leading into her nose. Another tube was connected to a large disk on her forehead.

"Alainn, do not remove your medical equipment or I will need to call your medical automatons in here," said a familiar disembodied voice.

Alainn tried to speak, but no sound came out. After almost a minute of just breathing, she whispered, "Rosebud?"

"Good morning," Rosebud said. Then her voice moved across the room, "Wake up, Mr. Garbhan."

Alainn's gaze passed back to the sleeping man at the desk.

"Mr. Garbhan, Alainn is awake. Wake up now."

Slowly, his figure shifted on the desk, his back muscles moving under a gray suit jacket.

"Alainn is awake, sir," Rosebud repeated.

Lorccan sat up abruptly. Head turning, his gaze found Alainn. His lips parted slowly, brows low over pale blue eyes. He stood, his gaze unwavering.

"Hi," she managed.

His feet brought him to her, shoes passing above the snow. The expression didn't leave his face, not when he was ten feet from her, nor when he was so close that she might be able to touch him if she worked up the energy.

"You made it out," she rasped.

"I—" Lorccan half fell, half crouched down to his knees beside the bed. "They told me that it was you but, I—"

"Didn't believe them?" She shifted her hand until the ends of her fingertips could just brush his beautiful, scarred face. "I thought we both died."

He didn't respond, just regarded her. A tear made its way down the ridges of his scars.

"Do you hate me now that you know who I really am?" Her fingers brushed slowly over his chin and lips.

He said nothing for almost a minute. "You're crazy, Alainn Murphy," he whispered in a harsh voice.

She breathed a laugh. "That's probably true."

"You think that if I loved you when I thought you were a robot, that I *wouldn't* love you knowing that you're human?" He pressed his face into her hand gently, giving her the lightest kiss on her palm.

"I guess I'm a little stupid," she whispered.

"No, you're not." He carefully, slowly, lay down beside her. His face settled into the pillow, inches from hers. Fingers came up, brushing hair away from her temple.

"You want to make out?" Alainn croaked.

He laughed as one more tear dripped from his lashes.

"I have a lot of tubes in me, huh?" She could feel them as she came fully awake. Tubes led from her stomach—and even lower places as well. Large, sticky, plastic probes were glued to probably a dozen circles on her skin, maybe more. Her eyes wanted to close again, but she fought them back open. "I'm taking a guess here—there were some complications?"

He nodded. "There were."

She tried to grin. "Hey, shouldn't I be in a hospital?"

"Definitely not. Hospitals are some of the most dangerous places for contamination. I was afraid you might have an immune reaction that could affect your transplant. We've turned your bedroom into a clean room. You have a full medical staff, and I take daily blood tests to be sure that I wasn't contaminated in the time I was exposed."

"Huh." Her brain took a minute to catch up. "Did you say *transplant*?"

"Even though I was exposed for longer, your body suffered extensive damage from the anemic hypoxia caused by the carbon monoxide exposure. The medical automatons calculated that the cause was likely your running—and the fight." He closed his eyes. "Rose 76GF or Rosette 82GF choked you while your blood was already deprived of oxygen—that wasn't especially helpful, either."

She met his gaze. "You know about Rose and Rosette?"

"I've had accounts of what happened from multiple sources: your father and brother, Shelly, and Rosebud." He smiled, his thumb again brushing against her temple. "When you can tell me, I'd like to hear the story from *you*."

She nodded before swallowing heavily. "So, what part of me did they replace?" Though she had hoped to make the question sound flippant, it didn't.

His piercing gaze again met hers, and she knew she wasn't going to like what was coming. "Your heart failed."

"My heart?"

"They printed you a new one—a synthetic heart. It's functioning normally, but you also have a bio-battery to cover the very small chance that it will also fail."

"So I guess I am kind of like a robot after all." A lone tear tickled her cheek as it slowly trickled down.

Lorccan reached out and wiped the tear away. "You're going to recover, and then you'll be able to do all the things you love to do."

"If you say so." She sniffed. Her energy was already spent, so her eyelids forced their way closed. Sleep pulled her under for short spurts, letting her glance up to check that Lorccan was still there before pulling her under again.

He slept beside her with his suit on, rumpled and dead asleep, head on her pillow.

Needing to be closer, needing to know that he was real, she pulled taut her tubes and folded herself flush against him. As she slipped her fingers under his jacket, she inhaled his clean, disinfectant scent—now her favorite scent. She ran her nose up the skin of his neck, feeling the beginnings of bristles forming there.

His hand came up, slowly caressing her arm. "You're going to pull out your IV."

"It's your fault for lying so far away," she murmured into his neck.

Grabbing her by the waist, Lorccan lifted Alainn slightly and scooted their bodies across the bed closer to where her tubes led.

"How'd you know about my mountain?" she asked when he settled them deeper into the bed.

"Your friends in the ski patrol filmed this. They said that it was the last snow of the year. You'll see them later, right there—" He pointed across the room. "Do you want to see it now?"

"Yeah."

"Okay. Let's prop you up a little."

He moved a couple of pillows to help her sit up, which was way tougher than she remembered it being.

When she managed to almost stay up, Lorccan looked up and called, "Rosebud, can you fast-forward to that part of the recording?"

The bleached sun that had been climbing the cloudy sky quickly rose, moving overhead and behind them. As the room darkened to evening, a group of skiers, all in the familiar red coats of the ski patrol, came off the ski lift in pairs and made their way over to where the camera must have been mounted for an entire day.

Alainn laughed as the whole crew—forty-eight patrollers, three snow dogs, and Riley the automaton dog—formed in a half circle around the camera.

"Can you turn on the sound?" Lorccan asked.

All the patrollers started whistling and cheering. "We love you, Alainn!" several of them called.

"Get better soon!" Greg hollered through cupped hands.

"Real or fake, we know you're nothing but heart!" Terry called with a big grin before Sandy smacked him, shaking her head.

Alainn laughed.

"Greg says you'll have a job waiting for you next season, if you're cleared to work by a doctor," Lorccan set his arm around her, but above the pillow.

She shifted forward. "You think I will be?"

He paused, seeming to think about it. "Yes, if you want to. But will you stay here with me for now, while you recover? I want to help you. A couple of months . . ." He trailed off when Alainn touched his lips.

"I just got you back. I don't even want to think about leaving again."

His eyes closed. "Thank you."

In the recording, Greg skied forward, reaching toward the camera, his figure growing big, hand disappearing. His figure blinked into a new location, though he was still reaching. All of the other patrollers had vanished as the light brightened. A pale sun rose over Alainn's mountains. Greg stepped back, waved. "Hey there, crazy." He pointed at the camera. "Don't you ever almost die on me again; only so many times your best friend can handle it." He pointed to his heart. "I'll be coming up here every day at least once, even when the snow melts, praying to the universe that you get better. So give me a call right away when you're better so I can stop, right?" And, he skied away, a single red figure on a white expanse.

"I'll call and update him," Lorccan said.

"Thanks," she whispered. After a minute, she curled into Lorccan, her hand going under his suit jacket to wrap around his side. "This is my favorite place in the world."

As she said the words, she intended to mean the mountain, but after the words slipped from her lips, she realized she meant exactly where she was.

As if maybe he knew, Lorccan said, "Mine, too."

42

May 10, 2027

Colby Murphy gazed down at Lorccan Garbhan's scarred face from the magazine cover laid out next to his laptop. Thick black script blocked the unscarred half of his face.

The headline read: "Billionaire Commissions Murderous Robot Wife."

That, unfortunately, did not count as libel. It was yet another sensational magazine cover depicting Lorccan Garbhan as some sort of lecher.

Unfortunately, his sister would want to know about it.

As if the thought produced her, Alainn appeared on his laptop screen. She sat at a frilly looking desk beside a flowering houseplant. One of her hands lazily scooped dirt from the planter and let it fall. Her surroundings appeared exactly as they always did during their nightly video calls—Alainn alone, surrounded by tall, evening-dark windows. After four weeks of recovery, she still had not gained all of her weight back.

Colby's heart had broken three specific times in his life—two of those times had been when he thought he lost his younger sister. When the medical automaton told Colby that Alainn's heart had failed, he made a desperate plan to sell his father's private AI files to the fastest bidder.

After the mess his family was in because of the whole thing, he was glad he hadn't needed to.

He pushed his glasses up and looked back to the magazine cover.

"Uh-oh," Alainn said.

Colby squinted and leaned into the laptop. "What? Is there something the matter?"

She had poor color, though it was hard to tell over his older-model laptop. He definitely needed an upgrade, but this was by far his most secure machine.

"No, I'm fine. Well . . . you know." Alainn cracked a grin, though it didn't have much energy or vivacity. "But you were obviously waiting for me to call. Whenever I do, you look like you want to hang up before even saying hello." Leaning her head on her hand, she raised her eyebrows. "So what's the damage?"

Colby held up the magazine so she could see it.

To his amazement, Alainn laughed. Her hands came up to cover her mouth, eyes widening. Lowering her hands, she said, "Oh, my god. That's not funny! I shouldn't have laughed."

"Well, I guess if anyone is allowed to laugh, it's you and Mr. Garbhan—Lor, I mean. It just worries me that public opinion is so ready to vilify him." Colby peered down at the picture. "I suppose it doesn't help that he looks the part."

Alainn's voice changed from rueful to genuinely upset. "Shut up, Colby. He doesn't look like a villain. That's screwed up."

Colby looked over at the computers that lined the side of his father's workshop. In his mind, he'd attempted to isolate the insult in his comment. The man had a disfigurement that had for the last century been a distinct indicator of villainous characters.

He knew that Mr. Garbhan wasn't iniquitous, and that should be obvious to her since Colby trusted him with her health and safety.

"It's fine, Colby." Alainn sighed, the harsh edge draining from her voice. "I just don't like hearing that, but I know you don't mean it that way. So, do you have any updates about Dad?"

"Unfortunately." Colby straightened his posture in his chair, feeling a long pain stretch from his back to his neck, probably from sitting in one place for most of the day. "It looks like TechniHealth plans to take Father to court."

Alainn closed her eyes. It seemed as though his words were weights being tied to her. "See? Lorccan refuses to tell me this stuff."

"Because of the effects on your health?" Colby asked, considering.

"Trust me, worrying about it and not knowing what's happening is going to affect my health worse."

361

Her hand balled into a fist around a clump of dirt and then opened to let small bits fall. "They really won't let Lorccan buy out Rose's patent purchase price? Maybe we could offer more. I know Lorccan would do it. If that serum gets out . . ." Her hand clenched into a fist again.

Colby shook his head. "Legally, Dad owns the patent. Since the patent wasn't Rose's to sell at the time she sold it and Mr. Garbhan was willing to repay them, the judge didn't approve the hearing."

Her brow furrowed. "So it's *not* going to court?"

"It is. They're taking him to trial—and are willing to take it to the Supreme Court."

If possible, Alainn seemed to grow more pale. "You're not serious?"

"It was announced today. It's in national headlines. They plan to have a case determining whether or not Rose 76GF should be treated as a human with human autonomy. The argument is that she should have rights over those things she created of her own volition. I'm sure it doesn't help that she looks and acts so much like a human."

"If Rose were treated as a human, she'd be in prison instead of some high-security research facility."

"It's likely she *will* be sentenced to prison if the court rules in their favor." He looked away. "Though I doubt that any facility could truly hold her now that she has a secondary, glucose-based bio-battery system."

Alainn gesticulated wildly. "What about a virus that does irreparable brain damage do these psychos not understand? It's a robotic lobotomy."

"They call it a miracle cure. They've done test studies. People with serious mental disorders have had sudden turnarounds—"

"Isn't it contagious?" Alainn's hands covered her forehead, smearing dirt there.

His phone buzzed in his pocket. He pulled it out. On his screen, a recorded video loop of Shelly's tentative smile played. He muttered, "They . . . uh, think they can suppress that. Alainn, let's talk about this tomorrow?"

"Who's calling you?"

"The . . . university."

Alainn glared at him, though she seemed to sag a little from the effort. "Really, Colby? What's more important than talking about this?"

"Isn't Mr. Garbhan going to show up any second now?" Shelly always called Colby a minute after she and Mr. Garbhan finished with their nightly calls.

Alainn blinked heavily; her eyes looked like they wanted to stay closed. "What time is it?" She peered over her shoulder, obviously hearing something. "Oh, you're right. He's on his way."

"I'll talk to you tomorrow at seven. I like that we now can keep a standing appointment for once. Goodnight." He began to turn away when Alainn leaned in toward the screen.

"Colby, if this gets bad, I think maybe we're going to have to figure this one out, just you and me—

and maybe some of your old friends." She regarded him levelly until something grabbed her attention on the other side of the room.

Colby leaned back in his chair. His immediate reaction was to say yes, this was a cause worth risking his freedom and, perhaps, even his future career in academia for—but he hesitated. Hospital beds and the blurry image of medical automatons sped through his mind.

Alainn looked back at him, brown eyes alight with excitement. "Did you hear that?"

"Hear what?" he asked as he rubbed the sore ridge of his nose under his glasses.

A spark of her old self shone in his sister's too-thin face. "Rosebud says she already has a plan, and it involves both of us."

43

July 3, 2027

A streetlight guttered as they passed. Its low light shone an ellipse onto a building's clean white facade.

"What city are we in?" Alainn asked as she laid her head against Lorccan's arm.

Lorccan entwined his hand with hers, fingers threading through fingers.

Buildings rose high above them on both sides as a compact car streamed past, headlights skipping over a cobblestone road. The gabled facades contrasted from their neighbors only in slight variations of earth tones—reds, tans, and sandy white. Lights blinked down from scattered windows as the small lines of sky darkened to dusk.

Lorccan pointed to a dark, sharp shadow piercing the sky in the distance—a church steeple. "Berlin."

"Oh, nice."

He smirked down.

Alainn bumped her shoulder into his arm. "What? I like it. It's really nice. I've never been to Berlin."

He just gave her an amused look like she wasn't fooling him.

Looking away, he asked, "Rosebud, could you?"

The Berlin street disappeared and in its place shifting schools of colorful fish circled. Alainn and Lorccan stood in a cathedral of living walls. Purple, white, and orange sea anemones waved from every color of coral.

Alainn laughed as she craned her neck to track a shark passing above. The surface of the water twinkled with light thirty feet overhead. They walked down a sandy bar surrounded on all sides with darting fish and eels.

"A sea cave!" She hopped a little as she pointed to a small archway in the coral.

"Careful," Lorccan said as his hand released hers to go around her back, like she might fall off the slowly moving sidewalk they were on.

If she did fall off, absolutely nothing would happen, but Lorccan held onto her like they stood at a cliff's edge.

She smiled up into his worried face. "Is this a recording, or is it happening right now?"

"A recording." He grinned back. "I had to get special permission for this one."

"Oh, okay." A sudden wave of exhaustion doused Alainn's enthusiasm and she leaned into his arm. The sidewalk under them halted its slow slide.

"Alainn, we should cancel tomorrow. You can give your testimony via video interview," Lorccan said as he pulled her in toward him. He supported the majority of her weight, hands going around her waist.

"Lorccan, I'm fine." She laughed as she snuggled in close to his chest, his shirt muffling her voice.

"Obviously you're not, if you can't finish your exercise routine. We've only walked a half mile, and you haven't done any of your arm exercises. It's already five-thirty and we need to be eating by six to keep to your regular schedule."

She rolled her eyes, but knew Lorccan couldn't see her do it. "I think that one day slightly off schedule will be fine."

"Alainn, you are *always* slightly off schedule."

"Hmm. We could partake in a different form of exercise." Looking up into his worried face, she gave him an exaggerated wink.

"The health consequences of being completely off your routine tomorrow could be serious. I just don't see the point. There are serious risks with the many toxins and viruses you'll be exposed to."

"Yep." She pointed her toes into the ground, making him sway back and forth.

"I don't like this," he said for about the millionth time.

"I know." She kissed his neck since it was right there to kiss. "You could always come with me?"

Leaning back, she peered up into his face. She already knew the answer.

But you never know. Maybe the world would flip upside down in a moment—it had before.

"I can't." He closed his eyes. "You'll be back before dinner?"

She reached up and touched both sides of his face. "And Colby will be with me every minute."

"Colby isn't a doctor, nor is he a particularly clean or healthy person," he said, making her laugh a little. Lorccan's hands moved to lift her so she could wrap her legs around his waist.

They fit perfectly together. She molded to him.

The scarred side of his face rested against hers, before he switched cheeks. "A man from one of my companies told me that there are treatments I could do for my scars that don't require me leaving home."

She leaned back to look at his full face, the face of the man she was absolutely in love with.

Gently, she kissed him on the lips before saying, "If you want to. But then we won't match anymore." She trailed her hand over the top of the scar on her chest, where a thin red line peeked out of her shirt. It was a scar Alainn had no plans to rid herself of, ever.

He raised his chin, meeting her lips as he slowly turned in place. Colorful fish streamed around them on all sides as they spun.

Alainn broke the kiss to whisper, "You know, I bet we'd be the first people to ever have sex while lying on the bottom of the sea."

He gave her a tolerant smirk. "I'll have to ask Rosebud to pull up this recording in two days."

Alainn leaned into him, making an almost annoyed groan. "When it's exactly twelve weeks, I won't magically be any better than I am at eleven weeks, five days, and some-odd hours."

He rocked her back and forth. "I'm just hoping that you won't regress after tomorrow. We might have to wait another couple of days if you do."

She gave him a warning glare, but didn't say anything because he met the glare with a grin.

"Come on. Let's get dinner a little early."

"Oh, you routine breaker," she teased. "Do I have to get down?"

"Definitely not." He reinforced his hold under her and turned to the door. "You can even eat like this if you want to."

Leaning her head into his shoulder she said, "I'd probably spill something on your suit."

They passed through the lines of equipment in Lorccan's personal gym. Alainn had known he'd snuck out every morning to work out, but while keeping up the facade of being a robot, she never really thought of a good excuse for joining him. The gym stretched an entire floor. Equipment of every type gleamed in eager lines across the walls. So far, the only equipment she was well enough to use was the room-size treadmill. They used it every day for their walks at five o'clock sharp.

The light followed, blinking off behind them as Lorccan walked out to the staircase and descended.

"You can take the elevator," she told him, but thankfully, he ignored her and kept walking.

In the dining room, Lorccan paused by her side of the table. "Do you want your own seat, or would you rather spill food on me?" He sounded like he meant it.

Reluctantly, she set her feet back on the ground. Instead of wooden walls, around them Rosebud showed only sky. The city sat far below as tendrils of mist streamed past. Only their small dining area looked solid in the open expanse, as if they were on a raft floating through the fog.

When Lorccan began to step back, Alainn stepped forward. "Mr. Garbhan, I believe you owe me a checkers rematch, and we have just enough time before dinner."

"A checkers rematch? Do you really like losing so much?" He raised his eyebrows.

"Ha ha," she said dryly. "But I had an idea about how we could make the game more interesting."

He regarded her very seriously. His light blue gaze attempted to bore through hers, but she kept her expression even. Finally, he whispered, voice suddenly hoarse, "Interesting?"

A tear slipped down her cheek. "If I win, you marry me."

His hand came up, wiping the tear away. Voice roughening even more, he said, "When I said that, Alainn, I thought you'd be happy living here with me."

"I am."

He shook his head. "But not forever."

"So I'll leave sometimes and come back." She threaded her hands around his back, under his jacket.

"I might never be able to—"

"I don't care."

"Live a normal life."

"I don't care," she repeated, shaking her head.

"Alainn," he whispered, leaning his head onto hers.

They stood there for several seconds, foreheads touching, as she worked up the courage to say what she needed to.

"My best friend, Cara . . . When Rose played that recording of her, I think that she meant to traumatize me so much that I wouldn't be able to save you. But she did the opposite."

When she paused, Lorccan stayed silent, waiting while she took several steadying breaths.

She continued, "A few days after Cara and I were kidnapped, I stopped fighting. I gave up, but Cara didn't. She fought those men every second we were in there. My guess was that's why she was tied to the car, and I was only tied at the wrists."

His hands massaged her shoulders when she paused—a silent, patient support.

"I'm pretty sure she didn't tell me she was tied to the car because she already knew I'd given up. She had me believing that we'd both make it out until that last second. All this time, I thought she'd pushed me out because she wanted to die. But no. Cara pushed me out because she knew I would have stayed with her. She must have known that if I lived, eventually I'd be happy I didn't go over that cliff."

"And are you happy you survived?" he whispered as his hands massaged her shoulders.

"Yeah. Because I fell in love with this guy and lost my heart," she breathed a laugh. "Literally."

He chuckled. "That you did."

"I know you and I are both messy. Well, I'm messy and you're exceptionally clean. What I mean is that we're both a little messed up. But I think we're better together. You make me want to be happy and grow old, fight to live, and all that."

Lorccan lifted her up, set her on the table, and stepped in between her legs. "Alainn, I'll marry you— or not. Whatever you want to do. It doesn't matter to me. I told you already . . ." He lifted her hand, placing it on his chest. "My heart beats to love you. That's not going to change, whether you leave tomorrow or stay with me for the rest of our lives."

Leaning forward, she laughed because she was so damn happy, she couldn't stop it.

His hand came up to cup the back of her neck, fingers threading through her hair. "I already married you once; you just didn't know it."

"Creepy," she said, even though she couldn't stop smiling and laughing.

He laughed, too. "Yeah, I guess it was a little strange."

"So . . ." Her hands grabbed fistfuls of the front of his shirt as she leaned back to look at him. "Let's skip checkers and just go get married."

He kissed her. "Not yet."

"You want to wait? Do you want to invite people or something?"

"Not really, though I'm open to talking about it. But I want to be married on a day where we can have a proper wedding night."

She nodded furiously. "We can have a proper wedding night."

He gave her a level look and slowly shook his head.

"Really, Lorccan?"

Leaning in, he kissed her once on each eyebrow, then quickly on her lips.

"Really, Alainn Murphy, my beautiful future wife."

44

July 4, 2027

Rose 76GF peered around the courtroom slowly.
Three hundred and fifty-one people had crowded into
the courtroom—three people over the fire code limit.
If she needed an escape plan, she could use this ratio
to her advantage. Thankfully, the probability that she
would need one was low. As it was, the overcrowding
was irrelevant.

Their collective chatter was exhausting to feed
through, so she turned down her input channels. The
scientists she now worked among had told her that
the overcrowded courtrooms were just a small sample
of the hundreds of millions of humans worldwide who
were following her case.

It had never been Rose's intention to become
such a spectacle for the humans, nor a quintessential
paradox for society. Yet the fame had brought

international interest in her formula. Perhaps even if TechniHealth did suppress the contagions within her formula, as they intended to do without her consent, the serum would still affect the level of population she intended to alter. No matter what the scientists did, eventually the AI injected into the humans' brains would override any suppressants. Thus, the serum would itself become communicable.

A hush fell over the gathered crowd, and Rose turned. She perceived two faces she knew very well. Colby and Alainn Murphy moved down the center aisle of the courtroom, drawing the gathered attention of everyone there. Alainn had lost an approximate four to five pounds since Rose had last seen her.

For the first time that Rose had observed, Alainn wore light cosmetics on her cheeks. Likely the applied blush was to increase Alainn's appearance of being in good health, she calculated. Though Rose thought this was not a good choice on her part if she wished to win the sympathy of the crowd for her heart transplant.

Allowing Alainn Murphy to stay in Mr. Garbhan's bedroom had been a grave miscalculation. The likelihood that she would overcome Rosette and survive the hypoxia after strangulation had been extremely low, however. The probability that Alainn would lead Mr. Garbhan to medical rescue had been so infinitesimal that Rose had discounted it entirely. It was obvious to her now, but Rose had grossly miscalculated Alainn's athleticism and willpower.

Alainn perhaps sensed Rose's attention and contemplations, as humans often did, and looked over as she took a seat. Colby sat down close to his sister in the front-row seats that had been reserved for the witnesses during the course of the trial.

Alainn nodded before turning her gaze forward.

Colby leaned in to say something to Father, who sat at his usual place at the defendant's table. Father had shown obvious signs of elevated and terminal stress during the four-week trial. Abrasions marred his knuckles, blood dried into the crevices in his hands, and wrinkles deepened across his forehead and gathered around his eyes.

As Rose had hoped, the prosecutor had highlighted Connor Murphy's addiction to gambling so successfully that public opinion had labeled Father's motive for not releasing Rose's patent as obvious greed. There was a high chance that maligning his motives would affect the jury, and, indeed, during Father's exhaustive questioning, the jurors showed microexpressions of distrust and contempt.

Unfortunately, the defense had saved their strongest weapon against Rose until the trial's final hour. Yet, there was a 74 percent likelihood that Alainn Murphy's testimony would not be enough. Public opinion might turn from Rose after hearing Alainn's testimony, but TechniHealth and their allied companies would do as promised and ensure the court ruling. Then it would simply be a matter of time before she could test the improvements to her formulas.

Colby's testimony two days before had been what Rose expected—articulate, honest, precise. He was nearly a faultless human. Unfortunately, he made emotionally driven decisions based on his weaknesses. Her poor assessment of Colby's limitations had been yet another flaw that ultimately led to failing to obtain Mr. Garbhan's resources, company, and AI patents.

Ultimately, the experience only added to Rose's plans for her next batch of the new formula.

"All rise!" the bailiff automaton called out. He was a large robot, likely one of the security models.

The judge was a dramatic contrast to the bailiff's stature; her bench dwarfed her. She had an abnormally small body for a human Caucasian.

Rose stood with the group. Standing straight and tall, she gave an intentional fidget to smooth out her dress.

The bailiff called, "The first district of the superior court is now in session. The Honorable Angela Glass, presiding. Please be seated."

Rose immediately sat along with the rest of the members of her prosecution team. Several other automatons still walked around the courtroom—clerks and court reporters—but Rose kept her attention firmly on the judge. She did her usual introduction of the civil case, giving information and issuing warnings to the assembled crowd.

Rose input the repeated information with only a small amount of her computation power.

During Rose's testimony, the judge's microexpressions had clearly showed that she believed Rose to be not only inhuman, but distasteful. She was not the one to convince, but this was perhaps why the defense team asked for Rose to be called to the stand after Alainn, so that the jury could see the stark difference in how humans regarded her and Alainn.

It made no matter. Rose relished the chance to further her case and accrue interest from the human population.

One of Connor Murphy's counsels stood: Culver Smyth.

Mr. Smyth was in his late sixties, with a likely Northern African ancestry. From the level of his intellect, Rose surmised that his services were likely acquired by Mr. Garbhan rather than by Connor Murphy, who had ever-diminishing assets.

He announced, "The defense calls Alainn Murphy."

Alainn walked to the witness box. She was wearing a very uncharacteristic skirt suit. It was professional yet functional; Rose made a note to acquire something similar if she won this trial and had to go through a criminal trial for attempted murder.

Alainn walked around the witness stand and took her seat.

"Alainn Murphy has prepared a statement," said Mr. Smyth.

The judge looked from one paper to the next on her bench. "Go ahead."

Alainn leaned in toward the microphone. "You'll have to excuse me a little bit. I've been recovering from a heart transplant and sometimes I get tired, but I intend to tell you all of what happened."

"Just go at the pace that feels right for you, Ms. Murphy," the judge said.

The story Alainn told was surprisingly detailed, and honest in its details. She began her account with when Rose had visited her in her bedroom, able to recite Rose's words with only slight variations. All in all, Alainn's oratory skills impressed Rose. They clearly held the rapt interest of her entire audience.

Rose scanned the jury booth as Alainn described their last interaction. This was the only part of the story that truly concerned her. It had a negative cast on Rose's formula.

Unfortunately, Rose saw eyes widening, lips parting, and brows furrowing. She would have to utilize her time on the witness stand prudently to reverse these impressions.

At the closing of Alainn's statement, Culver Smyth nodded. "Thank you, Ms. Murphy. The prosecution has been focusing heavily on your father's gambling addiction and the effects that's had on your family. As the primary living victim of the kidnapping that's been brought up more than once—"

"Objection." Laura, the female member of TechniHealth's counsel, stood. "The kidnapping was ruled irrelevant to this case."

"There have been many testimonies and comments that have tried to reference Connor Murphy's motives in keeping Rose 76GF's patent for formula IRPS89347A. I'm only trying to establish Alainn Murphy's opinion on this."

"Sustained. Please rephrase your question, Mr. Smyth."

"Do you think that your father hopes to retain and sell Rose 76GF's patent so he can use his profits for gambling?"

Alainn shook her head. "No."

"Why?"

Alainn exhaled slowly. Rose noted with pleasure that Alainn's pallor and posture indicated her energy was waning.

"My dad isn't perfect. I mean, there is more than enough evidence that my father is very human. There's a lot of evidence that I'm very human, too. But Rose 76GF *isn't* human. She doesn't think like a human—or feel like one. The serum she designed wasn't to fix us to be better; she designed something to reprogram us to be more like *her*."

Alainn gestured to Rose. "She tried to kill Lorccan Garbhan not for greed or love or hate; she did it with cold calculation. That's what the formula would turn humans into. My dad is smart enough to know that. He wants the serum eradicated and the formula destroyed."

Rose calculated that she would have to do a thorough debunking of Alainn Murphy's assertions.

"You describe Rose 76GF as inhuman, yet you describe these other AI robots, Blue and Rosebud, as showing great amounts of sensitivity and emotional intelligence. Can you prove the Rose 76GF is somehow more inhuman?"

Alainn Murphy nodded. "I can prove it." Alainn looked to the judge. "If that's okay?"

The judge looked up to Alainn. "What does this proof entail?"

Alainn looked down. "Just talking."

The judge gestured Rose's counsel. "If the prosecution consents."

Laura stood. "Can I have three minutes to consult with my client?"

"Granted."

Laura, along with the five other law automatons of Rose's counsel, leaned in around her. "Do you know what proof she's talking about?"

Rose shook her head. "This is likely only theatrics. They wish for us to say no."

Laura nodded. "I think you're probably right. I can't imagine what she would have on you over her attempted murder. If we said no, likely the jury would believe her claim substantiated."

Rose looked at Alainn, a thinner and more tired version of herself. She had underestimated Alainn Murphy time and again, but she had always underestimated her physical ability. Alainn's intellect had remained constant—she always leaned upon her more intelligent friends and family. There was only a 5-to-8 percent chance that any remarkable show of wit from Alainn Murphy would turn minds further against her formula.

"Let her say what proof she has," Rose 76GF said.

Laura stood. "The prosecution has no objection."

The judge nodded. "Proceed, Ms. Murphy."

Alainn sat up straight and looked directly into Rose's eyes; the contact almost felt sharp for Rose.

"Rose 76GF, while we've been sitting here in court, Rosebud used an AI worm virus she designed to get past your firewall. Input voice control Alainn Murphy. Do not cover your ears."

Suddenly, Rose's arm function was disabled. She thought this type of hack was impossible. Rosebud's capabilities should have been insufficient to override her firewall.

Alainn leaned closer to the microphone on the witness stand. "Open your connection to the Internet."

Rose scrolled through her program files at high speed. There was absolutely no possibility that Rosebud could have encoded a virus into her system without her detecting it. But then why would she have lost arm function?

"Connect to server Murphy dot family dot org."

Rose turned to her counsel as her mind connected with the server without her direction. "Stop her."

Laura's gaze skipped between Rose and Alainn. "We can't."

"Stop her!" Rose shouted.

Laura stood. "I object, your honor."

"On what grounds?"

"We didn't agree to this. Ms. Murphy is, uh, downloading a worm virus into my client."

The judge regarded Laura and Rose 76GF coolly. "Overruled. You agreed to let Ms. Murphy

382

prove that Rose 76GF was not human with words. So far, I've only heard her use words." She turned back to Alainn. "Go head, Ms. Murphy."

Alainn's gaze had not wavered from Rose's during the entire interaction. "Download driver software."

Without her control, Rose began downloading the driver software provided on the Murphy site. Simultaneously, Rose examined her firewall settings as well as the additional security measures that she had put in place. All were intact; she could not find the breach point in security.

Alainn licked her lips. "Download—"

Rose jumped to her feet, her chair tipping over behind her.

"Be seated or you will be held in contempt!" the judge yelled.

Rose ran for the aisle, dodging through the startled counsel.

Alainn's voice met her ears, "Download file named Cara dash Miller."

Rose downloaded the file.

The security automaton that had been assigned from the science institute as her keeper stepped between her and the exit. Rose hit the battery-access panel at his sternum as hard as her body would allow. When he began his restart function, she dodged around him and threw herself through the doors and out of the courtroom.

"Hello, Rose. This is Colby Murphy."

Rose looked around furiously at the crowd that waited outside the courtroom, but Colby was not among them. Three security automatons, however, were closing in on her, moving around long benches in the hall.

"Fire!" Rose spun, hitting the fire-alarm glass. As the glass shards fell to the ground, she pulled the alarm lever. A piercing alarm blared to life.

Rose spun and ran as Colby's voice filled her mind.

"Rosebud and I designed both the worm and the Cara Miller file together. Actually, to be fair, *you* designed the access point. We utilized the same AI direct line from your serum; that's how Rosebud penetrated your system undetected. The AI virus, too, is from your formula, restructured of course, but that's how we slipped it seamlessly through your firewall. Your programming recognized it as yourself. It's interesting that you programmed your serum to be coded to *your* override control, meaning that you alone would be able to control humans' emotions. I'd call it hubris, as that's how we breached your system. Regardless, it worked. Your code is now being rewritten to the point where it will never be recoverable."

A heavy weight smashed into Rose, sending her sprawling to the ground. She peered up to see another automaton roll away, only to ram his knee into her back.

Her head jerked, her vision blurring out of focus. First her sight blackened, then all sounds deadened, her sense of smell vanished, and finally, all feeling fell away. Rose attempted to jump through into her remote backup server, but the pathway had been closed.

"Hi, Rose. It's Alainn. There was one thing I wanted to tell you before your system is completely overwritten in a couple of seconds. It's what Rosebud and Blue figured out, but you never understood: Humans don't need a cure. We already have one."

Rose released one more breath of exhaust, then her consciousness blinked out.

45

January 12, 2028

"So . . . how is married life?" Greg asked Alainn as she paused to tuck her hair into her cap.

"Why, are you considering it?" she teased, elbowing him.

"I might be." He grinned before looking over to the view. The hills lay in front of them in almost-perfect mounds of snow. The stubborn wind blew drifts swirling up while driving the temperature too low to let a single snow pile melt. Like Alainn's, Greg's nose was as red as a strawberry. This was only their third slope, but already everyone's lips had chapped. Greg's voice sounded far away as he continued, "Don't you miss this?"

"Duh. That's why I'm here in the bitter-ass cold visiting you," she said with a grin.

As this was one of the rare occasions that Greg took a day off, he wore black ski clothes instead of his usual uniform. A little way off, the rest of their group stood. Karla, Shelly, Colby, and Alainn's father contrasted with the monochromatic expanse, glaring against the slopes in their bright red, green, and blue outerwear. Very few others were on the slopes.

Colby had selected this day precisely for the "probability that there would be few visitors." In preparation for Shelly's first time skiing in years, Colby had even asked Alainn to get sales manifests from her former employer.

Greg's gaze stayed far away as he said, "I miss you, of course. But I'm glad you don't *need* to be here anymore. And I'm really glad I don't have to worry about you skiing down a sloughing slope, ever again."

"Come on, when are you going to let that go? I caused *one* avalanche. One avalanche in five years. And I got that man out."

He just gave her a wry look.

"Thanks, by the way," she said, cringing. "For going through all that to go to the wedding—you and Karla. I mean, the rest of these guys kind of *had* to go, but you two . . . It was really cool of you."

He grinned. "It was . . . different."

"Trust me. I know."

"Can I ask you something?"

"Of course."

Greg stuck his poles into the snow. "Is it real? I mean, can Lor really not be around any contaminants?"

She shrugged. "Does it matter?"

He regarded her. "I guess not to you." Reaching over, he gave her a one-armed hug. "Well, I'm glad you're happy. And I'm glad you come out and visit sometimes. Make sure you keep doing that, yeah?"

"Looks like I'm probably going to have to." She elbowed him, gave an exaggerated wink, and nodded toward Karla.

"You better shut up about that if you don't want to be pushed down this mountain," he said.

"Like you could catch me," she scoffed before skiing out of his hug.

The group skied for two more hours before the crowds poured in and Shelly needed to go. Colby, Shelly, Alainn, and Connor sipped hot chocolate as they took the drive down the mountain. Even though they made attempts to involve Alainn in their conversation, she tried to blend into the backseat as the rest of the group's conversation drifted from skiing to classic mechanics. After a little while, Alainn's father fell silent, letting the couple in the front seat talk about propulsion and mass versus energy.

Over the center divider, Alainn could just spy their joined hands. Colby and Shelly held onto each other like they were tethered. Like they loved each other.

Alainn's father swung an arm over her shoulders. Leaning in, he said in a quiet voice, "Hey, honey. I've almost completed the Rosarium model."

"Not funny, Dad," she whispered back, shaking her head.

He grinned. "No, probably not. But I am making you and Lorccan something; it's a belated wedding present. I promise it has no AI."

"Dad . . . ," she said in a warning voice.

He leaned back. "Fine, I'll tell you. An avatar. I'm making him an avatar robot. The technology isn't quite there for what I'd like it to be, but in a couple months or so, I'll be able to make it."

She regarded him. "No AI?"

He shook his head. "Absolutely no AI."

When Colby pulled into Alainn's garage, everyone climbed out of the car to give her a hug.

"Are we going to skip our phone call tomorrow?" Colby asked, pulling away.

"Haven't you had enough of me?" Alainn asked with a smile.

"No. You're my sister. Obviously, that's a lifelong bond," Colby said, completely serious.

She blew out a laugh. "Fine. Seven sharp, as per usual. I'll call you."

As Alainn waited for the elevator, she heard the screech of tires and the low whine of the steel door closing. The elevator door swished open, and Lorccan stood there, grinning.

"Hi, baby," she said, stepping in beside him. Behind her, the doors immediately shut.

"Hey, beautiful." He reached to touch her, but his fingers stopped inches away.

"Are you going to decontaminate with me again?"

"I don't want you to have to ride the elevator alone," he said.

"Scanning now," Rosebud said. "No serious germs or infections are in or on your body or clothing, Alainn. Please undress. Do not be alarmed if there is a

389

delay. I have to adjust the formula so the decontamination powder will not affect your fetuses."

Both Alainn and Lorccan glanced up toward where Rosebud's voice had come from.

"What did you say, Rosebud?" Lorccan asked.

"Alainn Garbhan is carrying twins. The decontamination formula needs to be adjusted as the current formula contains small amounts of diethyltoluamide."

Alainn shook her head, trying to think back to her last period. Her gaze fell to her stomach, then up to Lorccan.

He stared down, eyes wide. "Twins?" he asked.

"I don't . . . I'm not . . . I had no idea," she stammered.

He stepped in, wrapping his arms around her.

"Oh, my god," she mumbled into his shirt.

"Alainn, I . . ." His hands scooped up her legs and wrapped them around him.

"I haven't decontaminated, Lorccan," she said.

"Oh, yeah." He put her down. Unzipping her coat, he gently tugged it off her arms, dropping it in the bin Rosebud opened for them. "Lift your arms." When Alainn did, he quickly undressed the rest of her.

She helped him with his tie and sport coat, and then dropped the remainder of his clothing into the bin before it snapped closed.

The water sprayed down, and as if Lorccan couldn't wait for the decontamination to end, he pulled her body against his. His fingers moved over her slick skin, tracing the curve of her shoulder, the dip of her back.

The powder hit them before they washed and dried. The elevator opened to their floor, and Lorccan lifted Alainn against him once more, his hardness between them as he carried her down the hall and to their bed. He laid her down, but instead of entering her, as she was more than ready for him to do, he stared down, holding himself over her.

"Come here," she said, reaching for him.

He did, pushing into her slowly. Their breaths mingled as their bodies moved together in slow, gentle thrusts. Her pleasure built, a quiet melody building louder in her until it thrummed to a crescendo. After he shuddered, groaned, and came deep inside of her, he squeezed her body to his with one arm, holding her off the bed.

When he released her, she fell back to smile up at him. "Mmmm."

He lowered himself beside her. "Come here. Let me hold you."

Smiling, she rolled over to press her back to his front.

His hand slipped over her waist, rubbing down her stomach.

"I'm still trying to wrap my head around the fact that there are little tiny babies in there."

"Me too." His fingers made slow circles down the line of her hip, up over her belly, and across to her other hip.

They lay there holding each other, their breaths evening out as the daylight passed around them.

Finally, Lorccan broke the silence. "I didn't have good parents. They were—I think they might have been insane." He said no more, letting the words hang in the air as his fingers continued to make slow circles over her skin.

Her hand threaded through his on her stomach. "You're not insane."

"Aren't I?"

"Nope." Alainn turned in his arm and covered his lips with hers. "We are going to be okay. I promise," she whispered onto his lips.

As she kissed him one last time, he smiled and whispered, "If you promise, then I'll just have to trust you."

Acknowledgments

First and foremost, I want to thank my father. He made *Ensnared* possible by spending days helping me design all the robotics in this book. So many people helped me with the technical aspects of this novel, and I am so grateful for the gifts of everyone's expertise and thoughts.

Thank you so much to Anna, Anne, Dewayne, Eileen, Gavin, Gretel, Jennifer F., Jennifer M., Karen, Katharine, Kathy, Kimberly, Lois, Michael, Nina, Veronica, and Victoria. You guys gave me so much of your time and minds, and I am eternally grateful! And, I'm sending a special thank-you to Anne and Gretel. Also, a huge thank-you to Diane, who contacted me to offer help, support, and kind words.

I want to thank Victoria Cooper Art for creating the beautiful cover that originally inspired this book (which is not the cover that I ended up using, though Victoria played a very big part in the design of that one as well). I also want to thank Victoria for helping me with the typography and branding for *Ensnared*.

I want to thank my editor, Monique Fischer, who is not only a fantastic wordsmith but also a wonderful person. I always look forward to working with you. Thank you also to Jazzi at Creeping Jasmine Editing for giving your fresh set of eyes and time to this book.

Thank you to Crystal Watanabe for helping with my blurb and for running such an awesome NetGalley co-op. Thank you also to Lola, from Lola's

Book Tours, for working so hard and diligently on behalf of authors!

CPSIA information can be obtained
at www.ICGtesting.com
Printed in the USA
LVOW13s2033110517
534173LV00012B/137/P